a budding romance, taut with terror at every turn, and delivering the goods, and how!"

—J. C. Patterson, *The Clarion-Ledger*

"Charles Wilson wows thriller audiences again with EMBRYO, a terrifyingly plausible book about the future of human fertilization and its possible consequences. Mr. Wilson's writing blazes across the page at the speed of light, hardly giving the reader time to catch her breath before he tosses yet another twist or surprise. However, in amidst all the terror and action and suspense, is a surprisingly poignant story of two people who are forced together by chance, then by adversity, and finally by love. . . . Excellent."

—*Affaire de Coeur*

"Thrillers are Charles Wilson's forte, and his past efforts have been winners. He is right on target again with EMBRYO, which is the kind of story you just might be reading about in a newspaper and discussing as to the ethics of reproductive research. No matter whether you want to consider future horrors of this sort or are just looking for a good book to take your mind off today's problems, it's a fascinating idea transformed into a novel that's hard to put down."

—Marie Beth Jones, *Brazosport Facts*

"Charles Wilson has once again set out to do something large, and ended up with something even bigger! His plot winds away to a finale that will keep you on the edge of your seat . . . Don't be surprised if Wilson doesn't stretch your thinking just a bit. Highly recommended."

—*Singularity*

"Charles Wilson, the bestselling author of EXTINCT, has created a story which provides the reader with far more than just another fast-paced thriller. Aside from losing sleep over not being able to put the book down at night, you will also lose sleep questioning the ethics of modern science—should man perform miracles of medicine simply because he can? . . . A tightly woven suspense thriller that will keep you on edge, as you struggle with the ethical dilemmas faced by the book's characters. We highly recommend EMBRYO for anyone wanting a fast-paced intelligent thriller from a critically acclaimed storyteller. If you've read any of Wilson's earlier works, this one will certainly find a place on your bookshelf."

—*Mystery On-Line Editors*

EXTINCT

"Eminently plausible, and highly entertaining straight through to its finale. The best work of fiction I've ever read about a sea predator."

—Dean A. Dunn, Ph.D. in Oceanography and Paleontology, and former shipboard scientist for *Glomar Challenger* expeditions in both the Pacific and Western North Atlantic

"Meticulously researched."

—*Entertainment Weekly*

"A better story better told than *Jaws*."

—*The Tupelo Daily Journal*

"A nail-biter that those planning a seaside vacation may want to save for beach-house reading."

—*Publishers Weekly*

"As always, Wilson delivers a page-turner . . . providing plenty of incentive to stay out of the water and safely ensconced on the sand."

—*Memphis Commercial Appeal*

"EXTINCT is summer reading at its best, but you will remember the story long after fall leaves turn golden."

—*BookPage*

"As in all Charles Wilson novels, the style is unique and original—and frighteningly real."

—*The Clarion-Ledger*

DIRECT DESCENDANT

"Move over *Jurassic Park*, the really dangerous prehistoric creature has been brought back . . . Man. A terrific read, one done better with your door locked—for all the good that would do."

—*The Clarion-Ledger*

"A story as technically correct as Tom Clancy, as terrifying as Stephen King . . . genetic experimentation that not only could take place, but will someday—with the results only to wonder about now. A surefire best-seller."

—Johnny Quarles, author of *Brack, Fool's Gold* and *Spirit Trail*

"Readers will be hoping for a sequel."

—*Memphis Commercial Appeal*

"Lean, tight, and compelling. You barely have time to catch your breath—and they're back again."

—Greg Iles, *New York Times* bestselling author of *Spandau Phoenix*

"Wilson is a skilled storyteller—carrying the reader from one dramatic event to another with lots of surprises in between."

—*The Mobile Register*

NIGHTWATCHER

"Splendid . . . A lean, tight, compelling story that was over much too fast. I wanted more."

—John Grisham

"Wilson throws one curve after another while keeping up the suspense like an old pro. The whole book rushes over you like a jolt of adrenaline."

—*Kirkus Reviews*

WHEN FIRST WE DECEIVE

ST. MARTIN'S PAPERBACKS TITLES BY CHARLES WILSON

DIRECT DESCENDANT
FERTILE GROUND
EXTINCT
EMBRYO
DONOR

DONOR

CHARLES WILSON

St. Martin's Paperbacks

DONOR

Copyright © 1999 by Charles Wilson.
Excerpt from *Game Plan* copyright © 1999 by Charles Wilson.

ISBN: 0-312-97028-5

Printed in the United States of America

St. Martin's Paperbacks edition/November 1999

St. Martin's Paperbacks are published by St. Martin's Press, 175 Fifth Avenue, New York, N.Y. 10010.

10 9 8 7 6 5 4 3 2 1

*To Linda, whose thoughts
formed the basis of this
story*

As usual, I am deeply indebted to all of those who gave of their time and advice that made it possible for me to write this novel. For their scientific help: William T. Branch, M.D., F.A.C.S., Clinical Professor, Department of Surgery, University of South Florida College of Medicine and listed in *Who's Who in the World Among Educators,* for his aid here as well as for the help he gave me on *Embryo.* H. Davis Dear, M.D., Jackson, Mississippi, cardiologist. Dr. Craig Lobb, Department of Microbiology, University of Mississippi Medical Center.

Thanks to Brian S. Haight, San Francisco, California, for his editing suggestions. Thanks to my youngest son, Destin, to my son-in-law, Cas Heath, M.D., and to Alison Orr, all of Brandon, Mississippi, for their reading the various versions of my manuscript and giving me their advice as I developed, rewrote, and redeveloped *Donor.*

My special thanks to Matthew Shear, Vice President, Publisher at St. Martin's. His support, both personally and professionally, has been an overwhelming factor in my sales continuing to increase nationally with each novel published. Certainly his including a personal statement of high praise for me and my works on the back cover of Advance Reading Copies of *Embryo* sent to book reviewers, wholesalers and bookstores, was both unexpected and highly appreciated by me.

Finally, a special, long overdue, deeply felt thanks to Jennifer Enderlin, executive editor at St. Martin's and, luckily for me, my editor. There is nothing I have ever written for St. Martin's that she didn't make better by her advice.

Thank you all.

DONOR

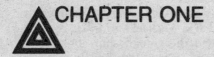 # CHAPTER ONE

"Help us, please."

The woman stood just inside the glass doors leading into the department. She cradled a little girl against her chest. The child's arms and legs hung limply toward the floor.

Michael Sims didn't take time to close the chart he had been writing in at the counter fronting the nurses' station. Slipping his pen inside the breast pocket of his surgical scrubs, he hurried toward the woman. Mary Liz hurried after him from inside the station. A second young nurse came across the floor from the direction of the trauma rooms. Behind the woman, the glow of the flood lamps outside the entrance illuminated her aging car. The driver's-side door stood open. Wind-driven drops of rain from the thunderstorm that had moved in from the Gulf shortly before midnight glistened like darting fireflies as they passed through the bright light.

Michael caught the little girl under her back and hips, lifting her from her mother's arms. "Are you a doctor?" she asked. He nodded as he turned toward the trauma rooms. The woman swayed. Her face was pale and it looked as if she might faint. Mary Liz caught her by the arm and shoulder.

The child's fever was spiking; she felt like an electric blanket turned on high in Michael's arms. He could feel her body jerking with her rapid, short breaths. He looked across his shoulder at the mother, who was following him across the floor, Mary Liz by her side. "I need to know how this started," he said. A nurse near one of the trauma rooms had started a stretcher toward him, but moved it back against the wall as she saw how light the child was in his arms.

"She's had a little temperature for a couple of days," her mother said behind him. "I don't know what happened."

He entered the nearest trauma room. The child's eyes, slitted and seemingly unseeing as he had carried her across the floor, began to open. She looked at him. Her long blond hair hung toward the floor. He smiled softly down at her as he laid her on the bed surrounded with emergency equipment. Mary Liz reached for the cardiac monitor leads. The nurse who had started to move the stretcher had come inside the room and now slipped a blood pressure cuff up over the child's thin arm.

"I work three to eleven," the mother said. "The baby-sitter said that Candice—that's her name . . ." The woman choked back a sob and took a deep breath. "The sitter said she had trouble getting her to sleep, but that she was resting peacefully. Candice hadn't slept good last night. I slipped into bed with her, but didn't touch her."

Michael felt the pressure around his thumb. The little girl had caught it in her small hand and somehow was smiling up at him through the anguish across her face.

He smiled back down at her.

"I didn't want to disturb her," the mother said. "I . . ." She started crying loudly, gasping out her words through choking sobs, shaking violently with each breath.

"Oh, God . . . I rolled . . . over . . . touched her arm . . . she was burning up. I . . . I couldn't get her . . . her to . . . wake up."

The child's finger relaxed around his thumb. He moved a stethoscope to her chest. "Has she been coughing?"

"No."

"Anything you can remember?"

"She . . ." The woman tried to stop her crying. "She said when she went to the bathroom it burned."

As he listened to the child's chest with the stethoscope, the nurse on the far side of the bed lifted Candice's legs out to the sides. In a moment she had done a quick in-and-out catheter, collecting a urine sample.

"Doctor," she said, showing him the tube. The liquid was cloudy with pus, displaying the sign of a urinary tract infection, more common in older women but capable of striking children, too, and able to race out of control much more quickly in a younger victim. Mary Liz had finished inserting an IV needle, drawn a blood sample, and connected the needle to a bag of normal saline solution hanging from a rack at the head of the bed. Candice hadn't reacted to the needle being inserted. Her eyes slowly closed now.

"Wake her up," her mother said. "Oh, God—*wake her up!*"

Michael felt the woman brush his side. A nurse caught the woman's shoulders and moved her back from the bed. Mary Liz placed an oxygen mask turned on high over the child's nose and mouth.

Across the department, a nurse said, "MVC arriving."

It was the motor vehicle collision patient that had been called in five minutes earlier by a paramedic in an ambulance nearing the hospital.

Michael looked across his shoulder and saw Daryl

Stillman, the other young physician on duty for the night, glance inside the doorway at the little girl, then nod that he would handle the incoming emergency.

Michael turned his attention back to the child. Above the bed, the cardiac monitor showed a blood pressure of eighty over forty and a heart rate of eighty beats a minute. Her respiration was displayed in rapid, roller-coaster-like up-and-down sweeps on the screen. "I want a gram of Rocephin."

Mary Liz already had the plastic bag containing the broad-spectrum antibiotic in her hand. She hung it on the rack, connecting it piggy-back to the line in Candice's arm.

The flashing red lights of the ambulance coming to a rocking stop outside reflected across the department. A paramedic in a yellow rain slicker hopped out of the blocky vehicle and hurried to its rear.

Seconds later, a nurse came backing through the doors, pulling one end of a stretcher as the paramedic and an orderly pushed the other end. Michael saw that the lanky teenager lying between them had his shirt open and three small EKG electrodes resembling round Band-Aids stuck to his chest. Blood was matted on one side of his head, mixed in with his red hair and smeared across his face, but he showed movement, opening and closing his hands under the webbing securing him to the spinal board, his legs squirming in his discomfort, indicating the lack of any serious back injury. That the paramedic hadn't inserted an endotracheal tube into the youth's throat indicated the breathing passage was clear. Daryl led the stretcher into the trauma room next to the one where Michael worked.

"Is she going to be okay?" Candice's mother called from the doorway.

Michael did not answer, using the excuse of his attention being concentrated on the child. He knew she was septic. The prognosis for a child her age, the prognosis for anyone septic, wasn't favorable at best—and the bacteria had obviously been building in her bloodstream for a long time, as listless as she was acting.

But he would eventually have to turn from the room and face the mother. He had to get to the laboratory computer to see what the blood work showed—to verify what he already knew so that he would be absolutely certain. He took a quiet breath and turned away from the bed.

"I need to get the results of the lab work before I'll know anything," he said. He wanted to be able to say something comforting as she stared at him with her tears now coursing silently down her face. But he couldn't.

As he moved past her and started across the department toward the computer at the nurses' station, he slipped his gloves off. He looked at his thumb. The one the child had clasped. In the three years of his emergency medicine residency and the year he had worked at the hospital, he had seen many children in serious shape. But he had never worked over a child who had forced a smile up at him though the anguish on her face—as if she were trying to tell him she trusted what he was doing.

And yet what had there been for him to do that warranted her trust? In this so-called age of modern medicine, what was there really to do but administer the antibiotic and wait? While it would only take seconds for the Rocephin to spread through her body, it would be hours before it would begin to fight the bacteria effectively—and there was no way to know if she had that much time. It didn't seem right that there wasn't more he could do.

He wasn't burned out on medicine. He still loved what he did. But there were times when he suffered a deep-down feeling. Certainly he wasn't as enthusiastic as he had been when he was starting medical school, before he had seen so many illnesses and injuries end in tragedy for want of a better medicine, a better technique.

The computer screen lit up with the message that the child's blood work hadn't been posted yet. It would be at least a few more minutes before it was. But he knew the computer wouldn't be where he got the word. He looked toward the red telephone mounted next to a pair of black phones on the wall.

It would be the red one that would suddenly start ringing. And not with the intermittent, sharp sounds of a normal phone, but with one continuous, unstopping ring. The loud, piercing sound would continue until someone lifted the receiver. It was the emergency line from the laboratory, known in hospital jargon as the 'panic' phone. It was only used when the critical values of a patient's blood work were dangerously off-kilter. In this case, a child deeply septic with a poor prognosis.

He knew he was right in his diagnosis.

And he almost hated himself for knowing that.

Now he noticed Candice's mother staring at him, a look of fear in her widened eyes—almost as if she knew what he was thinking, and what the ring would mean.

And there was nothing he could do about it—and nothing more he could do for the child.

Nothing more anybody could do.

Except wait.

For the ring.

And then the longer wait.

For the outcome of a child who had trusted him in a way it was going to be impossible for him ever to forget.

A FEW MILES AWAY

Blue rotating lights from police cars and sheriff's department vehicles reflected off the front of a sprawling one-story stucco house, flashed against a white Cadillac parked in the home's driveway, and illuminated the last drops of the falling rain. Harrison County Sheriff James Everette stood underneath the roof's overhang at the front door. Tall and heavily built, with dark hair, he wore a sport coat and slacks rather than a uniform. A shorter man in a jacket with FBI printed on its back stood next to him. They faced a third man, Dr. Joseph Marzullo. As tall as the sheriff, but with a leaner build, Marzullo's thinning, light brown hair, streaked with gray, shined brightly in the flashing lights. He had been performing emergency heart surgery at Coastal Regional Hospital when he heard the news of Congressman Donnelly's suicide. Still dressed in green surgical scrubs, he had driven to the house the moment he finished the operation. "I knew Lawrence was depressed about his health," he said. "But I had no idea he had reached the point where he would . . ."

As Marzullo let his words trail off, he looked at the door and shook his head. "I should have known. I was talking to him all the time. I was listening, but not hearing. I should have said something to somebody."

A sad expression across his face, he looked away from the door to his watch, and sighed. "I have surgery scheduled early, gentlemen. If that's all you need from me I guess I should try to get a couple of hours' sleep."

"Thank you for coming by, Doctor," the sheriff said. "You've been a big help."

Marzullo nodded, looked toward the door again, then turned and started toward a black BMW parked on the far side of the street fronting the property.

As he walked across the grass, a flood lamp flashed to life, bathing the house in its brilliant glow, and Everette looked at the WLOX-TV satellite truck in the street. A young cameraman focused a tripod-mounted camera lens on a tall brunette taping a story on Congressman Donnelly's suicide for the coming day's news.

"We're going to have media from all over pulling in here," Everette said in his deep voice. "Want to bet I'm going to get second-guessed on this whatever I do?"

"Call it like it is," the agent said. "He was feeling down, drinking heavily, and broke in here—between you and me I think he was probably coming back to a place where he used to find some kind of special warmth. It's A-B-C—straight down the line. Everything fits. You're going to get less speculation out of everybody if you just stamp it what it is and close the investigation—make it that cut-and-dried. That's my opinion anyway."

They both looked toward a silver Ford Expedition as it braked to a stop behind a deputy's cruiser blocking the driveway, and the Congressman's daughter, Shannon Donnelly, stepped outside the vehicle.

She hadn't wasted any time after being notified of her father's death. Her dark hair was noticeably mussed, unbrushed after she had climbed hurriedly out of bed. Her slim figure was lost in the folds of a gray sweatsuit that seemed a couple of sizes too big, and she wore a pair of tennis shoes with the untied laces flopping out to the sides as she hurried across the yard toward the house.

She began to slow as she neared the walk in front of the entrance. She raised her hand and nervously pushed her hair back from her shoulder.

"I'm sorry, Shannon," Everette said as she stopped in front of him.

"They said Daddy left a note," she said in a low voice.

Everette reached into his inside coat pocket and pulled out a small plastic bag. The wrinkled piece of notepad paper could be seen through the side of the bag. Shannon stared at the blood-stained corner of the note, then at the three words:

Please forgive me

Everette lowered the bag. "Shannon, Dr. Marzullo was just by here. He was talking about Lawrence's depression. Had you noticed anything in particular over the last few days that would indicate it had grown worse?"

When Shannon didn't answer, Everette said, "I know this isn't a good time to be asking questions, but it would help me if you—"

"Daddy didn't commit suicide," she said abruptly.

The FBI agent glanced toward Everette. Everette didn't say anything.

"He wasn't depressed," Shannon said. "I mean not enough to . . ." She shook her head. "He just wouldn't. I know."

When Everette still didn't say anything, she said, "Would you murder somebody, James?"

Before he could respond to the strange question, she added, "And that's just how certain I am Daddy wouldn't kill himself. Somebody made him write the note, and then they murdered him."

The FBI agent's eyes narrowed. Everette said, "Why do you think that, Shannon?"

"Because I know he wouldn't kill himself," she said. "I know," she repeated, and looked toward the front door.

As she did, it opened, and a young deputy carrying a bundle of small, plastic Ziploc bags stepped outside. When he saw her, he closed the door quickly behind him.

She turned her face back to the sheriff's. "Can I go inside?" she asked.

"I'm going to keep the house secured until I get a release from the governor and Washington."

Just his saying no was enough to make her want to cry. She knew anything anybody said would make her want to cry. It had been all she could do when she saw the flashing lights of the law enforcement vehicles around the house not to break out sobbing. But she had to go inside. She had to see for herself, see if there was anything that might give her an idea of who had killed her father. "You know I won't touch anything," she said.

"It looks pretty bad anyway, Shannon."

Though Everette's words created a vision she didn't want to see—and she knew it would be worse when she went inside—she forced herself to stay on course. "I can handle it," she said, not knowing whether she could or not.

Everette shook his head no without speaking this time.

"He was my father," she said.

When Everette still didn't say anything, she said, "There's nothing wrong with you *using* me to look inside. To see if I might notice something you missed—maybe something only a member of the family would notice. The news media would think you were smart if you did that—you didn't take a chance of letting something go unnoticed. And you know they're going to be talking to me."

As she paused, she made herself stare directly into his eyes. "I want to be able to tell them that I'm satisfied with the investigation you've done."

The FBI agent grinned at Everette. "Looks like you're between a rock and a hard place, James."

When Shannon glared at the man, his grin went away.

Everette was silent for a moment more, then he said in a low voice, "Okay, Shannon, let me see if the lab techs are about finished. Then I'll take you through—if you're certain you really want to see what you're going to see."

Shannon didn't say anything. She knew she had reached the point where she couldn't say much more without crying—and Everette walked toward the door.

TWENTY MILES WEST OF THE DONNELLY HOME

Two single-story buildings were encircled by a tall chain-link fence in a heavily wooded area. One was paneled with steel siding, a cavernous structure a hundred feet wide by two hundred fifty feet deep. The other was a much smaller structure of concrete block. Within the larger building, a bank of radio speakers stacked one on top of the other stood against a wall in a dimly lit room. A stocky man dressed in jeans and a dark windbreaker sat in a straight chair in front of the speakers. He reached forward and turned up a volume control knob. The sound of Sheriff James Everette opening the front door of the Donnelly home and speaking to a deputy came across one of the speakers. Another carried the sound of the deputy's footsteps as he walked across a hardwood floor.

Around the man, other electronic equipment lined the walls. A bank of glowing visual monitors displayed scenes of small, working robotics machinery mounted on tables that were arranged in long rows inside a wide area in the building; scenes of a darkened, quiet area in another part of the building; and scenes of a room lit only by a night light and lined with laboratory equipment and cages of small, white rats. A separate set of monitors showed the flood-lamp-lit grounds outside the building, a view of the smaller, darkened building two hundred feet away, and the fence surrounding the complex. On the wall behind the man, a single large screen measuring four feet by four feet remained dark.

The sound of the front door of the Donnelly home opening and closing again pulled his attention back to the speakers.

"Are we missing anything?"

It was the sheriff speaking again, the deep tone of his voice easily recognizable.

"What's there to miss, James?"

It was the FBI agent who asked the question.

"He was a congressman. I miss something, I couldn't get elected dog catcher."

"Yeah, and if it was Joe Blow you wouldn't still be

standing here wondering if you might have missed something, James."

"That's the problem—it's not Joe Blow. You about finished, Jackson?"

"Need to lift some prints off the cabinet in the kitchen, Sheriff. Give me about five more minutes."

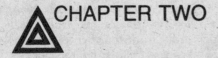 # CHAPTER TWO

Michael Sims looked at the stretcher carrying Candice's small, listless form toward the entrance of the hallway leading to the intensive care unit. The pediatric specialist he had called walked behind the stretcher. Candice's mother remained inside the room praying with the priest who had just arrived.

"You're pretty good," the youth lying on the bed before him said. He was the MVC emergency the ambulance had delivered fifteen minutes earlier.

"Thank you, Johnny," Michael said as he brought his gaze back to the laceration on the side of the boy's head, hooked a curved needle through the wound's borders, and pulled a suture tight.

He had taken over the stitching after Daryl had been called to the third floor on a heart patient coding.

"I mean I can't feel a thing," Johnny said.

"Give credit to the lidocaine."

"That's what you deadened it with?"

"Uh-huh," Michael said as he tied off the stitch. He looked back at the entrance of the hallway leading to the ICU as the door closed behind the stretcher. He looked at his thumb. The one Candice had clasped. He remembered back to when he had been a child himself, his father a physician in this very hospital, and how in staring up at the building he had imagined it a wondrous castle full of magicians performing miracles. Now he saw it only as a collection of aging two- and three-story buildings haphazardly stuck together as the hospital had expanded over the years. And the doctors within its walls, no matter how dedicated, no matter how hard-working, were only doing what little they could, constrained by procedures and medicines that were limited and improved ever so slowly. He raised his gaze back to the hallway. Scientists knew what the various bacteria were. They knew what the bacteria could do when they entered the bloodstream. Why hadn't scientists somewhere learned how to counter the problem? Some quicker-acting antibiotic that could be used. Some medical technique. Something. It didn't seem right that complications from a bacteria that had been around since time began could still lead to a child dying—to anybody dying—and modern medicine could do nothing about it. That was the very real possibility that Candice faced. And all they could do now was wait and see. Then Johnny's voice pulled him from his thoughts.

"I wouldn't *mind* being a doctor," he said, then added, "Better see if I can get through freshman English first, though, hadn't I?" and immediately crossed his fingers for luck. "You ever have a professor you knew you were in trouble with the moment you walked into his class? Freddy Krueger with an emphasis on grammar."

Despite how he felt, Michael smiled a little, hooked the last stitch into place, tied it, and snipped the suture with a pair of small scissors. "There—finished with that." He laid the needle driver on the plastic wrap from the suturing kit lying by the side of the bed, and reached for a gauze pad and tape.

The youth moved his hand to his chest and gingerly touched the ugly circular bruise that had been left there when he had been thrown into his car's steering column. "My X rays were all right?"

"Chest is fine."

"What about the . . . what did you call it?"

"The CT scan."

"Yes, sir. I have to get back to track practice—not to mention Freddy's class."

A telephone in the set of two on the wall outside the room rang, the black telephone ringing with a normal, intermittent ring, and Michael turned away from the bed. "That's the results now."

Johnny's parents stood a few feet outside the doorway. Mrs. Whitaker was a short, stocky woman with shoulder-length brown hair and dark coloring. The youth had gotten his red hair, pale complexion, and lanky build from Mr. Whitaker.

Michael lifted the telephone receiver. "Dr. Sims," he said, and listened as the neurosurgeon explained the results of the scan. He noticed Mrs. Whitaker clutch her purse nervously in front of her waist as he replaced the receiver and turned from the phone.

"There's no skull fracture. The scan *does* show a small frontal lobe contusion. We're going to keep him overnight for observation."

Then he parroted the hospital's policy of never misleading a patient or their relatives. A policy that had less to do with patients' well-being than with the hospital attorney's idea of what would help to alleviate liability. "There's always a possibility of brain swelling. But with the time that has passed since the accident and no evidence of swelling yet, I consider that highly unlikely. The neurosurgeon said he'll be by to see him in the morning."

Mr. Whitaker grinned. "I told Denise a little knock on the head wasn't going to hurt Johnny none," he said. His grin changed to a proud smile. "He's a heck of an athlete. He won the State Cross Country Championship just last spring—he's on a track scholarship at Southern now."

Mrs. Whitaker forced a smile, but only a feeble one.

Michael thought of Candice's mother in the next room with the priest. There was nothing that he could have said that would have made her feel better. He wanted to make at least one mother feel good that night.

"The observation is only a precaution," he said.

And then he went further than he should. "I'm certain he'll be sleeping in his own bed by tomorrow night."

Mrs. Whitaker's fingers quit moving against her purse. She took a deep breath. "Thank you, Doctor," she said in a soft voice. She glanced at her husband. "Fred here goes on too much about Johnny's athletics sometimes, but it's because we're so proud of him. We didn't have the money to send him to college. Johnny's not dumb, but he wasn't going to get an academic scholarship. He set his mind on a track scholarship. He ran during practice, then ran some more after his job at the grocery store."

As the woman paused, a smile as proud as her husband's crossed her face. "He's made two B's and an A on his first three tests at Southern."

"He's going to be fine," Michael said.

From the room next to Johnny's, the wailing sob of a mother who could no longer contain her grief filled the air and echoed across the department.

Mrs. Whitaker flinched.

Her husband looked toward the room's closed door.

A FEW MILES AWAY

Sheriff Everette opened the door to the Donnelly home and looked outside at Shannon, who was standing on the concrete walk leading up to the entrance. "Okay, you can come in now," he said.

She hesitated a moment, then walked forward.

A deputy coming outside with a set of fingerprint cards stepped aside as she approached him. She walked past Everette, and immediately stopped, staring at a living room scene out of a grisly horror novel—blood, turning black as it dried, streaked the easy chair, was splattered on the throw rug around the chair, and on the small lamp table beside the chair; there were even flecks on the lamp shade. Her stomach churned and she felt like she was going to vomit. She closed her eyes to keep from seeing what she was seeing. And yet even then, the vision remained so strongly in her mind it was all she could do to not turn and run from the house. But she couldn't let her father down. She couldn't desert him now when there was nobody else. She had to find something, see something that nobody else had noticed, something that would give her an idea who did this.

"You sure you want to do this?" Everette asked.

Slowly, she opened her eyes, forcing herself to look at the scene again. The only weapon in the house had been the one the deputy who had telephoned her said her father used, the twelve-gauge shotgun he had left behind after the divorce from her mother. The force of the blast had blown him to the side of the chair, but he hadn't fallen from it. Where his head had rested, blood had streamed down the backrest. She hadn't known that blood had an odor, but it did. So much blood. Her stomach kept turning.

"Shannon?" the sheriff questioned again.

She knew he could see she was pale. She had felt the color drain from her face when she saw the blood. But it didn't matter what he thought, or what anybody thought. She had to swallow to clear her throat before she could speak.

"What have you taken from the house?"

"The shotgun. His right shoe. It had glass in its heel. It came from when he broke out the door pane. There was no forced entry, except his. The front door was still standing open. He left the shoe off to . . ."

Everette didn't say any more. Everybody knew Donnelly had left his shoe off to reach the shotgun trigger with his toe.

"You're wrong, James," she said. "You're just wrong. Daddy wouldn't commit suicide. He wouldn't. I know."

Everette didn't reply. She ran her gaze around the rest of the living room. "I want to see if I notice something outside the obvious," she said as much again to herself as to him. "Something you might have missed."

At her words, the same ones she had already spoken outside the house, Everette replied this time: "We didn't miss anything, Shannon."

"You didn't?" she asked, looking into his face. She was starting to feel stronger. "You remember Gerald Clayton? He was the first felony case I ever defended after I graduated from law school. Five years ago, remember? Your people missed a lot, didn't they, or I wouldn't have gotten him acquitted."

Everette frowned a little, but didn't say anything. He followed her as she walked toward the kitchen.

She stopped at the door and looked across the tile floor at the open liquor cabinet above the sink. Black fingerprint powder had been patted around the doorknob and up the edge of the door.

"Looks like he came directly in here," Everette said. He nodded at a newspaper folded on the counter. "He left his coat in the car. I guess to keep it from getting wet. The paper was damp, so evidently he used it to shield him from the rain when he came from the car. He laid it down in here, got a bottle out of the cabinet. Then he went back to the chair. He wrote the note there—the pen and pad were on the floor. I don't think he waited very long."

Shannon ignored what Everette said. She knew he couldn't possibly know how long her father had been in the house. Couldn't know what he did before he was killed. What might have been done to him before he was shot. What happened afterward—who was there with him and how they had left. Somebody had been there.

"Who called you about the shot?" she asked.

"The Blasingames next door. They heard it—thought lightning had struck something, and looked out their window. They saw the strange Cadillac in the driveway and knew your mother was out of town."

"They're the ones who told you nobody came out of the house?"

"From their window they can see all the way around the house. Mrs. Blasingame stayed at the window while her husband called us. Nobody came out. All the windows are latched."

"How does she know they didn't come out before she looked?"

"It was only a few seconds before she got to the window," Everette answered. He was silent for a moment. "Shannon, I've been a friend of your family for thirty years. I saw you come up from a baby. I don't want to make you angry, but things like this just happen sometimes without us knowing why. Your father had too outstanding a life for you to dwell on this at the end. It would be better if you accepted what's happened—and how it happened. It's going to be hard enough for you and your mother when she gets here without your thinking that—"

"You're wrong, James," she said, not letting him finish. "Daddy didn't commit suicide and I'm going to prove it."

Her voice had not only been strong this time, but risen as she had spoken. But the effort had drained her. Now all the strength was gone. There was nothing to steady her. Her lip trembled and she felt her eyes moisten. A tear ran down one cheek, and she had to turn and hurry from the house before she started crying openly.

EMERGENCY DEPARTMENT
COASTAL REGIONAL HOSPITAL

Michael Sims leaned against the counter fronting the nurses' station. His gaze was focused on the open doorway of the trauma room where the little girl had lain. Candice. He couldn't get her name out of his mind. He rubbed his thumb with his finger, then took a deep breath and forced his gaze away from the room, trying to get his mind on something else. He saw Daryl coming across the tiled floor from where he had just finished working with an older woman. Her sprained ankle now taped tightly, she sat on a side of the bed, her foot resting in the seat of a chair next to the bed. Daryl's face was uncharacteristically expressionless at the moment—he was usually grinning or wisecracking. He was known as the clown of the emergency department staff, always pulling a joke on one of the other doctors or nurses—and with the kind of personality that caused everybody to come out laughing. Despite the down mood Michael was in, he couldn't keep from smiling at thinking how Daryl had been employed at the hospital only a month longer than he had, and yet always referred to himself as the "senior" physician in conversations between them. They were good friends, even similar in appearance at around six-feet-two, with lean builds and the same thick, dark hair. Daryl stopped beside him, glanced toward the trauma rooms and said, "What're you doing over here all by your lonesome, buddy?"

When Michael didn't immediately reply, Daryl added, "Just wanted to tell you what a joy it's been working the night with you, and tell you not to be too envious when you think about me sacked out in the middle of my bed as soon as I can get home—with you still here working your butt off."

"I'll try to constrain my envy," Michael said.

"What *are* you doing?" Daryl asked again, then glanced toward the hallway leading toward the ICU and said, "You thinking about the little girl?"

"Candice," Michael said, the crazy thought passing through his mind that if she wasn't referred to by her name it would be like she had died, as if he were jinxing what chance she had. "Yeah, it bothers me," he added, understating his feelings by a mile.

"I figured," Daryl said. He was silent for a moment, then said, "Buddy, let a doctor give a doctor a lecture. One an old professor of mine once gave me. Do all you can for your patients. Don't spare any effort. But after you have done all that is humanly possible and the results don't turn out like you would have wished, get it off your mind. Don't dwell on what might have been. If you don't, you'll go crazy—or end up on drugs trying to get to sleep at night."

Michael nodded. But how *did* he get her off his mind?

"You want to hear something you're not going to believe?" Daryl asked. "Dr. Marzullo just came back in to check on a post-operative patient. He'd been over at Congressman Donnelly's former wife's house—Donnelly committed suicide."

Michael realized his expression betrayed his disbelief when Daryl added, "You're not any more surprised than I am. One day you hear him being mentioned as a possible future presidential candidate, the next he kills himself. Broke into the house and blew his brains out."

Michael thought of his mother. She wouldn't just be struck with disbelief, she would be distraught.

And she didn't need any more to be upset about, he thought. *She didn't really need any more bad news of any kind.*

HIGHWAY 90

Her hair whipping in the wind coming through the Expedition's lowered window, Shannon drove in the direction of the funeral home. Sheriff Everette and his deputies and the other faceless figures wandering around her mother's house behind her now, she let the tears flow freely down her cheeks. She couldn't get her father's face out of her mind. It kept coming to her not like she remembered him looking, but as she imagined him now, bloody with huge chunks of flesh missing after the shotgun fired. No matter how she tried to visualize him, she kept seeing the horrible, damaged caricature.

And Everette and the FBI agent and Dr. Marzullo and all the rest, *knowing* he did that to himself.

The tears, driven now by frustration as well as sadness, began to flow faster. She guided the Expedition over to a wide parking lane next to the beach and stopped it, leaving the motor running. She stared out past the sand across the calm waters of the Mississippi Sound, already starting to lighten with the first glow of the rising sun.

Her father's face mingled with the view—the torn face once again. The shotgun barrel raised to his cheek as if it were going to fire a second shot. She shook her head to force the image away and stared hard at the water. She tried to think, tried to force her thoughts out from behind her grief.

There *had* been depression. First from the bypass surgery of the year before. Then, as it seemed he was about to conquer that depression, the discovery of the cancer in a lymph node. Her father had been down. He had reason to be down. But he also had started the chemotherapy and X-ray treatments the week after the discovery, and the cancer had gone into remission and he had seemed certain he was going to be all right.

He *was* certain. She didn't care what anybody else said. She knew. She talked to him nearly every week. She would have heard something in his voice if he had started crashing again. She would have caught something.

And above everything, if she was right about nothing

else, she knew that he wouldn't have killed himself in her mother's house, where her mother would have to come and go each day with the reminder of the horror that had happened there. Not with how regretful he had always been since the divorce. He had said he would never hurt them like that again. He had promised that over and over again. And he had meant it. He had never promised her anything, not once in her life, and then not kept that promise. He hadn't this time either. She knew that without any doubt; she knew that as much as she knew how much he had loved her.

She just had to think, to try to find out what had happened, and why. And who had come inside the house behind her father.

And murdered him.

She had to find that out.

Somehow.

But not now. She couldn't think logically. Not with his face passing repeatedly through her mind like a deck of cards being fanned in front of her eyes, with the carnage imprinted on each card.

But she would think later. She would think, and she would find out. She made a choking sound, a cross between a cough and a sob. She swallowed to clear her throat. She raised her gaze toward the sky. Somehow she steadied her voice.

"I will, Daddy. I will find out. I'll find who did this to you. I don't know how. But I promise you I will."

COASTAL REGIONAL HOSPITAL

Johnny Whitaker was the only patient other than Candice currently in the hospital's small Intensive Care Unit. Sedated mildly and sleeping comfortably despite the ugly bruise on his chest and the bandage covering the laceration at the side of his head, he lay on his back in one of the glass-fronted rooms arranged in a half-circle at the unit's rear. Olga Lindestrom was the only nurse in sight. Heavy-set in white scrubs, with her blond hair up in a bun on the back of her head, she stood inside the nurses' station at the center of the unit. As Dr. Marzullo walked past her, she raised a steaming cup of coffee to her lips and sipped from it. Then she walked to the door leading from the unit, stopped there, and looked up and down the hall.

A moment later, she turned back in Marzullo's direction and nodded.

He stepped inside Johnny Whitaker's room.

The cardiac monitor above the teenager traced evenly spaced jagged peaks across the screen, the high-pitched beeps coming from the monitor mimicking the sounds of the youth's strong heart. His blood pressure read one hundred ten over seventy-five. Dr. Marzullo reached into his scrubs' breast pocket and pulled out a small camera.

He took a shot of the youth's face from the side, and one directly above him. Then he moved to the other side of the bed and took several more quick shots. He took one with Johnny's hospital gown pulled down off his shoulders, centering the bruise on his chest in the camera lens.

Finally, Marzullo measured the circumferences of the teenager's lean arms and neck and used a pair of small scissors to take a sample of his red hair.

When he passed Olga as he left the unit he didn't speak.

She watched the tall cardiologist until he had passed out of sight down the hallway. Then she turned back into the unit and walked to the nurses' station. As she set her coffee cup on the counter, she glanced at the clock on a side wall of the unit, and looked toward the teenager's room.

△ CHAPTER THREE

The emergency department and his long shift behind him, Michael Sims drove his aging Jeep along Highway 90. There was no trace of the storm of the night before. The sky was a light blue, the sun shined brightly overhead, and he had taken the top and side panels off the Jeep, letting his hair whip in the warm wind. To his left, the white sand beach sloped down to the silty waters of the Mississippi Sound. Across the water, he could see the tops of the trees on the barrier islands, several miles in the distance. Ahead of him was the city limits line between Biloxi and Gulfport and he would soon be at the Gulfport Yacht Harbor. His yacht was berthed there. Not as pretentious a craft as the word *yacht* brought to mind, it was a thirty-year-old Gulfstar trawler that anyone daring to call himself a yachtsman would have been ashamed to claim. But at forty-three feet long with a master stateroom large enough to contain a queen-size bed, a small salon that served as his living room, and a compact galley where he fixed his meals, it fitted his purposes perfectly. With its payments only a little over a thousand dollars a month, it was much nicer than any apartment he could have afforded when he came back to Biloxi to take the emergency department position. *And what apartment dweller had the luxury of taking their bedroom and kitchen with them when they went deep-sea fishing?* he thought, and smiled.

Starting to feel more upbeat than he had in the last several hours, he turned into the marina and drove past the long lines of sailboats and motor yachts of all descriptions toward the last row of craft at the rear of the complex.

He parked in front of the Gulfstar's berth and walked toward the narrow wooden ramp between the trawler and the neighboring yacht, a gleaming-white, fifty-three-foot Hatteras motor yacht, backed stern-first into its slip, as the Gulfstar was.

The old man sitting in a folding chair at the Hatteras's bow wore only a pair of short khaki pants. His thin, heavily suntanned body was as brown as mahogany and his bare feet were propped up on the rail in front of him. He looked back across his shoulder. "Morning, Michael," he said. "You don't look too worse for wear. What is it, four days on and three days off?" The man shook his head. "When I was a kid like you coming up I was lucky to get one Sunday a month off. Of course some got life made and some don't."

"Morning, Howard," Michael said and smiled a little at what the man had said. He knew Howard's father had been an uneducated but hard-working timber man, already owning several thousand acres by the time Howard was born. Howard had been forced to work unusually hard under the man's thumb. Michael was aware of that from some of the stories he had heard Howard tell. But that dawn-to-past-dark labor had abruptly ceased when his father had died of a heart attack when Howard was thirty. He hadn't lifted a finger since, except when he had a deep-sea fishing rod in his hands or was tinkering on his yacht's engines. That was something he liked to do.

"Your Perkins sounded a little rusty when you wound them up yesterday," Howard said, reminding

Michael of just how highly attuned the old man's ear was to the sound of running engines.

"I'll keep that in mind," Michael said as he walked across the gangplank onto the *Cassandra*. The sliding door to the side of the salon stood open. He remembered closing it before he had left for the hospital the night before.

The sound of a vacuum running came from the master stateroom inside the boat's stern. He stepped inside the salon and walked to the small door that led down the two steps into the stateroom. His mother pushed a vacuum back and forth next to the queen-size bed that took up most of the cabin's compact space. Her hair, once as dark as his, but now streaked with gray, bounced as she accidentally ran the vacuum into the post at the foot of the bed. She was a diminutive woman. His height and build had come from his father. She glanced his way, and smiled when she saw him.

"What are you doing?" he asked.

She turned the vacuum off. "What?"

"I said what are you doing?"

"Pretty evident, isn't it?" she said. "I did a terrible job of raising you to be tidy."

But the stateroom was tidy now, the bed made, all the assorted coffee cups, glasses, and Coke cans that had been sitting on the small dressing table to the starboard side of the cabin gone. There was even a scent of pine in the air.

For the first time he noticed the smell of food cooking. As his mother came up out of the stateroom, he looked across the salon to the step-down galley toward the bow. Two grocery bags, crammed to overflowing, perched on the table in the small booth across from the stove.

"You were up early this morning, weren't you?" he said.

When she didn't answer, he said, "You couldn't sleep again?"

She hugged him from the side and he turned around and hugged her back.

"Michael, I forgot again," she said, laying her head against his chest. "I couldn't find my car keys for the longest time this morning."

He hugged her tighter to him. "We all forget," he said. "I lose something every day."

"But you don't have Alzheimer's."

He cupped her soft hair with his hand and patted her head gently.

"How much longer is it going to be before I forget everything?"

She had asked him that a dozen times since the geriatric specialist with the bedside manner of a baboon had speculated that she had started into the early stages of the disease. Maybe she had. There was no test to tell with certainty. She *was* experiencing noticeable cognitive problems. That had become apparent over the last few months in particular. But that slowing of her recall could simply be due naturally to age, and not destined to grow much worse over the years. But every time he told her that, her fears drowned out his words of comfort. And he wasn't going to hide behind his medical degree and try to con her into believing he was absolutely certain she didn't have the disease. He could never do that to her. What he had decided was that the best therapy was to get the problem off her mind when he could. "The food smells good."

She lifted her face from his chest. "You always change the subject," she said, and smiled softly. "But I'm not scared. It doesn't hurt. It's only that I have a hard time with knowing I'm not going to remember you."

She turned toward the galley. "I'll fix you a plate." She took a step, then stopped and looked back at him. "You've had three phone calls since I got here."

Her tone had completely changed. Almost as if she were suddenly irritated.

And he knew why. "And who were they from?" he asked, smiling.

"Women."

"You don't approve of women?"

"Michael, if you'd just look a little less in the casinos and more in church."

His cellular telephone rang. It lay on the dash next to the control station's steering wheel at the front of the salon.

"You want to get it or me?" he asked. "Might be another casino woman."

She frowned at him.

Smiling, he walked to the station and lifted the telephone to his ear. "Hello."

"Dr. Michael Sims?"

"Yes."

"This is the office of Senator Waymon C. Terry. Would you please hold for a moment for Mr. Terry?"

Michael wondered if he was about to get hit up for a campaign contribution. Terry was big in politics on the Mississippi coast—county chairman of the Republican Party as well as a state senator ever since Michael could remember. Then Jackson County Community Action Agency came to his mind. He had contributed some time to visiting bed-ridden senior citizens in the last few months. Terry was a big supporter of the agency. Michael hoped the man wasn't calling to ask him to do more. He simply didn't have the time. He had only to wait a few seconds before Terry's loud voice came over the line. "Dr. Sims, this is Waymon Terry. How are you doing?"

Michael moved the telephone slightly out from his ear. "Fine."

"You heard about Congressman Donnelly?"

"Yes."

"Pitiful tragedy."

"Yes, it is."

"I remember when your father was the county chairman for the party back when I was first getting started in politics. He made a great doctor, we all know that. But I was most impressed at how knowledgeable he was as a politician. He should have run for office himself—he would have done well."

"Thank you." Michael waited for the request for a contribution or to be asked to volunteer more time with senior citizens. His mother walked to his side. She had a questioning look across her face.

He shrugged.

"Dr. Sims, that's why I'm calling you. I would like to be able to announce that you're the one who's running to fill Congressman Donnelly's seat."

Michael was taken aback. He would have thought that a joke was being played on him except for Terry's serious tone. But he couldn't think of anything he could be less interested in. "I don't know who would have suggested me. But I'm afraid I'm just getting started into my practice, and that's all I have on my mind right now."

"You say who would have suggested you? Well, son, somebody is going to have to run to fill the spot. And who would be a better candidate than you? Your father's still held in high regard around here. You're going to look intelligent to the voters as a doctor. You're young and good-looking—and don't discount that helping with TV appearances nowadays. You're *not* a politician—and that is getting to be more and more of a plus these days. Politics is all hype, son, and you ring all the bells. And if it's money for campaigning that has popped into your head, I can guarantee you all the funds you'll need. Hype and money, that's the key. The mother's milk of all politicians—successful ones."

"Again, I appreciate the call, but—"

"Son, now don't say no," Terry said.

I just did, Michael thought.

"Think it over today, son, sleep on it tonight, and get back to me in the morning. Sorry to cut the conversation short, but I have to run to a press conference to express my condolences at Congressman Donnelly's death. Pitiful tragedy. Pitiful tragedy."

Terry hung up before Michael could respond in any way. He stood with the telephone in his hand.

"What in the world was that all about?" his mother asked.

"That was Waymon Terry. He wants me to campaign to fill Congressman Donnelly's seat."

"Terry's had a falling out with the Congressman?"

"Mother, Donnelly commit . . . died last night."

"Died? Oh, that's terrible. He wasn't much older than your father would be." She shook her head. "You know he was talked into running the first time by your father."

Michael nodded.

"You must have been three or four then," she added. "No, nearer five, because your father had his heart attack when you were ten and he had already supported the congressman for a full two terms then—and then that last year when they had a falling out."

Dr. Marzullo leaned over Johnny Whitaker's bed. The bruise where the teenager's chest had slammed into the car's steering column had darkened into deep shades of purple and blue. The tall cardiologist gently pressed his fingers against a side of the imprint.

"Does that hurt?" he asked.

"Little bit, sir. But really more up here." Johnny lifted his hand to the side of his head, where his red hair was shaved away and the bandage covered the line of stitches.

"Tender, or more of a headache?" Marzullo asked.

When the boy smiled and said, "A little of both," Marzullo smiled back at him and lifted a section of gauze rolled into a six-inch-long tubular shape into view.

"This will help you rest," he said.

The boy was surprised when he saw the gauze being unfolded and the syringe that it had been wrapped around. He hadn't noticed the doctor holding the packet until that very moment.

Marzullo glanced back at Olga Lindestrom, standing at the entrance to the ICU, then leaned forward and used his thumb and forefinger to raise the large antecubital vein in the crook of the boy's elbow. As the syringe came forward, the youth turned his head to the side rather than look.

A moment later a yellow, milky liquid was injected into the vein.

"That should help you," Marzullo said.

The boy looked back at the doctor, glanced down at the spot of blood in the crook of his elbow, and then nodded his thanks.

Marzullo folded the boy's forearm up against his bicep to keep the puncture from bleeding. "Hold it like that," he said.

The boy nodded and used his other hand to help hold his forearm in place. "How long will it be until I can run track?"

"Track?" Marzullo questioned. "Oh, yes. You should be able to return to your normal activities in a couple of days."

"Good," the boy said. "I'm afraid I was already behind the first day I arrived at school. Can't afford to lose my scholarship." He suddenly blinked, opened and closed his eyes for a moment, then tried to shake off the effect of feeling suddenly sleepy. "Excuse me," he said. "—And studying," he added.

Marzullo looked at the cardiac monitor mounted above the bed. The heartbeat was being measured in strong, slow steady thumps across the monitor's screen.

Almost immediately there was an irregular beat, and the jagged up-and-down peaks began to spread farther apart.

The boy's eyes began to close again.

A moment later he mumbled, ". . . Freddy Krueger." His hand relaxed around his forearm. The forearm slowly lay across his stomach.

Marzullo wrapped the gauze back around the syringe, glanced over his shoulder, slipped the packet back into his pocket, and turned and walked from the room.

△ CHAPTER FOUR

A nurse coming down the hallway from the direction of the emergency department looked up at the *click-click-click* sound of the dirty-linen cart rolling toward her. Soiled towels and sheets were mounded high at its center and hung over its sides. The thin man pushing the cart was in his forties, his skin dark from too much sun, and a day's stubble of dark whiskers across his face. She had told him only the day before that he needed to inform the housekeeping supervisor that the cart's loose wheels made too much noise on the floors and they needed to be tightened. He had obviously ignored her. Nevertheless, she smiled politely at him as they passed each other.

The man returned the gesture with a nod of his head, and pushed the cart on up the hall.

The clicking sound ceased when he stopped at the entrance to the ICU and turned the cart inside the unit.

Seconds later, Olga Lindestrom appeared in the doorway from inside the unit, and looked up and down the corridor.

Michael's mother came quietly down the two steps into the master stateroom. Framed in the dim sunlight filtering through the curtains over the small windows at the cabin's sides, Michael lay asleep on his stomach in the center of the queen-size bed, his face turned out to the side, his bare, lightly tanned leg sticking out from under the sheet.

She leaned over the bed and touched him gently on the shoulder.

As his eyes came open, she said, "Sorry, honey, but the hospital administrator is on the line. He said it's important he speak with you."

Michael rolled onto his back, grasped the cellular phone she held out to him, and moved it to his ear. "Clark?"

"Dr. Sims. Jonathan Waverly telephoned me a moment ago. He asked me if I would try to get you to come out to the research center to meet him."

Jonathan Waverly? "To meet him?"

"Yes. He said he had Waymon Terry call you about the congressional seat, but that you weren't interested. He thought if you would come out and speak to him at the center—take a tour of the place, see the research they're doing—you might acquire a different outlook on the matter."

Jonathan Waverly was behind the offer? Everybody along the coast perked up at that name, or when they saw his long white limousine with its darkened windows passing by. But almost no one had ever seen Waverly himself. Michael was irritated at being awakened about something he had already turned down, but at the same time he couldn't help but be curious about a man said to be the richest person in the country.

"Dr. Sims," Clark said, "I'm not expecting you to change your mind about running for the seat. You would be a difficult man to replace if you left the hospital—I don't want that. But I was hoping you'd simply do Waverly the courtesy of discussing this with him."

Michael swung his legs to the floor. "I just got off a swing shift and I'm due back in at seven."

"I've already made arrangements for Dr. Boykin to swap shifts with you so you can wait a couple of days to come in."

Michael frowned and glanced up at his mother. "I know Mr. Waverly is important to the hospital, but—"

"Important?" Clark exclaimed. "You're aware of what this hospital was before he offered to help us. How do you think we attracted doctors like Lipson and Sennet? Doctors as prominent as they are normally wouldn't give a small hospital like this a second glance. But they come because he pours hundreds of thousands of dollars a year into their research. Yes, Dr. Sims, Mr. Waverly is important to the hospital, he's important to the quality of care we're able to give our patients, he's important to the research we do, he's important to my position as administrator—and he's important to *you*."

Michael sat a moment on the edge of the bed without responding. He raised his gaze to his mother, who was staring down at him.

"Okay," he finally said. "I'll speak to him. But I'm not the least bit interested in accepting the offer."

"I have no problem with that," Clark said. "I just need a polite refusal out of you." He gave him Waverly's number. "It's to his direct line," Clark added.

As Michael laid the telephone on his bedside table, he thought about the profile of Waverly he had seen on *Biography*—a man who had come from a less-than-savory family background and risen above it, leaving home at an early age and becoming a near-instant success in the computer software world, and then the biggest name ever in computers. Michael had also entertained an intellectual curiosity about the research center ever since its construction on the site north of Biloxi at about the same time he went off to college.

"They tried to get your father to run once, too," his mother said. "He turned them down graciously—graciously, Michael."

He rolled his eyes up at hers. "You, too?"

"You know I wouldn't move to Washington, Michael, so I don't want you to move either. But it doesn't hurt to keep people in high places—so to speak—thinking you're at least polite."

Michael stood and stretched, and then smiled at his mother. "I can fool them into thinking I'm polite anyway."

She looked at the bed. "Well, I don't suppose there's any need to make this again," she said. "You'll be back in it in a couple of hours. I guess I'll go on."

When the cardiac monitor alarm sounded in the room at the rear of the ICU, the nurse who stepped from behind the nurses' station at the center of the unit didn't break into a hurried gait. Often an alarm went off when a cardiac lead pulled loose from a patient turning in his sleep, or even reaching for something. Sometimes, simply static electricity set the alarms off. She was even more certain than normal that the alarm had gone off accidentally, for the teenager in the room had suffered only a minor contusion to his left frontal lobe; nothing to do with the heart.

When she entered the room and saw Johnny, she brought her hand to her mouth. His open eyes blank, his mouth gaped, he looked without seeing toward the ceiling.

Back at the nurses' station, Olga stared at the look on the other nurse's face as she turned toward her—and then Olga lifted the telephone receiver, punched in Dr. Marzullo's pager number, and looked back toward the room.

Dr. Marzullo waited, leaning against the wall down the hall. When his pager beeped he didn't even bother to look at the number, but pushed himself off the wall and walked in the direction of the ICU.

At that moment outside the hospital, an aging truck with a wide, enclosed bed with COASTAL COMMERCIAL CLEANERS stenciled in block letters on its sides, backed into the shade underneath a large oak close to a door leading toward the hospital's intensive care unit.

The truck's rear doors opened immediately, and a narrow ramp was pushed down to the ground, creating a runway up into the bed.

A moment later, a heavily laden linen cart overflowing with sheets and towels was pushed hurriedly from the hospital and up the ramp into the truck.

When Michael had finished his shower and was dressing, buttoning his shirt as he came up the steps into the *Cassandra*'s salon, his mother sat on the couch, looking through a yachting magazine she had found on the end table. She stood. "Well, I guess I'll be running," she said, repeating what she had said before. But she didn't move toward the sliding door leading to the walkway outside the yacht, or reach to hug him good-bye. She looked toward the galley. The dishes were washed and back in the small cabinets. The stove had been carefully scoured. The coffee pot sparkled. "I don't see anything else I can do," she added.

She always said she could read him well. But nothing like he could read her, he knew. He had always been able to, but never said anything about it to her. "Why don't you stay here?" he suggested.

"Until you get back?"

"Why not spend the night? You can sleep on the bed in the stateroom and I'll bunk in the bow."

"Oh, no, I wouldn't put you out like that even if I could stay."

"Why can't you?"

"Well, I don't know—you don't want me around underfoot."

"When I get back, I'll sleep most of the afternoon. I would love to wake up to a home-cooked meal."

She nodded her head knowingly. "I knew there was some ulterior motive."

"It's a deal then?"

"It's a deal," she said.

"And you're going to sleep over?"

"Oh, well, I guess I can—this one time."

He smiled. But a thought made it go away. As he walked toward the cellular phone at the steering station he thought of crossing his fingers like Johnny Whitaker had. Or praying, like Candice's mother had done. He did both.

It took only a moment for the number he called at the hospital to answer.

"There was a six-year-old female who was admitted through the emergency department last night. Candice Schilling."

The nurse's voice came back as coldly professional as his had been: "She expired about two hours ago, Doctor."

In the ICU, a flat line traced across the cardiac monitor screen. Dr. Marzullo stood beside the bed. The expression on his face was one of someone deeply concerned, maybe even sad. He lifted a syringe equipped with a long cardiac needle over Johnny Whitaker's body.

The nurse standing behind him stared at the tall cardiologist as he pushed the needle deeply into the center of the teenager's chest.

She knew it was part of an effort to confirm Marzullo's opinion that the boy's sudden death had been due to the rupturing of his heart or aorta, brought on in the wake of his being thrown into his car's steering column.

When Marzullo pulled the plunger back, the syringe filled with the tell-tale red blood that had flooded the chest cavity after the rupture. Obviously the blunt trauma his chest had suffered during the car accident had been sufficient to cause a weakening of the arterial or heart wall, maybe even a slight tear in one of the walls, without being detected. The beating of the youth's heart as he had lain in the room would have kept sending surges of blood pounding against the weakened spot. Finally, the wall had dissected, the tissue giving way in a sudden explosion of blood, causing nearly instantaneous death. Dr. Marzullo's diagnosis had been correct. He turned to the nurse.

"Tell his family they can come in to view the body. And then move him to the morgue," he said, and then walked toward the unit's door.

The nurse noted that Marzullo, absorbed in his thoughts about the youth's sudden death, carried the syringe containing the proof of the rupture with him as he walked from the room.

But she didn't say anything to him about it.

Nobody was very talkative after losing both the teenager and the little girl in the last three hours.

They were especially mute when the parents, led by Olga, came slowly inside the room; the woman walking stiffly, supported by her husband's hands clasping her shoulders.

She remained that way, tears silently coursing down her cheeks until she reached the bed, and then she moaned loudly and fell across her son, hugging his head to her face, pulling his arm toward her, feeling the soft, unresponsive muscles give no resistance at all—and the terrible cool feeling of his skin, devoid of its warm life-giving blood that had flowed only a few minutes before.

And then Olga was gently but firmly pulling her back from the bed, moving the woman's hands from clasping her son. The woman resisted a moment, trying to hang on to her son, then let his hand go and turned her face against her husband's chest, and began sobbing silently.

Olga slipped the youth's arm back under the sheet, and carefully pulled the fabric up over his chest. His hair was mussed; one eyelid had been pushed partly open as his face had been pressed against the woman's head.

Olga closed it with a gentle motion of her fingers.

*   *   *

Outside the hospital, the truck with COASTAL COMMER-CIAL·CLEANERS stenciled in block letters on its sides began to pull away from the shady area where it had been parked.

Inside the rear of the truck, Johnny Whitaker stirred. His eyes opened. It was dark all around him—black. He felt the soft material surrounding him. He remembered the wreck—his car hydroplaning on a sheet of water left by the thunderstorm. He remembered being wheeled inside the emergency department. For a moment he thought he was dead and in a coffin—buried.

He screamed and stood up through the soiled linen and towels, wildly throwing them to the side.

Next to the cart, a white face stared at his. He started to scream again—and from behind him a hand clamped tightly across his mouth, and he was wrestled back down into the cart.

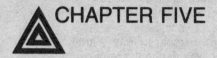

CHAPTER FIVE

GULFPORT-BILOXI REGIONAL AIRPORT

       Shannon, clad in a simple gray skirt and white blouse, sat with the Expedition's windows lowered, letting the warm breeze wash across her face. The last times she had cried had been after the man at the funeral home had told her it would be better if she didn't view her father's body until the damage done to his face had been repaired, and again after she had taken a shower and was dressing in her apartment. But she still had the deep, sick feeling in her stomach. Two charter flights had already come in since she had stopped next to the small terminal. But they had both been larger aircraft, one from Minneapolis, and one from St. Louis, bringing in gamblers to the glittering casinos that lined the beaches. The one bringing her mother back from visiting her sister in Tampa would be a small charter. She looked at her watch.

She heard the sound of the plane before she saw it. It was a twin-engine Cessna. Even before the craft landed, she started walking toward the tarmac.

Her mother came out of the door behind the pilot and co-pilot. Her still-slim figure was clad in a fashionable linen skirt and blouse. She wore high heels and her makeup highlighted her face perfectly. She appeared no different than she ever did. But she betrayed her nervousness by twisting her fingers against her purse as she walked across the runway, and then her lip trembled just before they hugged.

"Why, Shannon?" Despite the long years of divorce, moisture appeared in her mother's eyes.

"Daddy didn't commit suicide, Mother—he was murdered."

In the midst of a tear running down her cheek, her mother brought her hand to her mouth. "Who . . . ? The police said . . ."

"I know what they said. I know what they still believe. But do you? Think about it, Mother. Daddy commit suicide? I don't give a damn about the cancer or anything else."

Her mother stared at her for a moment, then shook her head no. She wiped the tear from her cheek with the back of her finger.

The stocky co-pilot stopped beside them. Two pieces of luggage hung in his hands and a small carrying bag was tucked under one arm. "Are you the daughter?" he asked.

"Yes."

"I'm sorry about your father. I don't see how anything could be much harder on a daughter."

He wore a wedding band. He was middle-aged. He might have a daughter close to her age. "Thank you," she said.

She reached for the luggage.

"I can handle them," he said. "Don't have anything else to do." It was a gesture of compassion, one that almost caused Shannon to lose her composure. But she managed, smiled softly at the man, and nodded toward the Expedition.

As he walked in its direction they followed along behind him. Shannon forced her strength to build again, waiting until she was certain her voice would come out okay, and then asked, "Did Daddy call you within the last few days?"

"No. I . . ." Her mother shook her head. "I wish he had."

"I didn't say anything to Everette, but Daddy called last week. You know how he always used me for a sympathetic ear. It was late, I had already been asleep. He was drinking—enough for it to be obvious. I told him what he had to say had better be important. He asked if I would consider it important if he had just heard about an old problem possibly resurfacing that could take him down in flames with it. You know how dramatic he was. Then he wouldn't go any further, as if I'd irritated him by saying it had better be important and he wanted me to beg him before he would tell me more. I told him to call back the next day. But he didn't, and I didn't think any more about it."

"That sounds like Lawrence might have been depressed. I was trying to remember if he had sounded like that and I hadn't noticed it the—"

"No, Mother. It sounds like last year when he said it was all over for him if he didn't get the added appropriation for the air base."

When her mother nodded without saying anything, Shannon slipped her arm around her and squeezed her shoulders gently. "Maybe it does mean he was depressed, Mother. I don't know. I don't know what anything means yet. Except I know he didn't kill himself."

Her mother smiled feebly and nodded. "Lawrence did sound better to me the last time I spoke with him."

Shannon returned the smile. "I'm going to take you by the house for your car, then I want you to go to the funeral home to make the arrangements. There isn't anybody else but us."

"You're not going with me?"

"I want to go inside the house again and look through it. Have some time alone simply to look. To think."

"Have you already seen Lawrence's . . . the body?"

The memory of what the funeral home people had

said about the repair work flashed through Shannon's mind. She didn't want to mention that. "I haven't seen him yet, and I don't want you to ask to see him either. I want to wait until we can see him together."

"You can't now?"

"I really want to go back through the house, and the sheriff has just released it so I can."

A sign on the door leading into the hospital morgue read CAUTION—FORMALDEHYDE IN USE. Dr. Bacon used his key to unlock the door. Short and balding, he wore thick glasses and was dressed in green surgical scrubs. He stepped aside as a tall, black, male orderly rolled the stretcher containing the sheet-covered body of the teenager, Johnny Whitaker, past him toward the freezer unit.

In a few seconds, the orderly had scribbled Whitaker's name on a tag, wired it to the youth's big toe, and moved the stretcher close to the freezer's four drawers.

He opened one, and was startled that he stared at a little girl's body, her flowing blond hair framing her face, her eyes closed, her mouth slightly agape, and a sheet pulled up around her neck.

Shaking his head with irritation, he pushed the drawer closed, lifted a small red card from the stand next to the freezer, and slipped it inside the holding brackets on the drawer, signifying the drawer was occupied.

Nobody ever did what they were supposed to, he thought, still irritated that whoever had put the child's body inside the drawer hadn't remembered to mark it. But such oversights had happened before, and it hadn't irritated him as much as it did now.

He realized his feeling came from having to be reminded that a child so young had died—a child about the same age as his little girl.

He opened the drawer next to the child's, positioned

the stretcher, and slid Johnny Whitaker's body inside the freezer. As he pushed a card into that drawer's holding brackets, he glanced once more at the drawer that held the child. When he came back toward the door, he left the stretcher behind him.

After Dr. Bacon stepped outside the room and closed and locked the door, he glanced at his watch. He was an early riser, preferring to come into the hospital at daylight, put in his allotted number of hours in pathology during the morning and early afternoon hours, and be gone before three. Today he wasn't even going to stay that long. His grandson's T-ball team was supposed to start playing in thirty minutes. He turned down the hall, walking at a brisk pace.

Any other bodies that might arrive during the afternoon or nighttime hours would be checked into the unit by a nurse, and refrigerated until he could check them out to the coroner or a funeral home the next day.

It was a job that didn't really warrant a pathologist anyway; most hospitals used a nurse or an orderly for such tasks. The extra stipend it paid was why he had volunteered for it, but it was only a small stipend, and he paid no more attention to the job than he had to.

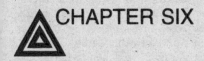# CHAPTER SIX

The luggage lay on the floorboard behind the Expedition's front seats. Shannon waited in the driveway as her mother backed her Lincoln out of the garage, past the white Cadillac.

Her mother lowered the window and glanced at the Cadillac and back to her. "Shannon, your father didn't marry me for the political connections my father had. I know some people think that. He certainly didn't marry me for the money I had; after father passed away Lawrence wouldn't spend a penny of my money on his campaign. That's when he met Mr. Waverly. Lawrence said it was the best thing that ever happened to him. But it was the worst. He didn't have to worry about funding his campaigns anymore, but he was already working sixty-hour weeks in his first two terms, and then when he met Mr. Waverly . . . Mr. Waverly was so demanding. But your father didn't see it that way. All he saw was somebody who might help him to be President someday. He was hardly ever home after that. You remember. We just fell apart, your father and I. Lawrence still loved you more than anything."

Shannon nodded. "I know."

Her mother glanced toward the house. "Are you certain that you want to keep going back in there? I know how it has to look. We could get somebody over here to . . . clean up."

"I'm all right, Mother."

Her mother stared at her for a moment, then backed the Lincoln toward the drive without saying any more. As she turned onto the street, Shannon stared after her for a few seconds, then walked to the Cadillac.

She parked it in the garage, lifted her father's coat from the passenger seat and carried it inside the house to the hall closet. She paused a moment, looking at the coat. Why would someone planning on killing themselves take off their coat and leave it in the car to keep it from getting wet? Why would they care? She stared at the garment a moment longer, then hung it at the far side of some winter clothes.

She looked toward the living room, and thought about her father sitting in the chair and somebody walking inside the house with a gun—the pane in the door had been broken out, so anybody could have come inside. What could he have done except for what he was told if that person had a gun?

But it wasn't just any gun he had been killed with. It had been his own shotgun. Somebody had to have kept him silent while somebody else went for the weapon where it was kept in the bedroom closet. So were two people involved?

She walked into the bedroom. Black fingerprint powder coated the closet's doorknob and ran up and down its front edge. The sheriff was trying his best.

Back in the living room she stared at the chair for a moment, and thought about her mother coming back from the funeral home to see inside the house for the first time. She used the wall telephone in the kitchen rather than the one next to the chair.

"Edgar, I wonder if you would mind bringing your truck over and hauling off a chair and a couple of other things . . . Oh, yes, Edgar, I appreciate your saying that about Daddy . . . Yes, I know . . . Yes . . . He thought a lot of you, too."

*   *   *

Thirty minutes later, Shannon watched the easy chair, throw rug, and the shade from the table lamp ride away in the rear of Edgar's old pickup truck. She had a fleeting urge to run after the pickup and tell him she had changed her mind about having the blood-stained pieces hauled to a dump. Was there some evidence of murder leaving with them? But she had forced herself to examine every inch of the rug, and ran her hands down past the hard, dried blood into the deepest recesses around the chair's cushion, carefully feeling for anything that might be there before she sent anything away. All she found were two pennies behind the cushion, a scattering of cookie crumbs, and a paper clip. The only evidence the sheriff had been interested in anyway was the note, the shoe with the tiny fragments of glass in its heel, the shotgun he thought her father had used on himself, and the bottle of Chivas Regal that showed her father was upset enough to be drinking heavily—the things that proved a suicide.

She looked toward the center of the living room. She had managed to mop almost all of the blood from the floor. There were a few dark streaks that had resisted her hardest effort. She walked into the kitchen to the cabinet under the sink and opened it, looking for the small can of paint remover she remembered being there, hoping it would be strong enough to dissolve the streaks.

She saw the can, but never reached for it as her father's phone call of the week before passed through her mind once again. On the surface, the call wouldn't have given her cause for a second thought, even with his having said something was going on that could cause his career to come crashing down—he was always so overly dramatic. Probably what kept the thought coming back was that he had hung up without really saying what he had called for. More particularly, he had hung up without arguing after she said she had to get back to sleep. Usually he would demand that she take the time to listen—and right then—no matter what else she was doing. She could remember times when he caught her in her office and insisted she listen to every last detail of his problem, even when she had clients waiting.

She tried to recall what he had said—not what she had paraphrased for her mother, but his exact words. She remembered "*an old problem possibly recurring.*" No, first he had said he had "*just heard.*" He had "*just heard about an old problem possibly recurring that could cause me as much trouble as the ones causing the problem—cause my career to come crashing down in flames. Is that important enough?*"

Her father was dead. That made anything important enough. Any little thing. Any big thing. Anything at all.

She walked to the telephone mounted on the wall next to the doorway leading back into the living room. As she reached for the receiver, she looked out the window past the breakfast table and saw a TV van with call letters she didn't recognize stopping on the street in front of the house. She turned back to the telephone and punched in the number of her father's Washington office.

"Congressman Donnelly's office," a woman answered in a soft Southern accent that sounded more South Georgia than Mississippi.

"Is Robert Samples in?" He would know better than anyone what had been on her father's mind—if there had really been anything serious about the call. Samples was her father's administrative assistant. His right-hand man ever since he had first held office. What one of them knew, the other knew.

"Mr. Samples is not available at the moment, ma'am. May I be of assistance?"

"I'm Shannon Donnelly, Congressman Donnelly's daughter."

There was a sudden dead silence on the line.

"Hello?"

"Oh, Miss Donnelly," the woman said in a voice

softer even than the one with which she had answered. "I'm so sorry about your father."

"I appreciate your saying that. Do you think when Mr. Samples comes in you could tell him that I have something I'd like to ask him? I'll be at my mother's home."

"Of course. He should be back at any moment. I am so sorry about your father. We didn't even know he had left Washington."

The staff hadn't known? Shannon thought. "Thank you," she said and slowly replaced the receiver. The staff hadn't known he had come to Biloxi? With all the committees her father served on—some of them he even headed—what would the staff have been able to tell other congressmen calling with important committee questions? Even when he went on vacation he usually kept a cellular phone close at hand.

To just up and leave?

To come to Biloxi unannounced?

And not even call me to say he was coming? He almost never came without calling her to ask her to pick him up at the airport whether he landed in Biloxi or New Orleans. It was one of the ways he got time alone with her to talk. He had done that ever since she had received her driver's license as a teenager.

Her thoughts paused for a moment as her gaze fell on the folded newspaper lying on the counter on the other side of the kitchen. It was something her mother would recognize as not being there when she left for Tampa. It was only a small reminder of the horror that had happened while she was gone, nothing like the reminder of the chair and throw rug missing from the living room. But it would be a reminder nevertheless.

She walked to the counter, lifted the newspaper, opened the cabinet under the sink, and started to toss the paper into the waste can. But she suddenly felt hesitant at disposing of something her father had held in his hands only moments before he died. It was only a thought born of emotion, but she pulled the paper back.

It was a copy of the *Sun Herald*, the coastal newspaper—actually only a section of the paper. She noticed the date showed it was six days old. Her brow wrinkled with her thought—had he brought it with him from Washington?

Thinking of him reading the paper caused another thought to pass through her mind. *A person calmly reading a newspaper only hours before he killed himself? Calm, and on the way back home to kill himself at the same time?*

She thought of her father's coat again. *Holding the paper over his head to keep the rain off? Leaving the coat in the car to keep it from getting wet?* She could visualize someone walking slowly, depressed, through the downpour, on his way to commit suicide—such a person wouldn't care if he got soaked or not. But a man . . . her father not only protecting himself from the rain but leaving his coat lying in the car so it wouldn't get wet— *so he could wear it again?*

None of it made sense. It showed even more he hadn't been contemplating suicide.

And then another thought entered her mind—one she really didn't want there. Her feeling a compunction at throwing the paper away had been caused by emotion. She had recognized that. But was emotion also giving undue importance to the thoughts that kept jumping into her mind about what her father had said and done? The phone call had seemed like it might be important; her father was upset over something he had heard. She wondered if it could have had anything to do with his murder. Maybe the call had been the reason he had left Washington without telling those he normally would. His sudden leaving in itself without telling anyone also seemed important. His reading a newspaper on the plane meant he wasn't in the frame of mind to commit suicide—she had decided that. And she had decided he tried to keep his coat from getting wet because he knew he was going to be wearing it again. All important thoughts. All told her something.

Or was his keeping the coat from getting wet simply an action born of habit? And why not glance through a newspaper during the trip from Washington? He would have done something to pass the time during the flight no matter what his state of mind. Was she making something out of even the most trivial things, of everything, and not wanting to face that it was emotion making her do so? Was she so upset over her father's death that she refused to accept what everybody else saw to be obvious?

"No," she said, and shook her head to drive away her doubt before it could harden into concrete. Maybe any one thing she had thought of could be explained away simply—but not everything. Especially his not calling her when he arrived in Biloxi. Most especially him killing himself in her mother's house.

She looked at the paper. It was wrinkled and stiff from the rain. It was folded. Its upper third was filled with columns containing a continuation of an article about family tragedy support groups from an earlier page. Its lower two thirds were filled with black-and-white blocks of advertising for flower shops and funeral homes and the like.

She unfolded the section and looked at the other side. It was the coastal obituary page.

Somebody Daddy knew had died?

She scanned through the listings of the deceased.

She didn't recognize any of the names.

The telephone rang.

She walked across the kitchen and answered it.

"Mrs. Donnelly?" a male voice asked.

"This is Shannon, Mrs. Donnelly's daughter."

"Shannon, this is Joseph Marzullo. I wanted to call and express my deep sadness at your father's death."

"Thank you, Doctor. I appreciate all you did for my father. I was going to call you. The sheriff said you mentioned his depression. I talked to him nearly every week. He didn't appear to me to be—"

"I'm sorry, Shannon," Marzullo said without letting her finish. "I feel guilty about that. I had only known Lawrence since the bypass surgery, but I'm proud to say he had allowed me to become his confidant. He was really down, Shannon, but he didn't want you and your mother to know how badly he felt. He said he didn't want to burden you with any more worry. I can look back on it now and see how depressed he was. I should have mentioned something to you or your mother. But I never dreamed he . . ." Marzullo's sigh was audible across the line. "I can see it now, though, Shannon. What he was going to do was written in everything he said over the last few days."

She wanted to ask exactly what her father had said. But what good would that do? And she had already heard more than she wanted to hear. She thanked Marzullo again for his call, and slowly replaced the receiver.

"I can see it now," Marzullo had said. *"What he was going to do was written in everything he said over the last few days."*

The doctor who had performed her father's bypass, the doctor who had talked to him nearly daily by telephone when her father was back in Washington and still suffering the depression from the bypass surgery. The doctor who she knew her father had called to speak with immediately after the cancer had been diagnosed. As a cardiologist, Dr. Marzullo hadn't been called for any expertise in cancer, but because of a friendship that had developed.

She could feel her ardent belief that her father's death was due to murder rather than suicide being tested more than she thought possible when she rushed to the house after receiving the call from the deputy. She wondered if she could be tested anymore and still be able to go on trying to find out what had happened. And she really hadn't learned anything yet.

And didn't know where to start. But she had to start somewhere. She had to do something.

She closed her eyes tightly to force the doubt from her mind once again—then looked back at the newspaper.

After speaking with Shannon, Dr. Marzullo folded his small cellular telephone and slipped it back inside the breast pocket of his scrubs.

Now he leaned over the linen cart, which was shaking from the motion of the van. He lifted a towel out of the way and felt for Johnny Whitaker's pulse. The first sedative he had given the boy had been so light it hadn't lasted as long as it had been meant to, and the youth had come awake while the truck was still at the hospital. There had been some danger in giving another sedative so quickly behind the first one, but the youth's pulse was pounding a solid, steady rhythm, evidence of how strong his heart was. That was especially good, Marzullo thought, as he straightened from the cart. Then he saw Johnny's eyes slowly open, and then close. The teenager stirred, moving his hands. Marzullo looked at the stocky man standing among the other linen carts and nodded down at Johnny.

The man stepped closer to the cart.

Marzullo walked to the small window in the side of the truck. They were passing the bayou. Tall cypress and willows rose out of the dark, algae-covered waters. A small alligator sunned himself on a sliver of mud grown thick with water grass. Then Marzullo looked ahead toward the curve where the narrow highway turned past the end of the bayou toward the complex. In a few minutes they would be safely inside the tall fence. It always made him feel better when they were.

The only difference this time was how quickly he was going to have to provide still another subject. It would be the last time he would ever have to provide a subject, but so many so close together was dangerous.

◭CHAPTER SEVEN

When Shannon's mother stepped inside the house after returning from the funeral home, she took one look toward the open area where the missing easy chair and throw rug had been, and walked immediately toward the kitchen.

Shannon stood beside the kitchen doorway, holding the receiver of the wall-mounted telephone to her ear. She covered the mouthpiece with her hand. "Mother, are you certain Daddy didn't say anything that you can remember about his being more depressed than we thought?"

"No. Nothing," her mother said.

Shannon nodded across the kitchen toward the newspaper section lying on the counter. "He brought that with him from Washington. Do you recognize any names?"

Her mother walked to the counter and looked at the obituary page, folded with the columns of death notices showing. A few seconds later, she shook her head. "Why do you ask?"

"I wondered if someone Daddy knew died." The number Shannon was calling hadn't answered, and she replaced the receiver.

"You know how Lawrence was, Shannon, always mailing birthday cards to voters in the district, sending them notes of congratulations on their anniversaries . . . sending out condolence letters."

Shannon nodded. She had known that was what her father would do—send out a condolence letter. As many people as he knew, there was always someone who had a family member die. To make a special trip here he would have had to be especially close to the person, or at least to someone in their family. But if it was someone that close, he wouldn't have to wait until the paper arrived in his office to know about their death. She lifted the notepad where she had scribbled down the telephone numbers of the next of kin in the death notices, looked at the next one on the list, lifted the telephone receiver and punched the number into it.

"What are you doing, Shannon?"

"I don't know."

Her mother stared at her for a moment, then walked to the door at the rear of the kitchen. Stopping before its glass panels, she stared out across the back yard.

"Mother," Shannon said, looking toward the door. "I really don't know what I'm doing. I don't know what happened, or why. I don't know why Daddy got his car from the apartment and came here instead of staying at the apartment. I don't know why he flew in here without telling anybody, especially not calling me. I don't know why he brought the obituary page with him. Its date means he probably received it in the mail only a day or two ago, maybe yesterday before he got on the plane. He might not have even read the newspaper until then. So is that all it is—he was catching up on the area news and had finished the other sections and left them on the plane? I don't know. But the way my mind is working right now, trying to understand what happened, if I saw a caterpillar crawling in the living room I'd call an entomologist and ask if he had any idea why a caterpillar would be in the house. I know I'm grasping at straws. But what else can I do? All I know for certain is that Daddy didn't commit suicide. Over cancer or anything else."

The number she had called kept ringing. "Damn," she said and disconnected the line. She looked at the next number on the list, and punched it into the receiver.

This time the line rang only once, and was answered by a female with a high-pitched voice.

"Ma'am, this is Shannon Donnelly. My father is Congressman Donnelly. I was wondering if you or any member of your family might be acquainted with him."

"We don't give contributions to nobody," the woman came back.

"This isn't about a contribution, ma'am. It's . . . my father passed away last night, and I'm trying to notify anyone who might have been a friend of his. He . . ." Shannon looked at the obituary columns. "He had Richard Johnston's name listed in his rolodex."

"Richard's? That was my husband. He passed last week. I sure'n hell don't know why his name would be in there. You sure it was spelled J-O-H-N-S-T-O-N?"

"Your husband didn't know the congressman?"

"If he did, I didn't know about it. Of course if you don't mind my saying so, I'm finding out about other people I didn't know about either, if you get my meaning—women. My next-door neighbor just this morning told me—"

"Yes, ma'am," Shannon said. "Thank you."

She replaced the receiver and looked at the next number on the notepad.

"Honey," her mother said, turning to face her, "maybe you should do as Sheriff Everette said—just let it go."

"Mother, Daddy was murdered."

Her mother turned back toward the glass panes in the door.

As she did, a light bumping sound came from the direction of the living room as the air-conditioner compressor kicked on. A moment later, there was another light, muffled sound and the unit's fan started, sending cool air flowing down from the ceiling vents in the kitchen.

Behind Shannon, a light fixture with a green shade surrounding two small bulbs hung above the breakfast table. A flow of air from a vent close to the table passed across the fixture, causing it to sway slightly.

In the small monitoring room twenty miles away, the flow of air blowing across the listening device at the base of a light bulb in the fixture in the Donnelly kitchen sounded much like the noise of a shallow stream meandering across rocks. A short, stocky man in a dark windbreaker leaned forward and adjusted one of the EQ slides on the speaker before him. He reduced the frequency of the sound of the air flow, lowering the noise, and increased the frequencies most prevalent in Shannon's and her mother's voices, making their words easier to understand. Then he looked up over his shoulder at a towering man, his wide shoulders slumping beneath the material of a similar windbreaker as he stood beside the chair.

"What do you think, Murphy?"

"What I think is how in the hell did you miss seeing the friggin' newspaper when you put the bulb in the fixture?"

"Hey, Murphy, I was hurrying all over the house getting them in—it was dark in the kitchen. I . . ."

He averted his gaze at Murphy's glare. "I just missed it."

Murphy stared at the man for a moment, then turned his gaze to the visual monitors.

The truck with COASTAL COMMERCIAL CLEANERS lettered on its sides was turning off the highway onto the narrow blacktop leading to the gate.

▲ CHAPTER EIGHT

The linen truck came slowly toward the gate fronting the research complex. To the gate's sides, an eight-foot-tall chain-link fence circled the ten acres of grounds, separating them from the heavily wooded area that surrounded the complex. Two structures rose within the fence, one of them a large, sprawling building of metal construction. The other was much smaller, built out of cement block, and crowned with a high-peaked roof covered with aging, dark shingles. This smaller building was the one the truck drove toward after it passed through the gate.

Nearing the blocky structure the truck turned in a short circle, then backed toward the building's front door. It stopped only a few feet away. The door to the facility opened.

A man in a white lab coat hanging open over jeans and a grayed T-shirt stepped outside. Of shorter than average height, he appeared to be in his late forties, with black hair and a narrow face made to seem wider by bushy sideburns extending down into his beard.

The driver hurried to the back of the truck and opened its wide double doors.

Dr. Marzullo, still dressed in his green scrubs and a lab jacket, and two men in khakis dropped to the ground.

They reached back into the truck, caught the

stretcher resting flat on the floor of the truck bed, and pulled it toward them.

The stretcher's legs popped down as it came clear of the blocky vehicle. Johnny Whitaker, his eyes wide, his head moving wildly back and forth, lay on his back on the stretcher, his arms strapped to its sides and his ankles to its end. A thick strap encircled his waist from under the stretcher.

"Pllleease," he muttered in a slurred voice.

Back toward the larger building, a tall security guard in a dark windbreaker kept watch on the employee parking lot to make certain no one came outside.

"Pllleeease," the teenager begged once more as Marzullo pushed the stretcher inside the blocky building. "What are you doing?"

The bearded man closed the door behind them.

The truck, with its driver and the men in khakis, slowly drove away from the building.

Ahead of the truck, the wide gates in the chain-link fence began to open again.

Johnny stared at the spacious area around him as the stretcher was rolled across the floor. It was like a hotel lobby. To his sides, wide windows were covered with tightly drawn curtains. The stretcher moved past a card table and an easy chair. A black orderly in khakis stared expressionlessly from his spot in front of the steel door they were approaching. As they neared it, there was a metallic click and the door swung open.

The bearded man stepped inside first, then Johnny was rolled through the doorway into another spacious area. His eyes narrowed when he saw the two barred cells off to the side, and then widened when he saw the short, blocky figure, dressed in nothing but a pair of gray shorts, standing inside one of the cells, staring at him.

The stretcher turned abruptly and swept under a bright overhead light toward another steel door. MED-

ICAL SUPPLY was printed across a placard on its front.

The door opened.

They entered a much smaller room. Three of the walls were lined with shelves packed with small boxes and bottles. The other wall was stacked waist-high with large cardboard boxes.

"Dr. Lobb," the orderly called from the open area.

The bearded man turned away from the stretcher and walked back out the door. Dr. Marzullo started sliding the cardboard boxes away from the wall.

Johnny tried to see back over his head into the other area. Dr. Lobb, scratching a side of his beard, stepped back inside the room. His dark, sunken eyes stared coldly into Johnny's. Johnny averted his gaze, tried to keep his voice level. "Please," he said. "What are you doing?"

Dr. Marzullo had finished moving the boxes from the wall. Dr. Lobb pulled a small, black oblong device that resembled a garage-door opener from his lab coat.

He pressed the button at the device's center.

A metallic click sounded, and a door-sized section of the wall slid back.

Marzullo caught the end of the stretcher and pulled it through the opening.

Directly in front of him sat two long operating tables. Medical equipment cased in black plastic covers surrounded the tables. "Oh, no," Johnny said when he saw the glass cabinet full of surgical instruments. "No."

Marzullo turned the stretcher past the foot of the operating tables and guided it toward a door in the far wall.

Lobb pressed a second button on the small black device.

Another metallic click, and the door swung open.

Two narrow beds, separated only by the width of a black, metal box the size of a large portable TV, sat just inside the door. Thick leather straps hung from their sides.

A screeching sound came from off to the left.

Johnny's head turned on the stretcher to see two cages the size of oil drums hanging from the ceiling.

Each contained a monkey within the confined space. Johnny knew animals. Under his bed at home was a stack of wildlife books he had been collecting since he had been a little boy, but he didn't recognize either of the species. One monkey's body was lean and covered with dark brown and black hair, almost identical to a spider monkey's build and coat—except its head was surrounded by light gray hair sticking out to the sides rather than the black hair of such a monkey. Its thin fingers hooked through the wire mesh, it canted its head to the side as it continued to stare.

The other monkey's slightly heavier body was completely covered with light gray hair, up to its neck, where the hair became abruptly black, and stayed that solid color as it ran up around the head and framed a light-complected face. A spider monkey's face?

For the first time it registered on Johnny that each animal had a shaved area around its neck, and lines of stitches following the shaved areas.

And then he understood.

The head on the gray monkey was a spider monkey's head. *The* spider monkey's head. And the head that had once sat on the gray-haired monkey's body, now belonged to the spider monkey.

Johnny's mouth gaped in shock.

Then out of the corner of his eyes he saw Dr. Lobb approach. The bearded man had pulled on latex gloves and held a syringe with a long needle.

"*No!*" Johnny yelled. He looked at the monkeys and shook his head wildly. "*No! No! NOOO! Please, God, no!*"

The monkeys screamed back at him, their fangs showing, the loud screams coming up from each animal's lungs through mouths they hadn't been born with.

"NOOO!"

Dr. Lobb laid his hand on the teenager's head above the bandage covering the laceration and shaved scalp, and pushed his face to the side. Johnny forced his head back against the pressure. *"NOOO!"* he screamed again.

The monkeys screeched louder and shook their cages.

"No, please!"

Johnny fought against Lobb's hand with a sudden increased strength born of terror. Lobb gestured with a sideways motion of his head for Marzullo to help him.

Marzullo grabbed the boy's face in both hands and violently twisted his head to the side.

Dr. Lobb pinched the needle just behind its point and pushed it into the skin.

"No, God, no! Please!"

The monkeys screamed.

Lobb slid his fingers an inch back up the needle's length and slowly pushed it farther into Johnny's neck.

"God, please! Please!"

Shannon held the telephone receiver to her ear as the number rang. She was about to hang up, when an answering machine came on.

"DUE TO THE REDUCTION IN PERSONNEL AT THIS HOUSE, THIS PHONE IS NO LONGER BEING CONSTANTLY MONITORED."

A light chuckle followed the words.

"NO, ME AND MARIE HAVEN'T UP AND GOT A DIVORCE, JUST OUR NIECE FROM CALIFORNIA'S GONE BACK TO WHEREVER IT IS SHE'S OFF TO THIS TIME. SO IF YOU'VE GOT A MESSAGE FOR JOE OR MARIE, JUST LEAVE IT AT THE BEEP AND WE'LL GET BACK TO YOU AS SOON AS WE CAN."

A series of short chirps began. The sounds went on and on. Shannon lost count.

Then the beep sounded.

"This is Shannon Donnelly. If anyone receives this, if you would please call me back I would appreciate it."

She gave her number and slowly replaced the receiver. The number of chirps she had heard, indicating the number of messages already on the machine, told her no one had retrieved the Englands' messages in some time—maybe since their deaths a few days before. Maybe no one was staying at the house and the telephone hadn't yet been turned off. The only next of kin listed in their obituary notices had been two small children; Ryder, six, and Cash, three. There must have been the niece and the niece's parents—but they hadn't been listed. The funeral home would know who made the arrangements for the burials. She lifted the receiver and punched in information.

As she waited, she lifted the newspaper section and looked at the Englands' death notices. Joe England was listed as having been employed by the Waverly Research Center west of Gulfport, while Marie's occupation was listed as housewife. They were the last names to check on from the columns. All but one of the people she had already called had known of her father. Several had met him. Two claimed to have had old ties, but hadn't spoken with him in years. But what if they had? What would that tell her anyway? She thought of Dr. Marzullo's words: *What he was going to do was written in everything he said the last few days.* She felt it all slipping away.

Jonathan Waverly was sixty-four years old, but looked more like an ailing man in his eighties. The suit he wore was custom-tailored. When he had first donned it a year before, it had fit his thin body perfectly. With the additional weight he had lost since then, it now hung loose across his frame. He didn't care. The two-day growth of whisker stubble covering his hollowed cheeks showed how little he cared about his appearance. His thinning, white hair was uneven where it hung down over his ears, as if it had been trimmed with hedge clippers, and not in weeks at that. But a smile lightened his face

He leaned over Dr. Katie Dethloff's shoulder. Her dishwater-blond hair hung down the back of her lab coat nearly to her waist. She wore thick glasses. She had been staring through a double-barreled stereo microscope. She slipped a slide from underneath the lenses and held it up for him to see.

"Noticeable regeneration," she said. "More noticeable every time."

Waverly's smile broadened.

They were in a laboratory that measured fifty feet square. She sat on a stool at a long counter running down the wall. Various kinds of equipment ranging from Bunsen burners to small racks full of old slides to an autoclave sat on the counter. A glass cabinet full of surgical instruments stood against the wall at the end of the counter. Across the concrete floor behind her, a wide arrangement of wire cages the size of shoe boxes were layered one on top of the other against the far wall. Each held a single white rat.

Waverly glanced at the cages, but walked toward the far end of the laboratory.

He used a magnetic card from his pocket to unlock and open the steel door there.

The smile still on his face, he stepped inside the room and flipped a switch on the wall just inside the door, turning on the overhead light.

More cages lined the walls of this much smaller room. Each of them held a rat. A small white card on the side of each cage listed the occupant as female or male by the letters F and M. Each of them had an identifying number before the letters, and each had the notation ONE HUNDRED PERCENT to the right of the letters.

One rat, its hindquarters slumping lower than would seem normal, moved forward inside an exercise wheel attached to the inside of his cage, going nowhere as the little cylinder turned at a pace that matched the rodent's slow strides.

"Looks like 10–M is enjoying himself," Waverly said in a raspy yet soft voice as Dr. Dethloff stepped up beside him.

She nodded and smiled. "He's our champion," she said.

None of the other rats were so active, though some were walking slowly across the sawdust that lined the bottom of the cages. All the rodents seemed to be slumped on their hind quarters. All displayed a tail that hung noticeably straight down, trailing along behind them in the sawdust. Waverly's smile broadened when he saw that even the two rats displaying the least amount of movement nevertheless had the muscle control to hold their front shoulders up and their heads erect—and they were the two that had enjoyed the least amount of recovery time since surgery.

Waverly's smile suddenly disappeared.

He had noticed the rat that seemed to be stretched out lazily, its forepaws and hindpaws extended to the limit—but in fact was dragging itself forward with its front paws, its rear legs and back half of its body dragging uselessly behind it.

"Which one is he?" he asked sharply.

"Surgery before last," the woman said in a low voice. "He seems to be an aberration that isn't responding to—"

"Dispose of him," Waverly said.

"Mr. Waverly, there's always going to be the tiny percentage that doesn't respond properly. I wouldn't let it worry—"

"*Kill him!*" Waverly roared so loudly that Dethloff flinched. She stepped immediately toward the cages.

Waverly turned from the room.

The color had drained from his face.

He looked frightened.

◭ CHAPTER NINE

The funeral arrangements for the Englands had been made by Ronald and Barbara McAffey, a couple who had been friends with them for years. They were currently acting as foster parents for the two minor England children, and planned to adopt them. Mr. McAffey was the one who answered Shannon's call. He responded in a compassionate tone when she said she was the daughter of Congressman Donnelly. "I'm real sorry about your father. Me and Barbara thought a lot of what he had done for the people down here."

"Thank you. I hate to bother you, but I was wondering if you happen to know whether the Englands knew my father?"

"Knew him well, Miss Donnelly. Years ago your father pulled off a favor for Joe. Joe's been hammering up signs for him in every election since then. Actually spoke on the phone with him every once in a while." McAffey chuckled softly. "Liked to brag about it."

So there had been someone who died that her father had been close to. Maybe close enough that he would have come back to Biloxi for their funerals. But that didn't make sense—the Englands had been buried days earlier. Yet he had come back, bringing the column showing their funeral notices. *Spoke on the phone with him every once in a while*, McAffey had said.

"You don't know if Mr. or Mrs. England spoke to my father recently, do you?"

"No, wouldn't have no way of knowing that. I hadn't spoken to Joe in days myself. He'd been out of commission—down with a bad back. In fact, he had been in the hospital right up to the day before the accident. I was surprised that he had gone back out to the center to work. Uh, why do you ask?"

"I'm, uh . . . trying to retrace my father's connections of the last few days. To see if somebody who talked with him heard him mention anything that might have been on his mind."

"Oh, I see. I understand, Miss. You can't keep from wondering, can you? Sorry I can't help you out none there. But, like I said, I hadn't talked to Joe myself in days. You know he was coming back from there when the accident happened—the center. Him and Marie. It was one of those horrible coincidences that they was together. He had car trouble and she had gone out there to pick him up. She lost control of their pickup and went into a bayou. Thank God she had left the children with us."

"Yes," Shannon said. "They had a niece."

"Sandra? Yes, but she won't be able to help you none, either. She left for somewhere in Europe last month and we weren't able to get ahold of her for the funeral. See her so seldom we even forgot to give the funeral home her name for the obituary column. And Joe's sister and brother-in-law were killed in a plane crash years ago. It's just Ryder and Cash now and us praying we can do as good a job bringing them up as Joe and Marie would."

Shannon thanked the man, told him she appreciated his taking the time to speak with her, and replaced the telephone receiver. She felt disheartened. She had finally found someone who had known her father well but had learned nothing of use. What had she expected to hear? She had been just wildly grasping at straws.

Then McAffey's words went through her mind again. *Actually spoke on the phone with him every once in a while.* Somebody *had* to have spoken to her father, either in person or on the telephone the day he had called her late at night. Somebody who had given him the information he had *just heard* that upset him, something that had led to his calling her. She glanced at her watch and frowned. The receptionist had said Robert Samples would return at any moment, but had never called back. She lifted the receiver and punched in her father's office number in Washington again.

This time the administrative assistant was in.

"Shannon, I just tried to call you and the line was busy. I tried your mother earlier this morning, but there was nobody there then."

"We've been in and out," she said. "Mr. Samples, I . . . Daddy called me last week. He—"

"Please call me Robert," Samples said. "As long as we've known each other. It has been a long time, hasn't it?"

"Yes, it has. And I appreciate all you meant to Daddy. Robert, he seemed upset about something when he called, but he never really told me what it was. Do you know of anything that might have been bothering him?"

"You mean something bothering him to the point that he . . ."

"No. Not that way. It was more like he was worried about something political. He often called me when he wanted to get something off his chest. But he really didn't get into anything specific this time, only that something had upset him. The only concrete thing he said was that whatever was bothering him was something he had *just* heard from somebody, like maybe that night or earlier in the day, something about an old problem maybe recurring."

"I can't imagine him upset about anything that he wouldn't have mentioned to me," Samples said. "But then, on the other hand, he kept from me how . . ." Samples was silent for a moment. "He really did a good job of keeping how depressed he was from me. I mean, I know he wasn't happy with what he was facing. But he seemed to be able to keep his mind on what was going on here. It was one time I was glad he had so much to do."

"Robert, did Daddy keep a log of his conversations?"

"Pardon me?"

"Did Daddy keep any kind of record of his conversations?"

"Well, he had a notepad where he kept up with appointments. He wrote in that once in a while to remind himself of what the meeting was going to concern. Sometimes he wrote a note there after a meeting—if it was something he needed to remember. But there was nothing in it about him being upset or anything."

"Excuse me?"

"I said there was nothing in it about him being upset, depressed, or anything like that. The FBI came by early this morning. We looked at the notebook. Anywhere Lawrence might have made a notation about anything out of the ordinary. They went through his apartment, too. They questioned the staff."

"You don't recall him being upset after anyone came in the office?"

"I don't see any way I would have missed that. When somebody was in a meeting with him I was usually there. Even when I wasn't, I was usually in there right after the meeting."

"But you might not have known about a phone call."

"One that upset him? I believe he would have mentioned it to me."

"But you can't be certain. Robert, there's something you can do for me."

"Certainly."

"I don't believe Daddy committed suicide."

The aide didn't respond.

"Robert?"

"Didn't he leave a note? The FBI said he did."

"You knew him better than anybody. Do you really think he was the type to commit suicide?"

There was another silence.

She spoke into it without waiting for an answer. "The night Daddy called me was last Monday. I want to see his office telephone records from a couple of days before that up to when he left Washington—every number he called. I want the records for the phone in his apartment, too. The telephone company wouldn't produce them for me, but they will for you; the bill would come to the office anyway."

Her father had come hurriedly to Biloxi. He had been murdered in Biloxi. It stood to reason that what had caused him to be upset was in Biloxi, or close along the coastal area. It was possible that somebody had called him from the area and told him whatever it was that caused him to be upset, that initiated everything that followed. He might have called back whoever it was. The telephone records would contain the numbers of everyone he had called. Maybe among them would be the person she was looking for.

"Are you going to help me, Robert?"

In the small monitoring room twenty miles away, Murphy, his wide shoulders slumped under the material of his windbreaker, reached for the telephone next to the wide bank of speakers. He pushed a button at the phone's base and lifted the receiver.

The sound of a receiver being lifted came through the telephone from the other end of line, but no one spoke.

"She's asking for her old man's telephone records now," he said.

"That won't mean anything," a voice on the other end of the line said.

"What about the telephone call?"

"Lawrence called here a dozen times a month. It won't mean anything."

"At midnight?"

"What difference does it make what time he called?"

And then there was the clear sound of the receiver being replaced at the other end of the line.

Murphy frowned. Dr. Lobb was always so short. Arrogant. Probably sniffing one of those little rocks up his nose again. *Crazy bastard.*

And doctors were supposed to be smart?

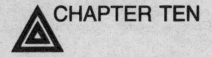

CHAPTER TEN

The **Waverly Research Center** consisted of two single-story buildings located within a ten-acre complex surrounded by an eight-foot-tall chain-link fence. Michael knew the largest building, a structure sided with wide sheets of metal paneling, was where the manufacturing and testing of experimental medical microrobotics machines and instruments took place. The smaller building with the high-peaked roof and dark shingles had originally been the barn and tractor storage facility of the family who lived there when the acreage making up the complex and the surrounding woods had been a small cattle farm. Now it was the building where a handful of mental patients were housed.

They had been selected from mental hospitals across the country. Their common characteristic was that each of them suffered from spinal cord damage in addition to their mental illnesses. The states that had allowed the patients to be transferred had welcomed being relieved of the financial burden of caring for those both physically and mentally ill. The patients' relatives had been only too happy to see their loved ones moved into a facility that provided much better care than they had ever known before.

Michael stopped his Jeep at the entrance gate. It was

a few seconds before it slowly began to slide back alongside the fence.

Jonathan Waverly had said he would be waiting in the front offices located on the far end of the larger building. Michael turned the Jeep in that direction. As he drove toward the building, he noted that despite its size, there seemed to be far fewer workers than he would have expected on a daytime shift; there were only four cars and a single pickup truck in the big parking lot.

Back to his left, a camera hanging under the eaves of the mental health facility swung its lens in sync with the Jeep's movement.

A half dozen cars were lined side by side in the parking spaces in front of the offices. Waverly's white limousine was parked there. Michael parked in the open space next to the long vehicle. The response to his arriving at the offices was even quicker than when he arrived at the gate. The building's front door opened immediately and a towering man with wide slumping shoulders walked outside. He wore jeans and a dark windbreaker with WAVERLY RESEARCH CORPORATION emblazoned down its back. The front of the windbreaker had a patch that stated GROUNDS SECURITY. He had a can of mace strapped to his belt, but otherwise bore no weapons. He smiled pleasantly. Michael noticed the long scar running through the man's left eyebrow up into his hairline.

"I'm Murphy," the man said as they shook hands. "Mr. Waverly is pleased you decided to speak with him."

He had a Massachusetts accent.

Jonathan Waverly waited in a large, carpeted office down a hallway behind the building's reception area. The first thing Michael noted when Murphy showed him into the office was how different Waverly's appearance was from his appearance on *Biography*. He had looked much younger and had been clean-shaven. Now, a two-day growth of beard spotted a gaunt face. He reminded Michael of the photographs he had seen of the emaciated Howard Hughes the last weeks of his life, except Waverly's coloring appeared even paler than Hughes's had been. He didn't look like a well man.

Waverly came to his feet, smiled pleasantly, and nodded toward a straight chair in front of his desk. "Dr. Sims," he said in a raspy but soft voice. "I apologize for inconveniencing you. But I am pleased you decided to listen to what I have to say."

What Michael wanted to tell the aging billionaire was that it really made no difference what he had to say. Michael felt like he had spent what seemed like most of his life getting a medical education, and now he had nothing else on his mind except getting on with his career. But he didn't say that. "I really appreciate your interest in me. I wish I felt I was capable of—"

Waverly cut him off by holding his palm up. "We'll get around to our discussion about the congressional seat later, Doctor," he said. "But for now, let me give you the tour—I think you will find it enlightening."

The Shannon Donnelly law firm had once been a modest single-story home in D'Iberville, a small community joining Biloxi on the north. What had been the shallow front yard now served as a parking lot large enough for a half dozen vehicles. The receptionist's desk and clients' waiting area had been the home's garage. The rear half of the building contained a small conference room, an empty office that used to be the master bedroom, and a kitchen and breakfast room area still serving its original purpose. Shannon's spacious office had been the home's living room. Off to one side of her desk, a fireplace was sunken into the wall. She was turned around in her chair, watching the paper containing the telephone records from her father's Washington apartment come slowly out of the fax machine mounted on a small table behind the desk. Her secretary, Carol, a short, dark-haired woman in her mid-thirties, stood in the office doorway. The machine stopped after the first page.

"That's all?" Carol asked. The copies of the pages Robert Samples had sent containing the calls made from the Washington office in the last ten days had filled a dozen pages. They had listed numerous calls to the coastal area, but all to the local congressional office in Biloxi. They told Shannon nothing. She stared at the fax for a long moment before picking it up.

She saw her number where her father had called her.

A sense of excitement went through her when she saw he had called two other numbers immediately after he spoke with her. *Calling someone after midnight,* she thought. That had to be for an important reason. Then she realized the first number below hers was the Bay St. Louis number of the Englands' residence.

She turned her chair around, lifted the telephone receiver from its base at a side of her desk and punched in the number below the Englands'.

It rang only once.

"Waverly Research Center."

She opened her mouth to speak, but then didn't say anything, and slowly replaced the receiver.

"What?" Carol asked.

"After Daddy spoke with me, he called the Englands, then the Waverly Center. Why?" She looked at the numbers. "Carol, Daddy had been drinking, more than I remember him doing before. It was noticeable. For the alcohol to have taken effect, he must have started drinking at least a couple of hours before he called me. He said he had *just* heard from someone. So somebody called him earlier? That wouldn't be on his bill. I think somebody called him and told him something that worried him enough he started drinking. He called me, then the Englands, then the center." She shook her head as she tried to think. But one thought kept blocking any others from coming through: "The Englands died the next morning."

Carol's brow wrinkled. "What are you saying?"

"Daddy brought the Englands' obituary notices with him when he came in. From the paper's date, it probably arrived in Washington either the day before or the day he left. Maybe their notices are why he came here. What had he told them? What had he told somebody at the Waverly Center?"

"Call and ask," Carol said. "There couldn't have been too many people available to answer the phone that time of night."

She couldn't do that, not with what she knew—and her father calling the Waverly Center after he was worried about an old problem. That's why she had replaced the receiver without speaking when the center's receptionist answered. "Daddy said something about an old problem resurfacing. The Waverly Centers had an old problem."

"Excuse me?"

"When Daddy called me, he said an *old problem* was resurfacing that could take him down with it. Years ago, the Waverly Centers had a serious problem. It's how he met Mr. Waverly. Daddy was on a congressional committee that investigated the Los Angeles Waverly Center. Now he's been supported so closely all these years by Mr. Waverly that if the corporations had another problem, the bad effects could rub off on him— maybe an old problem resurfacing that could take him down with it."

Shannon moved her thumbnail to her teeth.

"Go ahead," Carol said. "Or tell me you're going to leave me hanging so I can get on back to my work."

"No, you're not going back to work. You're going to Daddy's apartment in Gulfport with me."

"Why?"

"Daddy always hoped he could end up being part of

history. He told me once it would be nice if he had a library dedicated to his life's work. He kept a record of everything he was involved with so that it could be in a library someday, or he would have it for his memoirs. The originals are in Washington, and copies of everything are in his apartment here in case there's a fire or something in Washington. The hearings had to do with the theft of unembalmed tissue, an unethical pathologist, and a million-dollar bonus. The media hyped it for weeks."

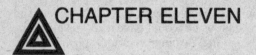

CHAPTER ELEVEN

Jonathan Waverly pushed the double doors open at the rear of the hall and stepped inside an area filled with the low hum of working machinery. Michael looked down a walkway extending back to a partition wall a hundred and fifty feet away. To the sides of the walkway, row after row of stainless steel work tables were mounted with small robotics machinery of varying shapes and sizes. In the row directly to his right, mechanical arms stamped down on small baseball-shaped, glistening containers, turned them over, stamped them again, and lifted them onto a conveyor belt running down the middle of the tables.

"This line of robots is making experimental sensors for use by the Defense Department," Waverly said in his characteristic raspy tone. "This is the only thing we're still doing that's not related to medical research. Frankly, I begrudge the loss of the space for something other than medical technology. But if those small globes you see live up to the expectations we have for them, they'll eventually be made available to the general public for home and business security—and the good that will come out of that will be significant. Inside each of them is more programmed intelligence than a computer the size of a refrigerator could have contained only a few years ago. Someday a homeowner will be able to mount one of those little balls in his back yard and have a monitor let him know if anything ventures near the rear of the home, from another human, to a dog or cat, even down to something as small as a bird flying by—if he desired that function. He could be warned if a child or animal falls in his swimming pool, could even have it tell him which child, if the ball had been exposed to that child's profile before."

They continued down the walkway, Waverly describing different robots and what they were working on, mostly various medical instrumentation he had patents on and had sold to hospitals and research institutes worldwide. "Except this particular table," Waverly said, walking toward a table distinguishable from the others by a basketball-shaped robot with multiple thin mechanical arms bending this way and that, looking much like a giant, metal spider as it lifted and probed a four-inch square, flat piece of metal. As Waverly drew close to the table, the arms suddenly stopped their movement.

"A safety precaution," he said, nodding at a small red light that had started flashing on the table. "If a supervisor gets close enough to the tables that he might be harmed by the movement of the arms, the sensors shut them down until he's a safe distance away again."

Michael realized why there had been so few vehicles in the employee parking area. Only one supervisor was in view, a man in khaki shirt and pants standing next to the near wall several tables down. All that machinery and only one supervisor. Michael recalled a program on the Discovery Channel that featured a Japanese assembly plant where not only was robotics machinery performing all the work, but when one of their own parts became stressed from repetitive movements they could turn away from the assembly line and replace the part from the materials contained in a motorized cart that whizzed their way. Technology was heading toward the day when even the supervisors would be replaced. As Waverly reached for the small section of metal the robot had been working on, Michael looked to the left toward a set of three wide windows along the building's far wall. They didn't afford a view to the outside. It was another work area, brightly lit with several rows of larger robotics machinery at work. Another supervisor, this time a man or woman garbed in a bulky, white protective suit complete with headgear resembling a space helmet stood at the room's rear wall.

Waverly held out the small, flat plate. "This is experimental. We hope to put enough intelligence in this to direct a probe into the groin and up through the circulatory system into the heart. I'm not speaking of the kind of fiber optics used to view arterial obstructions. I'm speaking about a free-standing probe under its own propulsion, directed by this." He laid the plate back on the table.

"And I'm speaking about not only self-propulsion," he added, "but enough intelligence to clear the obstruction itself. It's like the motorized probes that run inside the Alaska pipeline, finding leaks at the same time they're scouring the pipe clean of sludge buildup. In fact, the probes used in the pipeline are where I came up with the idea of a probe cleaning the arteries and veins."

Michael was impressed. It was an exciting medical concept.

Waverly turned his eyes toward the double door in the partition wall at the end of the walkway.

"Now for the fun part of the tour," he said. "Think Disney World and theme parks."

When they walked through the door into the next area, it was dark. Waverly reached to the wall and flicked a switch. Overhead flood lamps bathed the room in dazzling light, revealing an area that appeared more like a large artist's studio than the area of glistening machines they had left. Paint cans sat on the floor, and wooden rather than stainless steel tables were streaked with various dried colors of all shades. But what caught Michael's eyes were the heads and legs and arms lying on the tables. They were so realistic they would have startled him if he hadn't known what he was viewing couldn't be actual body parts.

"Meet Ralph," Waverly said, gazing past Michael's shoulder to the wall behind him. Michael turned to see a man facing him. He was dressed in a blue jacket over a white pullover and jeans. It took Michael a moment to realize the smiling face was that of a mannequin. He had never seen one so realistic in appearance—down to a few hairs spiraling out of place in the eyebrows.

"Feel him," Waverly said.

Michael touched the mannequin's shoulder. It felt soft, and not only soft from the material of the jacket and pullover, but softer deep down, where the substance serving as skin gave beneath the pressure of his touch.

"I've been rich ever since designing my first medical software package when I was twenty," Waverly said. "But my name only became known worldwide when I started constructing robotic mannequins for theme parks. My plant in St. Louis does the manufacturing for the parks now, but I occasionally come in here and work with a couple of my engineers on new ideas—for fun."

Michael looked at a head sitting on a nearby table. The face had a slight frown. There were dark circles under the eyes, and the cheeks sagged. If he had first seen the head lying on the beach during one of his morning jogs, he would have looked out over the water for a fin.

"This isn't all fun though," Waverly said. "In a way it does tie into our thoughts for the future of health care. Not too many decades from now there will be an *actual* bionic man. When that happens it will be the start of long, long life for humanity. We'll merge robotics parts into our bodies. The brain will remain solely ours, though perhaps even part of it will be mechanical. We will have blood pumping to the human organs, while synthetic lines implanted in our bodies will carry the lifeblood of the future, a high viscosity oil or a hydraulic fluid. We already use lengths of rod for bones, plastic for hips, why not replace the lungs' alveoli sacs with tiny, almost micron-sized bellows? The only problem comes in the part of the circulatory system that it's likely we're not going to be able to replace—in the brain. The maximum life of a circulatory system is estimated to be a hundred ten to a hundred twenty years. The veins and capillaries simply begin to disintegrate after that. We will have to improve on that, or anything else we do to lengthen the human life span won't mean much."

Waverly looked at the mannequin as he paused.

"We will *have* to improve on that," he repeated.

Now he started toward the wide double doors at the far end of the room.

"The next area is the last one in this building. You've heard the saying 'last but not least'? You'll see that is especially true in there." He grinned proudly back over his shoulder. "We're concentrating much of our resources nationally on nerve research. All of our medical research here is directed at spinal cord regeneration in particular."

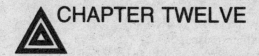# CHAPTER TWELVE

When Michael and Waverly passed through the doors from the mannequin area into the area at the rear of the long building, they were back in a sterile-appearing environment. This time the faces in the room were of real humans, a man in his mid-forties, dressed in a knee-length lab coat, with his brown hair cut in a short military style, and a bespectacled, middle-aged woman in a lab coat with dishwater-blond hair hanging nearly to her waist.

"Doctors Herreld and Dethloff," Waverly said.

The two smiled politely.

"Doctors," Waverly said. "This is Dr. Sims, soon, I hope, to be our new congressman."

Michael felt awkward. Waverly walked toward an arrangement of wire cages the size of shoe boxes stacked one on top of the other against the far wall. The doctors turned back to their work, the woman slipping off her glasses and lowering her eyes to a double-barreled stereo microscope, and the man lifting a test tube in front of him and staring at a yellow, milky liquid. Waverly stopped in front of the cages. They were filled with white laboratory rats, one to each cage. Each enclosure had a small white card attached to its side with identifying letters and numbers printed in black.

"Do you see anything unusual about the rodents?" Waverly asked.

Most of them lay quietly in the sawdust that covered the bottoms of the cages. A couple moved slowly across the cages.

"Well, Dr. Sims?" Waverly said.

"No. Nothing unusual."

Waverly's voice rose with his next words: "You are witnessing the beginning of what someday—and not far in the future—will be a miracle, Dr. Sims. Not a miracle of the supernatural, but one of science. A miracle, Dr. Sims. Each rodent in those cages has had its spinal cord partially severed."

Michael looked back at the small creatures.

"The identifying placards that say *five percent* after the letters refer to five percent of the total thickness of the rat's spinal cord cut. Those with *ten percent* on their cages likewise have had a cut made ten percent of the way into their spinal cords all the way around its circumference."

There were a half dozen of the latter cages. In four of them the rodents lay quietly in the sawdust, unmoving, but displaying the nerve control it took to hold their heads up and their shoulders erect. In one cage, a rat actually walked, though its hind quarters were noticeably slumped and one forepaw seemed to flop out of line before coming back in time for the rat to take its next step. It was hard to believe they had returned to that much locomotion after such a serious injury to their spinal cords. There were humans who had their cords barely nicked and found themselves paraplegics. The miracle Waverly had spoken of was a lot closer than Michael could have imagined.

"Are you aware of the spinal cord study at the University of Vanderbilt?" Waverly asked.

"With CM101?" Michael had heard about that only months before.

"Yes. Using that cancer drug, the doctors there were able to take rats with crushed spinal cords and get most of them back to a state of nearly normal to normal locomotion."

Michael looked back at the cages. "That's what you have done?"

"No. The Vanderbilt studies were done with injections of the drug immediately after the damage to the rats' cords occurred. We're working more with spinal cords that have old damage—where scar tissue has already formed, tending to block the possible paths of nerve regrowth. The next steps for all of us are primate studies and, hopefully, eventually human trials.

"Some scientists are confident we're reaching the end. Some are not so confident this will work. You can count us among the most confident, for even in the worst cases of spinal cord damage, scientists, in an unusually dramatic sense, have already demonstrated that all that is necessary for continued life can be maintained. Years ago, researchers conducted an experiment in which monkeys' spinal cords were not only severed, but their heads transplanted to other bodies. The study was published in 1971 as *Cephalic Exchange: Transplantation in the Monkey*. That the animals lived, though paralyzed, demonstrated that the arteries that supply the cord and the other vital links between the cord and the brain could be successfully reattached. There's been rumor that subsequent similar experiments with monkeys by a European research institute succeeded in reestablishing some of the nerve connections. Whether this later advance is true or not, my not inconsiderable resources have been unable to track it down to an actual institute."

"How is what you are doing different from the other research centers?"

"They're using the CM101; some, like the University of Florida, New York University, Georgetown Medical Center, and others engaged in a study called the Multicenter Animal Spinal Cord Injury Study have had some significant advances using high-dose methylprednisolone. We're using embryonic cell transplant. We take cells from the spinal cord in rat fetuses and inject them into the area of the damage in the adult rat. Being fetal cells, they are in a state of rapid growth. There's some crossover of this property into the adults, causing a spate of axonal regeneration in the area of the damaged tissue. In fact, we have reached twenty-five percent in some rats by not only using the fetal tissue injections but combining that with nerve tissue implants taken from the spinal cord of very young rats. We hypothesize that this added success is partially promulgated on the vigorous growth of the baby rats' cords transferring over to the damaged tissue. Our task now is to first build on this success rate, and then, hopefully, be able to move our experiments up from the lower order animals to humans."

"It's amazing," Michael said, his words mimicking his thoughts as he looked back at the rats.

"We're doing all we can," Waverly said. "Many researchers are doing all they can. But a serious problem works against us all. So many times the doctors working on any one particular project aren't privy to the information from other scientists involved in the same type of research. There's the jealousy between competing scientists at universities. Private corporations purposely hold the results of their research secret, hoping for a breakthrough they can patent—possibly that's why I was unable to track down the rumors of success in Europe with monkeys.

"Dr. Sims, the breakthroughs that are now vitally needed will only come about in a reasonable time if the top scientists in each field can be drawn together in a unified common effort. Not just those at Vanderbilt and in the Multicenter Animal Spinal Cord Injury Study that are willing to share their results, but all places involved in this kind of study. In any kind of study. What I envision is the establishment of a half dozen major research centers with each center's goal the conquering of a particular problem or disease—and each center willing to share whatever they learn with all other research centers. Each center should have unlimited funds—a hundred-million-dollar budget a year even for the smallest center—billions in all. The only place from which that much money can come is the national Congress. That is why I need doctors like you as members of Congress, rubbing elbows with other representatives and senators, doctors who understand the need for such research, and have the ability to scientifically explain the great benefits that will ensue."

Before Michael could respond, Waverly added, "But I am certain you'd like to see our last facility before we get into any discussion about the congressional opening. It's in the other building."

He started toward the door they had entered. "We will have to go this way. There's only one entrance or exit from this building, the same way you came in. For security purposes—you understand there is a lot here that's not for simply anybody's eyes."

COASTAL REGIONAL HOSPITAL

She had come to the automatic glass doors leading into the emergency room. They had opened, but she had just stood there. Her eyes had swept every area inside the department. Then she had walked to the doctors' parking area and had been waiting there ever since in the hot sun, despite the perspiration building across her face and her dress beginning to stick to her broad shoulders.

Inside the department, a security guard glanced through the door in her direction as he spoke with the police.

"A Mrs. Whitaker. She made threats earlier against Dr. Michael Sims, an emergency department physician here. Now she's just standing there—waiting for him to come back is my guess."

CHAPTER THIRTEEN

Walking beside Waverly, Michael passed the end of the robotics plant and looked toward the mental-care facility a couple hundred feet ahead of them across the mowed grass. He thought of Waverly's dream of billions of dollars available to eradicate some of the world's worst diseases. He thought about Candice. If Waverly accomplished his dream, the next little girl might return home to her parents. A lot of children might return to their parents. A lot of adults might go on to live longer lives. The billionaire, based on the research his corporations had already done, was a much bigger man than his physical size alone would indicate. Were he to accomplish his dream, he could grow even bigger—maybe grow in history books into the biggest man who ever lived.

When Waverly reached the door leading into the blocky building, he stopped and looked up at the camera monitoring their presence.

A moment later a black orderly in khakis opened the door.

Michael stared into a lobby that looked more like a motel than a medical facility. Two easy chairs, a long couch and three card tables surrounded by straight chairs were arranged across the tile floor in the spacious area. Two big-screen TVs sat positioned where they could be seen from the area's sides, where big windows faced inward from rooms behind them. There were six of the wide glass openings in all, three to each side. Through one of them, Michael could see an older black man wearing pajamas and leaning on a crutch at the center of his room. Past a window on the other side of the lobby, a young white man with blond hair, wearing similar pajamas, lay asleep on top of his bedspread. There were heavy curtains on the outside of the windows.

"The incurable miscreants that society would rather forget," Waverly said. "And those beset with physical infirmities as well as mental difficulties. We try to make them as comfortable as possible. The windows are to keep them from feeling overly confined. And, incidentally, afford us the only punishment we administer when a patient becomes unruly. We simply close the curtains so they can't see inside to the TVs or the movement of others in the recreational area. It's a quite effective punishment when you consider how little the patients enjoy in the first place. Sadly," he added.

"Each of them, by the way, are related to our nerve research due to the physical damage they have suffered to their spinal cords. We are studying those injuries in combination with their mental difficulties. The brain is, after all, the control tower, so to speak, of the nervous system. We do have one criminally ill patient," Waverly added, walking toward a door at the rear of the lobby. It was made of steel rather than wood, like the one which had graced the entry to the facility.

As they stopped at the door, Waverly looked up at the surveillance camera mounted above the door frame. A buzzing sound preceded a metallic clank, and the door swung open.

The area they entered was completely different from the one they had left, Spartan, with a bare concrete floor. Three ceiling lights enclosed in metal grids ran across the ceiling. A heavy wooden desk with a straight chair sat to the left side of the maybe fifty-feet-square area and two barred cells were built against the wall to the right. At the very back of the area a wooden door and a steel one leading to other rooms stood twenty feet apart. The man who had pushed the button to let them inside sat at the desk.

"This is Dr. Lobb," Waverly said, nodding toward him. "Our resident psychiatrist—and Blue's caretaker."

Lobb came to his feet and walked toward them. He was of smaller-than-average height, with black hair and a beard. The T-shirt under his lab coat was so grayed it almost appeared to be dyed.

"This is Dr. Sims," Waverly said.

"Welcome to our facility," Dr. Lobb said, extending his arm to shake hands.

"Thank you," Michael said as he clasped the man's hand. He noticed how deep Lobb's dark eyes were set back in their sockets, and how the pale skin around them was puffy. His handshake felt clammy, almost as if his temperature was running high. Waverly had mentioned the name Blue. But from where Michael stood he could see only the fronts of the cells. Inside one, a heavy wooden chair was set against the bars and turned around backward. Leather straps hung from its thick arms.

Now, an unusually stocky man around five-eight or five-nine with pale skin and wearing only a pair of gray cotton shorts, stepped into view beside the chair and stared toward them.

"Good morning, Blue," Waverly said.

Michael had noted the thickness of the patient's muscled arms with a little surprise. His shoulders were massive. His bulging thighs stretched the shorts to the point it looked as if the material was about to rip. Most criminally insane patients confined for interminable periods not only grew pale, but quickly lost their muscle. The bulky man he stared at now couldn't have been more muscled.

Waverly walked toward the bars. "Blue, this is my guest, Dr. Sims," he called ahead of him.

Michael noticed the patient's eyes locked onto his, and he averted his gaze, looking at the accommodations inside the cell—a sink, a toilet without a lid, and a bunk at the rear of the cell below a slitted, barred window high on the wall. When he moved his gaze back to Blue's, the eyes still bored into his.

Waverly stopped several feet short of the bars. "Blue is our only patient with physical damage to both the brain and spinal cord. As a youth he was fleeing law enforcement when he lost control of his car and slammed into a bridge. His left side was partially paralyzed—it's not totally recovered yet."

Michael now noticed the slight difference in the thickness between Blue's left arm and right. There was a difference in the legs, too. While his right foot was planted firmly on the concrete floor, his left foot seemed to barely be touching it, as if his leg had drawn up in length.

"Even injured as he was," Waverly continued, "Blue attacked and killed a police officer trying to extract him from the wreck. The state sought the death penalty. But during his trial he got loose from the policemen in the courtroom and broke a juror's neck before he could be wrestled to the floor. He was obviously insane, though whether the cause had to do with latent mental difficulties or the injuries he suffered in the car accident is unclear. He was sent to an institution for the criminally insane. It took a great deal of pressure on my part to have him transferred here. He works out religiously— if that is a proper word to use in his case."

Michael knew Waverly must have noticed him staring at the heavy chair against the bars when the aging billionaire added, "We test Blue's brain waves from time to time to compare them against earlier readings, hoping that some of our medications might show particular promise—of course, they're the same medications every other psychiatrist uses," he added, "but with some variance in their dosage and timing. So far, we have done little if any good—but we keep trying."

As the bulky man continued to stare at him, Michael nodded his head and said, "Blue."

"He has no ability to speak," Waverly said. "He has been that way since birth—it's likely it has to do with his other mental deficits, but we haven't been able to ascertain why."

As Waverly turned away from the cell and walked toward the steel door they had entered, Michael nodded a good-bye to Blue, who was still staring at him. Then he glanced toward the rack of shelves that ran up the far wall. They were packed tightly with leather straps of various sizes, straitjackets, handcuffs, mace and pepper spray and other control chemicals, and a long pipe with a U-shaped pinning device at its end lying lengthwise between two supporting pegs.

On the desk, there was a computer and a TV-size video monitor. The monitor's screen glowed with the scene just outside the steel door, fed by the surveillance camera they had stood under before entering the area. Michael noticed the monitor had screens both on its front and rear, where anyone who approached the door from the outside could be seen from anywhere in the detention area.

Shannon stood at the entrance to her father's apartment in Gulfport for a long moment before she inserted her key in the lock, turned it, and pushed the door back.

A musky, warm odor wafted by her.

She turned on the living room light by the switch panel next to the door. Carol stepped inside behind her.

Her father had rented the apartment ever since the divorce from her mother. It was a small, two-bedroom with a tiny kitchen and dining area. She knew the walls of one of the bedrooms were lined with filing cabinets stacked one on top of another. She noticed filing cabinets she hadn't seen before, lining one wall of the dining area.

"I hope those things are labeled," Carol said, "or we'll still be looking next year. Where's the air-conditioner thermostat?"

Shannon noticed that two of the drawers beneath the TV in the entertainment center across from the couch were cracked open. Probably from the FBI's hasty search of the apartment. They had obviously found nothing her father had written or anything else that would explain his death, or she would have heard about it.

For only a moment she wondered if somebody had been in the apartment before the FBI had.

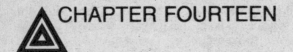

CHAPTER FOURTEEN

Waverly walked alongside the robotics plant on the way back from the mental-care facility. Michael walked next to him. As they neared the parking area at the front of the building, Waverly's eyes came around to his. Michael knew the time had come for the aging billionaire to make his final offer, and Michael, with his newfound respect for the man, wanted to make a special point to be polite in his refusal.

"Dr. Sims, what you have seen and heard here only scratches the surface of what I wish to do. It's unlikely I'll ever benefit from the research as far as my own health is concerned; not at my age, and with what's already wrong with me. Yet, before I die, I would like to know that others are not going to end up as I am at a mere several decades of age. If my joint venture funding passes Congress, I'll know my research is going to pay off even if I don't actually live to see the long-term results. But to acquire the funding, I need—the country needs—national office-holders who can plead my case in Congress and before the American people. A doctor in those halls of power can do that. Someone who knows what he's speaking about."

"Why me in particular?"

"Your father was respected both as a doctor and a politician. Your family *is* respected. You're handsome, you're articulate. You're the perfect candidate. And with my financial backing I can guarantee you will win."

Michael shook his head as they stopped beside his Jeep. "I can't visualize myself stepping into Congress and impressing anyone with my opinion. If you feel a doctor is necessary, I'm certain there are others maybe nearer the end of their careers who would jump at the chance."

"More mature-looking doctors?" Waverly questioned. "A little gray around the temples?"

Michael nodded.

"And all the fire gone out of them?" Waverly came back with almost a frown to his expression. "No. I want a man who will work twenty hours a day if necessary to help me accomplish my dream."

"Sir, I'm sorry, but . . ."

Waverly held his palm up. "Dr. Sims, business as well as politics is to a large degree based on compromise. I realize if I want something, then I must give up something in return. As the bill is now structured, ten percent of the funding will be primarily devoted to diseases that spring from an aging mind. I've been pondering whether the percentage of funding devoted to that kind of research should be greater. Especially with the graying of the population. If you agree to run for the seat, I'll make my decision now. I'll change the percentage that is devoted to the diseases of the mind to twenty-five percent—with a large portion of that budgeted to Alzheimer's research. That's twenty-five percent of ten billion dollars, Dr. Sims. Two-and-a-half-billion dollars. What can't be accomplished with two-and-a-half-billion dollars?"

Michael was quiet for a moment. "How did you know my mother might have Alzheimer's?"

"I know all about the doctors at my hospital—all there is to know about them."

Michael found the offer not the compromise Waverly had called it, but a bribe. A bribe that was way too personal. And the arrogance of the term "my hospital." The feeling of respect he had gained for the man was suddenly gone.

"I'm not interested in the job, Mr. Waverly," he said, not caring that his irritation showed in his tone.

Waverly's expression didn't change. "Dr. Sims, I apologize if I struck a sensitive chord, but the fact is I can make you the offer I did for the simple reason that Alzheimer's is one of the diseases that we have some promising science on at the moment. But we also have promising science on a half dozen other serious diseases. Even if we get the funding, we are not going to have enough money to make all of these diseases priorities. Some research will be put on the fast track, some will be put on the back burner. Alzheimer's could well be one that is put on the fast track in any case. But with your cooperation I can promise it will be. How can you fault me for that?"

As Michael started to respond, Waverly said, "And I can guarantee you one immediate financial benefit. I will pay off all your school loans—which I understand approach a hundred thousand dollars—if you simply say you will run. Win or lose—though losing is not in the cards."

As the frail man had spoken, Michael had felt his irritation at his mother being used as a bribe wane— until the additional bribe of the hundred thousand dollars was offered. "I'm sorry, but I can't help you."

Without waiting for a response, he turned to the Jeep and slid behind the steering wheel.

Seconds later, as the Jeep backed from its parking space and turned toward the gate, the door to the robotics plant opened and the bearded Dr. Lobb and the towering security guard, Murphy, walked to Waverly's side.

"How did he react?" Lobb asked.

"He's young and worked hard to get where he is. He's not going to make any sudden decision to give that up overnight. But we need him. We need his family name and his abilities. He'll come around."

As Waverly paused, he watched the Jeep head toward the gate for a moment, then turned his gaze back to Lobb's.

"Get Blue ready."

Lobb nodded.

Shannon sat on the floor in her father's apartment bedroom with her feet crossed at the ankles, her knees splayed out to the side, and her skirt halfway up her thighs. Her lap was full of papers. She was flipping through them rapidly.

"I wish I had a camera," Carol said, looking at Shannon's awkward position. Shannon ignored her and kept sorting.

Carol lifted a legal-size sheet and stared at it. "What's this? Your father's talking about working on living tissue? Gives me the creeps. I thought you said the pathologist in Los Angeles was caught working on unembalmed tissue."

"When I was a child, Waverly was trying to get a medical research bill passed in Congress. At the same time, the doctor at the Los Angeles center was caught bribing a deceased man's family to let him remove a spinal cord sample before the body was embalmed. Evidently the doctor did so in trying to learn something that would result in his earning a million-dollar bonus Mr. Waverly had offered to any scientist who made a breakthrough in nerve research. Daddy was on the congressional committee that investigated the incident. A second autopsy the committee ordered indicated the possibility that while the man had been in the hospital in a coma on life support, his spinal cord had been injected with some kind of chemical. Though it was never proved conclusively, it was what got Daddy's name known nationally. In questioning Waverly at the hearings, he suggested the Waverly Center might have been experimenting on the tissue through this pathologist by the use of injections while the man was still legally alive. He used the phrase 'experimenting on living tissue' and the media jumped on it. Waverly's bill never had a chance after that."

Carol's brow wrinkled. "And Waverly started supporting your father after he did *that* to him?"

"Have you seen the Waverly feature on *Biography*?"

Carol shook her head no.

"Waverly's father was rumored to be engaged in racketeering. But Daddy said that Waverly made a clean break from him while still a teenager, moved to Los Angeles, and started living with an aunt. Then he came up with the software that started him on the way to where he is today. Daddy respected that and didn't bring up the background during the hearings. Waverly came to him right after the hearing and thanked him for that—and his support started shortly afterward. Have you seen on the news about the bill Mr. Waverly wants passed now?"

Carol shook her head again.

"Carol, do you ever watch TV or read newspapers?"

"Not the news—it's too depressing."

"It's the same kind of bill Waverly pushed originally. It's taken all these years to have a chance again."

The wrinkles deepened across Carol's forehead. "Shannon, I'm going to get the net out if you tell me you're suggesting that this sneaky doctor might have struck again."

"Not him. He lost his license."

"But you *are* thinking somebody at the center is doing something like that again?"

"I don't know. But I'm not aware of any other old problem that could rub off on Daddy—cause him a problem."

"Joe England worked at the center. You think he saw something going on out there, called your father, and . . . somebody killed him and his wife? Then your father saw they had been killed and came in and . . . Shannon, why don't you tell the sheriff what you think?"

"What, that Daddy made two phone calls to people he's probably called a hundred times before? You know he's called the center. So what do I have that's any different than always except that the Englands had an accident the next day—and the calls were made late at night?"

Carol had the wrinkles across her forehead again. "So if you already know everything that happened in the hearings, and you know you don't have enough to go to Everette with—what are we doing here?"

"I'm trying to find something I don't know about."

Jonathan Waverly stood in the open doorway at the rear of the laboratory. He stared into the small room at the cages filled with white rats. The cage that had contained the rodent that hadn't responded well to the treatments was now empty. Waverly smiled at that. Despite the lingering knowledge that not every one of the rodents always came back to adequate movement, not having to actually look at one that hadn't still made him feel better. He looked over his shoulder.

"I apologize for raising my voice earlier," he said, once again speaking in his raspy but soft tone.

Dr. Dethloff, sitting on a stool at the long counter, smiled politely.

"You have so much pressure on you," she said.

Waverly nodded at her words.

Then he looked across his other shoulder at the rat cages. He looked at the placards on their sides stating that five and ten percent of the thickness of their spinal cords had been severed. He looked at the rats inside the cages. Some sat unmoving but were able to hold their heads and shoulders erect. A couple of the rodents moved haltingly across the sawdust at the bottom of the cages. They were the ones for display to anyone curious enough to wish to visit the center.

Then he looked back at the cages before him. They all had numbers indicating a hundred percent severance. Despite the much greater damage to their spinal cords, they moved more freely. No one outside the center had ever seen them. He couldn't prevent a grin from spreading across his face.

The phone sitting on the counter rang. Dr. Dethloff picked up the receiver and listened for a moment.

"Dr. Lobb says he's prepared for Blue now."

▲ CHAPTER FIFTEEN

Dr. Lobb and Murphy stood in front of the barred cells. Murphy had a tranquilizer-dart pistol in one hand hanging down by his side and a straitjacket in the other.

"You know the routine, Blue," he said.

Blue stood at the far end of his cell. His dark eyes, set far apart in his wide forehead, stared at the straitjacket. A drop of perspiration trickled from under his mop of thick hair and ran down to his eyebrows. The large security guard stepped forward and stuffed the straitjacket between the crossbars next to the big wooden chair. Then he stepped back a safe distance from the enclosure. He raised the tranquilizer pistol slightly out in front of him.

"You know how sick this makes you," he said.

Blue slowly stepped forward. He hesitated, then took another step and then another, stopping in front of the chair. His gaze never left Murphy's. Now he looked past him at Waverly, who was smiling from the chair behind the desk. Still staring at the frail billionaire, he caught the straitjacket in his big hands and pulled it through the bars.

In a moment he had slipped it across his shoulders and pushed his arms into its long sleeves. The heavy garment gaping open across his back, he turned and sat in the chair, leaving a few inches of space behind his shoulders and the chair's thick wooden back. He stared toward the rear of the cell.

Murphy handed Dr. Lobb the pistol and stepped to the bars, running his hands inside them around the sides of the chair.

In a few seconds he had pulled the leather straps protruding from the sleeves around Blue's thick waist to his back and buckled them. Next, he pushed a wide strap through the bars, snaked it around Blue's chest and pulled it tight around the rear of the chair, forcing Blue against its backrest.

From where he sat at the desk, Waverly pushed a button on a metal panel. The cell lock buzzed and made a metallic sound, and the door swung open. Murphy stepped into the cell, knelt off to the side of the chair and attached the shackles that hung from its legs to Blue's ankles.

Waverly pushed a black box the size of a wide suitcase toward the enclosure. Mounted on rollers that clicked noisily across the concrete floor, the box had loose wires coiled on its top and running down its front, connecting to instrument panels crowded with dials and gauges.

As the box was pushed inside the cell, Dr. Lobb followed behind it, carrying a shiny, plastic headpiece that resembled a football helmet with short wires protruding from its crown and back.

He placed it over Blue's head, covering his ears and pushing it down low around his thick neck, then buckled it under his chin. He connected its wires to the longer wires of the instrumentation panel. Blue's eyes began to dart back and forth across the rear of the cell.

Murphy now carried an armful of what looked like blood pressure cuffs into the enclosure. Each of the soft cuffs had a long wire hanging from it. Each of the wires ended in a plastic, rectangular-shaped plug similar to the type used to link computer equipment.

It took several minutes for Dr. Lobb and Murphy to

get all the cuffs into place and plug them into the parallel ports on the black box. In the end, Blue's arms and legs were banded every few inches with the cuffs. A cuff wider than the others was wrapped around his thick neck and locked in place by a Velcro clasp.

Waverly flicked a switch on the instrumentation panel at the side of the black box. A narrow strip of graph paper began to click out of a slot at the box's front. Below that slot, a second wider ribbon of graph paper began to emerge in rhythm with the intensity of the electrical discharges coming from Blue's brain.

Murphy held a rubber mouthpiece toward Blue.

Blue didn't open his mouth.

Murphy slipped a small pocketknife from his windbreaker. He opened it and stared down at the eyes glaring back up into his. The mouth still didn't open. Murphy moved the point of the blade toward Blue's lips. Blue tried to move his head to the side, but was prevented by the heavy leather strap across his forehead. He still didn't open his mouth.

Murphy pushed the tip of the blade between Blue's tight lips, and angled the point down into his gum. Blue's cheek ticced. His eyes blinked. The graph paper measuring his brain's discharges began to click faster from the slot. Murphy pressured the blade.

For a moment, Waverly's face took on a look of irritation, more at Murphy than Blue. Then Blue's mouth came open.

Murphy slid the mouthpiece between the wide teeth and quickly secured it in place by slapping a piece of two-inch tape across Blue's lips. He finished his work by wrapping a second layer of tape around the back of Blue's neck and across his mouth again, then stepped back from the chair.

A red stain soaked through the tape, discoloring it at a corner of Blue's mouth.

Waverly reached toward a panel of switches at the

top of the box. His forefinger stopped on the only one painted red.

"This won't last long, Blue," he said. "It's for your own good." And he flicked the switch.

Blue's body jerked. His eyes clamped shut. He shuddered. One eye popped open then snapped closed again. Perspiration broke out across his face.

The graph paper recording the brain waves was pouring out of the slots now.

Below those slots, a sheet of green, lined paper containing closely spaced, jagged, up-and-down lines like those registered by a polygraph machine began to emerge.

Waverly flicked the switch off.

Blue's eyes remained closed.

He shuddered again.

Perspiration dripped off his wide chin onto the straitjacket.

The graph paper resumed the slow, measured pace it had shown prior to the switch being flipped on. The wider sheet of paper continued emerging at its normal pace. The jagged peaks being traced across it slowly lessened in height.

Seconds later, the peaks had dropped to a flat line.

Blue's eyes slowly opened. He glared at Waverly.

Waverly flicked the switch.

Blue jerked. His eyes clamped shut.

Waverly flicked a second switch.

Blue's body seemed to swell, his chest pushing forward and up; his heels kicked repeatedly against the legs of the chair. A sound like the hiss of air exhaled from a pressurized tank came through the tape.

The graph paper coiled about the floor.

Waverly flicked the second switch off.

The graph paper slowed.

Waverly flicked the first switch off.

Blue shuddered. Perspiration soaked his face as if he had been dowsed with a bucket of water.

One eye popped open, blinked.

His other eye popped open.

He stared straight ahead.

The graph paper had slowed again. Blue gave a convulsive shudder, and slid his eyes up toward Waverly's.

Waverly smiled softly back at him.

It was for Blue's own good.

△ CHAPTER SIXTEEN

GULFPORT YACHT HARBOR

Michael parked in his reserved space in front of the *Cassandra*'s slip. He didn't step from the Jeep immediately. Mixed in with his irritation at Waverly's attempts at a bribe, he couldn't help but feel a twinge of guilt at turning down what had been offered. Two-and-a-half-billion dollars at work trying to find a cure or prevention for the problems of an aging mind, with a large portion of it used to try to find a cure for Alzheimer's disease.

But Waverly would find a doctor who would run and win, and funds would be spent on the disease anyway. Meanwhile, he knew his place was here as he had planned, with his medical practice and his boat and his mother. Here where she and his father had lived, where she would be happy—for as long as that was possible. He stepped from the Jeep to the blacktop. Howard smiled at him from the port rail of the *Howard*. He was still garbed in his normal dress of nothing but a pair of shorts and a great deal of exposed, heavily tanned skin.

"Short nap you took earlier, Michael," Howard said, grinning across the rail. "I didn't mean to make you feel guilty talking to you about your generation not working as hard as mine. Notice you do put in more than your fair share of time at the hospital. Why's that—you short some money?"

"Yeah, Howard, about a hundred thousand dollars in school loans. You want to pay them off for me? And be quick with your answer. I just turned down someone who made that offer."

"You think I'm made of money?"

"That's why I asked you if you wanted to pay them off—I know you wouldn't miss it."

"You've got me way overfigured, son."

"You'd just have to cut down to making one yacht last a few years."

"Hard as I worked, son, I don't want to make any sacrifices now. I like to know that's all behind me. I could afford to buy you a beer or two, though. Guess I owe you, with you treating me last time. But here on board, out of a six-pack—don't want to be throwing down three or four dollars a whack at some bar."

"I'm off this weekend," Michael said.

"I'll have a six-pack ready then."

Michael walked across the gangplank and through the open door at the *Cassandra*'s side into the salon.

His mother smiled up at him from beside the stove in the galley.

"That took longer than you expected," she said. "Were you polite?"

"Bit my tongue every time I had a bad thought." *Almost every time.*

"Another girl called."

"Who?"

"Guess."

"The one you don't like?"

"Who says I like any of them?"

"Who, Mother?"

"One named Mary Jo. Sounded like she was trying to talk around chewing a sandwich."

"Were *you* polite, Mother?"

"I bit my tongue at every bad thought I had," she

said, mimicking his words. "I have some tide-you-overs ready—gumbo and sandwiches."

"You fed me before I went to the center."

"Since when have you turned down food? When you were in high school I couldn't keep you in groceries. Remember when you started bringing the whole football team over for hamburgers after practice on Thursdays? I didn't know if the season or my money was going to run out first." She glanced toward the galley. "So what is it, you're going to turn down the best cook on the coast, or are you going to make your aging mother happy?"

"That's a choice?"

"Good," she said. "And after you're through eating, your bed is made with the sheets already turned down. I have the air conditioner going. How's that for service— unpaid? Do you want to eat in the galley or the salon?"

The cellular telephone rang.

"How do you ever get any sleep?"

"I turn the ringer off."

The telephone rang a second time.

"Are you going to get it?" she asked.

"Let it ring. Let's eat."

The phone rang twice more as they moved into the galley. Then it stopped.

The sandwiches were already prepared, on paper plates on the table in the small booth at the left of the galley. They were thick enough for a full meal in themselves—layers of lunch meats and cheese divided by pickles, lettuce, onions, and slices of green pepper. The gumbo simmered on the stove.

The telephone started ringing again.

"Women," his mother said under her breath as she started ladling the gumbo into a bowl.

The phone rang three more times before stopping.

"How do you ignore that?" his mother asked.

"That's what's great about being an emergency department physician," he answered. "No calls—I work a shift and when I'm off, I'm off." He lifted a spoon as the gumbo was set in front of him.

Long strips of graph paper lay across the desk and hung toward the floor. Waverly ran a strip slowly through his hands, looking at the peaks and valleys representing the electrical discharges that had emanated from Blue's brain. Dr. Lobb, scratching a side of his beard with one hand, worked at the keyboard of a computer on his desk with his other. His fingers typed in the numbers corresponding to the peaks traced on the sheets of green, lined paper that had recorded the movements of the muscle masses picked up by the pressure cuffs around Blue's limbs and neck.

He hit the enter button and waited a moment as the screen filled with thousands of numbers, flashing, changing, repositioning.

A series of vertical bars appeared side by side across the screen.

"The discharges are traveling three percent faster across the synapses," Lobb said. He smiled broadly. The bars gave a picture view of all of the muscle responses. When Blue had first arrived at the center, no matter how much they had agitated him, no matter how strong the discharges emanating from his brain, no matter how much he tried to move his extremities to help alleviate the pain of the electrical shocks being transmitted through his body, there was at best only a seventy percent response in most of his muscle masses. "Altogether ninety-five percent of normal now in his shoulders and arms. The nerves are responding nearly twenty-five percent better than when we first started with him."

Waverly looked at the computer. *Twenty-five percent better than when we first started*, he thought. Two long years before. The improvement in the responses, the signals managing to find their way from Blue's brain through his injured spinal cord to his extremities, had come slowly at first, barely a three percent improvement in the first year. That had been depressing.

But then the improvement seemed to build upon itself. As one signal found a path where it could slip past the obstruction of the injury, it not only seemed to lock that route in for future travel, but it was almost as if the other electrical discharges trying to find their way toward different muscles were drawn toward the same path. And Blue's improvement was now growing rapidly. Most importantly, his nerves had been damaged years before in the car accident—it was old damage. The nerves had been dead for years. And their experiments with the rats and monkeys had shown them that if the fetal tissue was injected as soon as the damage occurred—and especially when the injections were used in combination with the fresh live tissue implants from baby rats—the regeneration was even more rapid. It had worked at all levels, the rats, the hamsters, the monkeys. He looked at Lobb and nodded.

Lobb slipped a pair of latex gloves onto his hands, reached for a thick gauze pad at the side of his desk and opened it, revealing a syringe fitted with a three-inch needle and filled with a milky liquid.

He lifted the syringe from the pad, stood, and walked toward the open cell door at the other side of the room.

Blue sat secured firmly in the chair, his ankles chained to its legs, the wide strap across the chest of the straitjacket, and the other wide strap holding his head in place. His eyes slid in Lobb's direction as the doctor stepped inside the cell.

Lobb pinched the needle just behind its point and leaned forward over Blue's shoulder. The point touched the thick neck. Blue's eyes were locked on the rear wall of the cell.

The needle pierced the skin.

Lobb moved his fingers an inch farther up its thin length and pushed the needle slowly forward. Blue's

cheek ticced and his arms pulled against the straitjacket's sleeves.

Lobb slowed the needle's penetration as its tip neared
the spinal cord.

He felt the resistance of the cervical vertebrae.

He depressed the syringe's plunger.

Blue's eyes clamped shut. He shuddered. His arms
pulled harder inside the straitjacket.

"It's for your own good," Waverly said.

He always said that. He felt he had to. Now he saw
Blue's eyes pop open and stare into his.

And for once, Waverly experienced a feeling he
didn't even know he contained. And he averted his gaze
from Blue's.

From his son's stare.

They had loaded a dozen folders full of files into the
back seat of the Expedition. Carol walked from the
apartment with her arms wrapped around more folders
at her chest. Shannon stood beside the open driver's
door. She noticed a man staring at her as he drove
slowly by on the street in front of the apartment building, his head turning until he was looking back across
his shoulder. She was used to men's stares. They usually
just irritated her, if she paid any attention to them at
all. This one bothered her in a different way. She looked
at the car's license plate as it moved on down the pavement. She made a mental note of the numbers—and
that the car was from Jackson County, a few miles
away, east along the coast.

She wouldn't forget the man's narrow face, either.

◢ CHAPTER SEVENTEEN

Michael laid his spoon by the empty bowl, looked across the galley table at his mother, and said, "I eat again before Thanksgiving, I'll be a patient in my own department."

The telephone began ringing again.

It had rung once more while they were eating. This time he slid out of the booth and walked up the two steps into the salon and across it to the steering station where he picked up the phone.

"Hello."

"Michael."

"Daryl, was that you who kept calling?"

"Four times, buddy. Why didn't you answer the damn thing? The Whitaker boy who came in with the head injury . . . his heart or aorta ruptured."

"What?"

" 'What?' is right. I mean, how in the hell do you get a warning about something like that? The kid's lying there in the ICU with no stress, no nothing, and bam . . . it blows. Like you hear about someone walking out of a cardiologist's office after a physical, and keels over an hour later."

"When did it happen?"

"Earlier this afternoon. Jeannie came by when she got off her shift. Do you feel as inadequate as I do? I mean, hell, I'm glad I'm not the one who had to explain it to his parents."

How could *you explain it?* Michael thought.

"You think there might've already been a weakness there—from birth?" Daryl questioned.

But Whitaker had been a track athlete. His heart had been tested way beyond the norm by his participation in the cross-country running his father had spoken of, and he had shown no problem in the past.

"Are they doing an autopsy?"

"Jeannie said the mother didn't want someone cutting up her child," Daryl answered. "She went all to pieces. Dr. Marzullo said the cause of death was obvious. The coroner didn't see any need in one."

Dr. Marzullo saying the death was obvious was nearly as good as an autopsy. Only arrived at the hospital from California two years before, he not only brought with him the most experience of any cardiologist on staff, with over thirty years in the field, but was also now involved in cutting-edge cardiac research at the facility—the reason he had been recruited to the hospital in the first place.

But, still, Michael wished there *had* been an autopsy.

"Buddy, that's not the entire reason I'm calling. I said the mother went to pieces. Well, she was screaming you promised her that her son would be back in his own bed by tonight. She said she was going to get you if it was the last thing she ever did."

Before Michael could respond, Daryl said, "I'm not sweating a liability case for you. It's more than that. I just wanted you to know how really pissed she is. Hopefully this'll be the last you hear of it, but I wanted you to know what was going on so you could keep a lookout over your shoulder when you come back here."

"Yeah, Daryl, I appreciate it. But she's just—"

"No, Michael, not *just* anything. Mary Liz came by here. She said that when she got off her shift the woman was sitting outside waiting for you. Security was getting ready to call the police. But she can come back, you know."

"Yeah, Daryl, I appreciate it," Michael said again, and laid the telephone back on the steering station.

His mother came up into the salon. "A problem?" she asked.

"A teenager who came in last night died today. I didn't expect that."

"Oh, that's terrible, honey." A sad expression crossed her face. She caught her lip in her teeth, then shook her head. "I don't see how you deal with that all the time. I know how it used to affect your father."

When he didn't say anything, she turned back toward the galley. "I'm going to have to get on back home," she said.

He barely heard her—adding to his shock at Johnny's death, Candice's smile was back in his mind now. A moment later he walked through the sliding door out onto the deck.

At the bow, he rested his hands on the rail and looked out across the boats docked in the marina. The low sound of a fifties tune drifted his way from an old, wooden-hulled Connie. The loudest sound was that of lines clicking in the wind against tall sailboat masts. A twenty-foot runabout with skis lying across its stern seat carried a pair of teenagers out toward the Sound. Mrs. Whitaker *should* be angry. There should have been some way to tell the damage was there. It didn't make sense that there hadn't been.

But what sense was there in people still dying from cancer after decades of research aimed at stopping it? He thought about Waverly's dream of united research. Maybe with enough money and the sharing of information, cures would be found. He recalled his mother talking about his grandfather's brother. He had died from the complications springing from a simple abscessed tooth when he had been a child of only seven. His mother had said his grandfather often had remarked sadly on how it would have taken only a handful of penicillin tablets at the time and his little brother would still be alive.

But penicillin hadn't been known at that time, despite it having been around forever in the form of molecules synthesized by common mold, just lying in wait for its magical properties to be discovered. What else might be lying before researchers' eyes that hadn't been discovered yet? Why hadn't there been the money for more research, or the combined effort of other scientists to help a cure come to realization? Maybe if there had been, something could be done for the next little girl who was septic. Maybe a technique could be developed that would warn doctors ahead of time when a teenager had a hidden problem with his heart.

"Michael."

He looked back at his mother, making her way alongside the rail toward him. "Michael, I know how you're feeling. I've seen your father like that after losing a patient. But if you're going back in tonight, don't you feel you should get at least a little sleep?"

"Mother, Clark said he had Dr. Boykin trade shifts with me, remember?"

At the word *remember*, his mother dropped her gaze and was silent. He felt terrible as he realized what he'd said. Now she looked up at him again.

"Michael, I am scared."

"Mother, don't—"

"So scared," she said and a tear dropped from a corner of her eye.

He walked to her.

She shook her head. "I'm sorry. I need to go home. You have better things to do than to worry about a whiny mother who—"

He silenced her by placing his fingers against her lips, pulled her to him, and slipped his arms around her back.

She began to cry silently against his chest. "I'm

sorry," she said. He could feel her tears dampening his shirt.

It didn't last but for a few seconds before she pulled her head back and wiped her eyes with her knuckles. "Okay," she said. "I got it out of me. I promise you won't see that again."

She forced a smile. "Let me go wipe these silly tears out of my eyes." She turned toward the salon door.

He watched her until she had disappeared from sight.

Seconds later, he walked into the salon, lifted the cellular telephone from the control dash, and punched in the Waverly Research Center's number.

It took only a moment for the receptionist there to connect him to Jonathan Waverly.

"Mr. Waverly, I'm going to accept your offer to run if you accept my conditions."

"What are they?"

"I want the first dollars in any funding to go to Alzheimer's research. I want you to give me your word on that, and that I be kept apprised of everything that takes place in that research no matter how confidential you or any scientist might think the information."

"Agreed."

"I'm not finished."

"Go ahead."

"You and I both know, Mr. Waverly, that if one of the centers does come up with what looks like it could be a cure, or even a medication that might slow the progress of the disease, that the FDA will require years of testing before the public will gain any benefits. I want your word again that if something looks promising enough that I, in my medical judgment, am willing for my mother to try it, that you will agree to that—even if we have to do it where nobody knows."

"Is that all?"

"Except I want you to be aware that while I am going to work as hard as is humanly possible to try to get your bill passed, if I decide that it doesn't look like it ever will, if I don't at least see promising movement in the direction of added research, I'm resigning from Congress and going back to my practice. I don't give a damn how it looks. You'll have to get somebody to take my place then."

"Welcome to the Waverly Research Corporation, Dr. Sims," Waverly said. "We'll talk about your resigning later—if it comes to that."

As Waverly replaced the telephone receiver after speaking with Michael, a grin spread across his face. *FDA approval.* The young doctor had been correct in what he said about that—it took years and years to get approval before human trials could be conducted for even the most promising of new techniques and medicines.

They never would have given approval to him. Not with the religious groups and the medical ethics committees that were around. There was no question but that their outcry would have been shrill. Congress would have passed laws to ban the process forever.

It would have been a waste of time to try.

And he had no time to spare.

He looked at the package of Oreo cookies his driver had just brought him. His smile broadened.

◭ CHAPTER EIGHTEEN

Two folders full of the Waverly hearing files sat on Shannon's desk. Several more sat on the small table behind her. The copies of the phone records from her father's Washington office and apartment lay in front of her. She listened as the voice of the man in the telephone security office came across her speakerphone.

"You're not going to owe anything but the normal monthly service charges—Congressman Donnelly didn't place any calls from his apartment this month."

She thanked the man, told him to make certain the billing address of the Gulfport apartment was changed to her address, and cut the speakerphone off. So her father hadn't called anybody from his apartment the night he had come into Biloxi—at least long distance. He hadn't called anyone from her mother's phone either. She wished there was some way to find out if anybody had placed a call to him at his apartment—if he had even taken the time to go inside the apartment when he had been there to pick up the Cadillac. But she had known the telephone company wouldn't give that information out without a reason, and she didn't want to give them one right now.

"What next?" Carol said.

"I want to know if the Englands called Daddy earlier that day. If they did, and what they told him is what upset him—that could be the reason he called them back so late. Then, when he saw that they had been killed, if he suspected their death might not have been an accident, then he could have been nervous when he came here. He would have talked to somebody to find out more about the accident, or about whatever it was he had originally been told, or both. Maybe what he learned caused him to be more worried. He could have even become frightened. That could have been why he came to my mother's house—so whoever he talked to wouldn't know where he was. He knew he wasn't putting Mother in danger because she was out of town." *He didn't endanger me by coming to my apartment, either*, she thought.

"That's a lot of 'could'ves,'" Carol said. "And if there's anything to this mysterious something you think might be going on at the center or wherever, how come it couldn't be someone at the center who called your father and told him about it instead of the Englands telling him—that's why he called the center back so late."

"Maybe that's right. But nobody ended up dead at the center and the Englands did."

"If he was worried that the deaths weren't an accident, why didn't he call the police?"

"If he was certain, he would have," Shannon said and reached for her telephone. "We can eliminate one possibility, or find out I'm right—if I'm a good enough talker."

She punched in a number.

It only took a moment for the congressional office in Washington to answer, and then just a few seconds more until Samples was on the line.

"Robert, I apologize for bothering you again, but I wondered if you would help me with something else?"

"If I can."

"I know I would normally have to get a subpoena to see somebody's telephone records. But it takes too much time to go through that process." And she knew she had no reason a judge would consider adequate to ask for the records in the first place.

"Pardon me?" Samples said.

"A Mr. and Mrs. England from Bay St. Louis were friends of Daddy's. Do you know them?"

"No."

If Samples didn't know them, they weren't too close to Daddy, she thought. But if he wasn't close to them, then that would make it all the more unusual that he would call them so late at night.

"Shannon?"

"Yes, excuse me. They were friends of Daddy's, but they were killed in an accident, so I can't go to them. But I need to see their telephone records."

"Shannon, I just don't believe I can afford to get involved with—"

"Robert, I'm nearly positive Daddy was murdered. But I have to have proof. I know—if you can accept that he was murdered—that you don't want anybody to get away with that either. You've known me ever since I was born. You know you can trust me not to say anything, no matter what happens."

"Why don't you have the sheriff call me and make the request, Shannon? It would be a lot easier for me to grease the—"

"Robert. Please trust me. I can't tell the sheriff yet. I have to get everything lined up where I'm certain how and why it happened."

"Is there . . ." There was a hesitant tone in the administrative aide's voice. "I don't mean to sound cold, but I . . . uh, with you being Lawrence's daughter I discounted what you said earlier about thinking he was murdered. Is there something solid you are aware of down there that I need to know about?"

"I promise you I'll let you know as soon as I know," she said. "Now about the phone records? It *is* really important. Maybe the most important thing I need."

Samples's sigh was audible over the phone.

She spoke quickly, trying to get him while he was still undecided. "Please, Robert—for Daddy's sake." She closed her eyes at using her father's memory on his closest friend in trying to get her way. But she *had* to see those records.

"Okay, Shannon, for you. Out of respect for Lawrence . . . and how he would want me to treat you. No, he wouldn't. You could get in serious trouble. I could get in serious trouble. Damn, I can't believe I'm going to do this."

"Thank you, Robert."

She replaced the receiver.

Carol shook her head and grinned. "Remind me to hire you if I ever need a case pled before a judge. Want to know something silly? I'm beginning to wonder if maybe you're right about your father. So welcome to the crazy farm, huh?"

Shannon nodded her thanks. But it was so hard, she thought. Even if turned out that the Englands had called her father before the later calls during the night, what could she do next? Daddy, she thought, I'm trying as hard as I can. Maybe if you could just help me a little. She felt her eyes moisten.

Carol cleared her throat, turned away from the desk, and walked toward the hallway.

Shannon stared after her for a moment, then dropped her gaze back to her desk. The biggest question still in her mind was why whoever committed the murder didn't make it look like an accident. That would have been much easier for everyone to accept than her father killing himself—depression from a heart bypass just wasn't that kind of depression, not even with the burden of cancer, not before he would at least try to have it treated.

Maybe they didn't make it look like an accident because they had no other choice. They had to act quickly—didn't have time to make it look like anything else. That would mean he was getting ready to do something, and they knew it. Call the police?

He couldn't have known for certain that the Englands had been murdered, or he would have already called the police. But he had thought something, or he wouldn't have hurried to Biloxi. He had thought something, but didn't want to believe it. He came to Biloxi, and then he *knew* something—or *they* thought he did.

Somebody at the Waverly Center.

The monkeys made small talking sounds in the darkness. Johnny Whitaker tried to move his arms, but they were strapped too tightly to the sides of the bed. A thick strap around his middle was also attached to the bed. It was belted so tightly, it made breathing an effort and kept him from sliding up or down to loosen the tension on his arms. He twisted his wrists again and felt the straps cut into them. But this time he also felt a new, warm slippery sensation against his skin—too slippery for perspiration. He realized blood was beginning to seep from the raw areas where he had chafed his skin. He twisted his wrists harder, faster. The dark was what was so bad. And the constant sound of movement and low talking coming out of the darkness. He could hear the monkeys' fingers working against the wire of their cages now—each with the other's head. He shuddered.

He twisted his wrists harder.

They burned as if a torch were being held to his skin.

The monkeys chattered in low voices.

In the detention area, Dr. Lobb had divided the meals properly, a protein-vitamin mixture to be fed to Johnny Whitaker via a plastic squeeze bottle, and two paper plates with solid food. He placed an Oreo cookie on each plate.

Waverly reached to the pack for a half dozen more

cookies, piled five into a little stack on an empty plate, and slipped one inside his mouth.

Lobb looked at him, and Waverly shrugged and grinned.

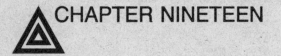# CHAPTER NINETEEN

GULFPORT YACHT HARBOR

Michael came quietly down the steps into the *Cassandra*'s stateroom. His mother lay asleep at the center of the queen-size bed, illuminated in the dim moonlight shining in through the narrow windows at the sides of the cabin. He stared down at her small, silent form for a moment. Her cheek ticced, and her expression tightened, as if she were having a nightmare. Slowly, her face relaxed. He pulled the cover further up around her shoulders. He held his hand up to the air-conditioner vent in the overhead, then walked to the unit's control on the far bulkhead and adjusted the thermostat.

At the bottom of the steps, he looked back toward his mother for a moment, then moved up into the salon to the small couch where he had been reading *JAMA*, the journal of the American Medical Association. It contained an article an Alzheimer's research.

Settling into the soft cushions, he lifted the magazine into his lap. From out of nowhere, a vision of Johnny Whitaker's and Candice's faces mingled. He stared across the salon for a long moment, then forced the images from his mind as best he could, and looked down at the journal again.

MENTAL-CARE FACILITY
WAVERLY RESEARCH CENTER

The top sheet and cover hung off the foot of the bed onto the throw rug covering the concrete floor. Dr. Lobb sat in a straight chair at a table across his small room. A Bunsen burner cast its low blue flame against a crack rock stuck in the end of a five-inch-long straight-shooter made of glass. Dr. Lobb's full lips were clamped around the tube's other end. He sucked deeply, his thick sideburns moving with the in-and-out motions of his cheeks. His eyes were slitted and seemed to have recessed even further into their sockets. The skin around them was puffy, swollen to the point that it almost looked like air had been injected under the skin.

Past the closed door to his side, out in the detention area, Blue faced his cell bars. Wearing only the gray, cotton shorts, his hands at the sides of his neck, he swayed back and forth. A low hiss of air coming up a throat absent vocal cords escaped his clenched teeth. He arched his back. He reached over his shoulders and tried to touch down his spine. He brought his hands around behind him, again trying to reach the spot where the burning sensation hurt him. Then he suddenly lunged to the bars and clasped them with his big hands, staring at the closed door to Lobb's room. He tried to shake the bars, but they wouldn't move. He whirled around and threw his back against them, bending his legs and rubbing his spine hard up and down the bars like an animal trying to scrape ticks from its hide against a post. He took a sudden step forward, stopped, and whirled in a circle. His hands went over his shoulders again. He ran to the rear of the cell, jumped onto the bunk and grabbed the ledge of the slitlike, horizontal opening above him on the wall.

His muscles bulging, he dragged his face up even with the bars. He let go of the ledge and grabbed the thick steel rods, hanging from them, shaking them and kicking his feet against the wall. He pushed his hand past the bars and pressed it against the steel screen covering the opening from the outside. He pushed harder. A corner of the screen pulled loose, and he wiggled his hand through the slight opening. He caught the stiff wire and tried to tug it the rest of the way loose. His weaker left hand, holding him up to the bars, began to quiver. His shoulder twitched and his fingers came open—his other hand jerked back through the wire, and he fell heavily to his knees on the bunk.

He looked at the blood seeping from his hand where the sharp ends of the wire had pierced the skin.

Above him, a light fluttering.

It took a moment to register.

He slowly raised his eyes.

A moth circled above the ledge, flew back toward the bars, then came out into view again and flew to the cell's overhead light, its bulb dim and covered with a thick grid of steel.

The moth began to circle the illumination, slowly, then faster, throwing its body against the grid, bouncing off, circling the light again, then flying farther out from the grid, and coming rapidly back at it again, throwing its body once more against the source of the glow.

Blue's head perfectly steady, he forced himself to ignore the burning sensation running down his spine. His pupils moved back and forth as his gaze kept pace with the silent insect's flight.

A moment later, Blue slipped quietly off the bunk, and began to pull its cover and sheets into his arms.

Shannon's Expedition sat off to one side of the highway, a hundred feet away from its intersection with the narrow blacktop road. The one that turned toward the chain-link fence surrounding the research complex a quarter mile away. Bright lights shined from the large building. A half dozen cars and pickup trucks sat in the parking area at the near side of the long structure. The remainder of the complex was cast only in the dim illumination from the moon. No vehicles were parked next to the smaller, blocky building housing the mental-care facility. The side of the structure was completely darkened.

She had been there over an hour, aimlessly looking, not seeing anything that would spark a thought, unable to imagine anything she hadn't thought of already.

She lifted her gaze and stared into the sky. A wispy, slow-moving cloud was beginning to pass across the moon. She looked at the bright North Star and the other stars twinkling above her. She searched between them, wondering.

"I will," she said, the strength of determination in her tone.

Simply that and no more.

In a locked room to a side of the hallway leading from the front offices in the robotics manufacturing plant, a bank of monitor screens glowed different hues. The screens fed by the surveillance cameras within the area where the robots worked glowed with a white light. The screens from the cameras in the nerve regeneration laboratory glowed green. Most of the rats in the laboratory were asleep. One moved slowly across its cage, the small rodent's chest and head high, its haunches low, its rear legs bent and quivering, its tail dragging along behind it through the sawdust covering a cage's floor. A larger rat seemed to be stretched out resting. But as the screen continued to glow it became evident from the animal using its front legs to pull its body across the enclosure floor that it was one that had been operated on earlier that day.

The bank of screens being fed by the cameras outside the building were separated from the bank of interior monitoring screens by a distance of only a couple of feet, and were arranged in three levels of four screens each. The top two levels displayed the views captured by the slow movements of a series of cameras panning the fence and grounds within the complex. The lowest level showed a field of view, not moving, but riveted in place. Each of these screens displayed Shannon's Expedition.

Outside the building, a lens of a camera hanging under the eave of the roof revolved slowly, extending its range. Inside the surveillance room, one of the screens in the lower bank now showed an extreme close-up of the Expedition, even Shannon's shadowy form through the windshield.

Murphy stared at the screen as the camera changed to an infrared lens. Shannon's face glowed a light green.

On the wall opposite the banks of screens, a single large monitoring unit the size of a big-screen TV suddenly came to life with a bright white glow. The screen's left half displayed a close-up of the Expedition. A moment later wording started scrolling up the right side of the screen.

VEHICLE: FORD EXPEDITION
COLOR: SILVER
ADDITIONAL INFORMATION
OCCUPANT: FEMALE
SUMMARY
FEMALE OCCUPANT: UNIDENTIFIED
INITIAL ARRIVAL OUTSIDE OF COMPLEX
22:37 HOURS
INITIAL DEPARTURE FROM AREA OUTSIDE COMPLEX
SUBJECT REMAINING
VISIT DURATION: 1 HOUR, 11 MINUTES,
18 SECONDS AND CONTINUING

The screen dimmed and went blank. Its lower right quarter suddenly glowed a light green. Bold black letters began spelling out a message:

MONITOR SCREEN VISUAL UPDATES
CONTINUING EVERY TEN MINUTES
TIME OF NEXT AUTOMATIC VISUAL
23:58 HOURS
PUSH ANY KEY FOR INSTANT UPDATE

At the side of the highway, Shannon started the Expedition and guided it back up onto the blacktop.

A few seconds later the vehicle's red taillights disappeared over a slight rise in the pavement.

At the complex, the cameras that had been focused on the Expedition made a clicking noise and resumed their slow, wide-sweeping surveillance in sync with the other cameras mounted around the buildings.

Inside the surveillance room, Murphy pushed a button at the base of the telephone and lifted the receiver to his ear.

Inside the detention area, a second moth had joined the first one circling the grid-covered light at the top of Blue's cell. Blue had folded his blanket and sheet into square pads nearly an inch thick, and stood on them directly under the light. The pillow he had placed under the sheets gave him another inch or so. The mattress off his bunk gave him the most added height. He had forced it into a thick roll, mashed it down flat, and held it compressed in place as he laid the sheet and cover and pillow on it. Then, carefully balancing himself, he had stepped onto the makeshift platform. Even with his head tilted upward, his thick hands reaching as high as they could, the tips of his fingers were still an inch or two from the paths of the circling insects.

He cupped his fingers, making a curling motion indicating the moths should come to him.

They kept circling the light.

He flattened his hands, moving them slowly around under the insects' flight, so they would have a place to land.

They kept flying without paying any attention to him.

Out of the corner of his eyes, he caught movement at the barred window in the rear wall.

A translucent bit of material floated slowly down toward his bunk. A praying mantis sat on the ledge in front of the bars. Nearly three inches in length, with the ramrod-straight upper half of its body not much larger than a pencil lead, it sat angled up on its four support legs. Its two thicker front arms cocked in front of it in a prayerful attitude, it clasped the small white body of a flying insect with only one wing remaining dangling at its side. The other wing, torn loose and floating down toward the bunk was what had caught Blue's attention. The mantis's head was buried deeply, unseen inside the insect's soft parts.

The triangular-shaped head suddenly popped out of the body. The mantis dropped the empty husk of the insect to the ledge. The long, skinny predator moved closer to the edge of the ledge. The two widely spaced eyes seemed to stare directly at Blue.

Blue came down from his platform.

He stepped slowly up onto the bunk.

He raised his face as high as he could.

The mantis didn't move. Blue stared a moment at the obviously unfrightened creature, then slowly extended his forefinger toward the sticklike predator.

The mantis jumped.

It landed on Blue's thick nose.

Blue's eyes drew together as they stared at the insect. The creature's head cocked to the side. The eyes continued to stare back at him.

For the first time in memory, a grin crossed Blue's face.

He raised his forefinger to the side of his nose, and ran it slowly up the skin. When the finger started under the mantis, the insect, instead of flying off, climbed onto it.

Blue's grin broadened. He looked back at the moths.

Seconds later, moving slowly, holding his finger as steady as he could, he climbed back up onto his soft platform, raising his hand and the mantis toward the bulb.

He was still an inch or two short. Balancing his thick bulk on the unstable material, he raised slowly up onto his toes.

A moth swept directly past his finger. The mantis's arms struck in a blur too fast to see—the moth struggled desperately to free itself.

Blue lowered his finger and watched.

The moth quit struggling as the mantis severed its head from its body. The head bounced off Blue's hand and fell toward the floor.

Blue grinned.

A moment later the mantis's head began to bury itself into the opening where the moth's head had been, and Blue's grin broadened.

Dr. Lobb stepped from his room.

"What in the hell?" he said when he saw the flying insects circling the three overhead lights running across the ceiling. He looked at Blue standing on the folded garments from the bunk.

"You broke your damn screen out," he muttered.

The telephone in his room rang. "You crazy bastard," he said, staring at Blue, then he turned back into his room.

Blue looked at the praying mantis clutching his finger. The predator's thin upper body was now pushed halfway up inside the moth, burrowing ever deeper with each motion of its sharp jaws. Blue, being careful not to disturb the insect with too quick a motion, slowly reached down and lifted the blanket and pillow from his platform.

A moment later, bunching the material at his chest, he slid under his bunk, and glanced back at Lobb's open door.

The last thing he pulled into the dark shadow was his finger and the ravenous mantis—the first companion Blue had had in years; the only thing that dared to come into the cell when Blue wasn't bound to his chair.

Shannon guided the Expedition off to the side of the road fronting the bayou a few miles from the research center. Thick trunks of cypress and tall water oaks stretched out across the water into the darkness. A mist hovered above the water. Smears of floating green algae and patches of water grass, black in the dim moonlight, covered most of the bayou's surface. A series of tiny ripples from something moving out in the darkness washed gently against the bank. She stared at what remained of the ruts the Englands' pickup truck had left in the soft dirt when it had left the blacktop and sped into the bayou. Almost on top of the same spot was the torn and plowed ground where the pickup had been wrenched by a tow truck back up onto the bank. She wondered if the Englands had been autopsied or if the coroner had simply determined that they were victims of a tragic accident.

Joe England had worked as a robotics machinery supervisor at the complex. He had seen something. Something there that had gotten him killed. And her father killed. She was as certain of that as she was that she was sitting there staring into the water where the Englands died.

Someway, somehow, she had to get inside the complex and look for herself.

"No," Lobb said.

"I'm telling you," Murphy said. "She knows about the Englands. She was sitting out here for over an hour. What's she going to do next? You want her to keep on until she gets lucky?"

"She doesn't know any more now than she did when

she started. She'll get tired of thinking; it'll wear off and she'll give up."

"She could be made to quit thinking."

"After her father? Why don't you get out and wave a red flag so the cops will know where to look?"

"It doesn't have to be a red flag. What's one more car wreck? There's car wrecks all the time. People fall down and go into comas all the time. You got some stuff that can make that happen."

"Murphy, I have work to do," Lobb said, and hung up the telephone.

Blue stared at Lobb's closed door from underneath the bunk. The praying mantis dropped the empty shell of the moth, then suddenly flew from his finger, landing a few feet out on the concrete floor. Blue stared at the insect for a moment, then slowly crawled out toward it. He felt a sharp pain race up his spine. That triggered the raw nerves surrounding the cervical vertebrae. The pain lanced back down his spine and radiated through his arms and legs. Soon he was in nearly as much agony as he had been before.

But he ignored it.

Still on his hands and knees he crawled up to the mantis. He lowered his head close to the insect.

The triangular head was focused up toward the light, the two hairlike antennae standing erect.

Blue slid his finger under the mantis and gently lifted it off the floor.

It didn't fly away.

A grin spread across Blue's face, and he said something pleasant, but no sound came from his lips.

A moment later, he pulled the erect creature back under the bunk with him.

Dr. Lobb, a tall can of insect spray in his hand, stepped outside his room.

He moved under the first ceiling light, lifted the can, and pressed down on the nozzle. A misty spray sped toward the bugs circling the steel grid. A cloud enveloped them and they began to fall, spinning one by one toward the floor.

In seconds, he had stood under each light in turn, spraying until every insect lay on the concrete floor.

Now he walked to the cells.

He stared at Blue's dark figure in the shadow under the bunk. Two moths and a flying beetle spun around the light at the top of the cell. Lobb stuck his hand between the bars, raised the can, and held down on the nozzle. The spray shot toward the grid, the cloud began to form.

A bug spun slowly down from the light toward the floor.

From under the bunk, a fluttering.

The mantis flew out from the shadow toward the falling bug. The thin predator climbed into the air, faltered as it entered the billowing mist, hung for a second, then abruptly glided down to the concrete floor, landing close to the bars.

Lobb pointed the can downward and pressed the nozzle; the spray shot forward in an enveloping cone, dampening the floor and mantis alike.

The insect arched up on its four supporting legs, and fell over on its side. Its triangular-shaped head turned away from the bars toward the rear of the cell—and stayed in that direction as it quit moving.

The loud hiss of anguish coming from underneath the bunk caused Lobb to jump backward from the bars.

Angered, he stared at Blue's figure.

Then he stepped closer to the cell again, reached his arm through the bars, aimed the spray can underneath the bunk, and pressed the nozzle.

The mist traveled rapidly halfway across the open space, then began to dissipate, only traces of it floating on toward the bunk, and Blue, now with his head out from under it, staring toward Lobb.

Slowly, Blue slid out onto the concrete floor and

came to his feet. His expression relaxed. He took a step toward the front of the cell.

Lobb waited no longer, rapidly back-pedaling away from the bars and staring at the wide face with its eyes glaring back into his.

△ CHAPTER TWENTY

The Jonathan Waverly home was an eight-thousand-square-foot brick and stucco structure sitting behind a circular drive. A manicured yard thick with bushes and beds of flowers spread out to the sides. The double doors at the front of the house opened into a wide marble-tiled foyer leading to a huge living room decorated with a mixture of fine antiques and contemporary furniture. At the rear of the room, sliding glass doors afforded a view of a brightly lit, oversized swimming pool surrounded by neatly trimmed hedges, rosebushes, and Grecian statues.

But nowhere was there evidence of any more luxury than in Waverly's bedroom. Its focal point was a specially designed bed, larger than king-size, covered with silk sheets and a bedspread embroidered with a brightly colored replica of the American flag that had flown over Fort McHenry during the War of 1812.

Jonathan Waverly, dressed in a silver-colored silk robe over blue silk pajamas, sat back against two thick pillows at the head of the bed. A giant-screen TV standing alone a few feet from the foot of the bed was tuned to WLOX, with the sound turned off. The screen displayed a background scene of an oil rig in the Gulf of Mexico beyond the barrier islands. An environmentalist, a stern look across her face, her thin lips moving rapidly, stared into the camera. The host was nodding with her words. The channel changer lay beside Waverly.

Also lying around him and strewn across the foot of the bed were copies of various daily reports from his medical research centers across the country.

The report he stared at through a pair of glasses rimmed in eighteen-carat gold was from the Los Angeles center, the largest nerve research facility under his corporate umbrella. He glanced over the top of the report toward the TV just as an overweight, balding man in a suit and red bow tie stepped up to a set of microphones. Waverly lowered the report, caught the channel changer, pressed the volume button, and waited for what the Senate Majority Leader had to say.

The senator started by lifting his hand in front of him to silence the reporters who had already started shouting questions. He read from a prepared statement.

"I want to add my thoughts to those who have already expressed their sadness at the death of Congressman Donnelly, and say how much I will miss him, too. He was a hard-working member of the House who will be remembered for many achievements, but none more important than his constant struggle to improve the medical health-care system in this country. In particular, his constant urging of the Congress to adequately fund medical research.

"To that end, there will be a bill soon introduced in both the House and the Senate. A bill designed to provide funds for medical research in this country in an amount that has never been dreamed of before, for the benefit of every man, woman, and child in this nation, and eventually in the world. I want to say now that I intend to join the sponsorship of this bill, and will do what I can to ensure its passage in the Senate."

Waverly grinned.

At a sudden pain in his chest, the grin left his face. He reached for the bottle of nitroglycerin pills on the bedside table. As he groped for it, he knocked two other small bottles to the floor. He got the lid off and dumped one of the tiny pills into his mouth, moving it under his tongue.

It took a couple of minutes for the pain to begin to subside.

It wasn't fair, he thought. He had never smoked a cigarette. He had quit drinking years ago. He had tried to jog until his lungs wouldn't allow it anymore. He had done everything, and yet his health had grown steadily worse. It wasn't fair.

For a moment, self-pity moistened his eyes. Then he remembered it wouldn't be much longer—and a smile came to his tired face.

At Shannon Donnelly's name being spoken, he looked back at the television, and the smile disappeared. The screen was now filled with the faces of Lawrence's daughter and former wife.

Waverly stared at Shannon. In her likeness, so similar in its features to her father's, he saw all that had been destroyed, all the wasted years—and the pain and suffering that had been endured.

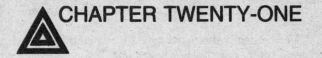

CHAPTER TWENTY-ONE

The cellular telephone rang at 7:00 A.M. Michael had forgotten to turn it off. He leaned across his bed to the lamp table and lifted the telephone as it rang again.

"Mr. Waverly said to tell you he hoped you enjoyed a good night's sleep, Dr. Sims, and he would like to see you for breakfast."

Fifteen minutes later, through with his shower, Michael shaved in the head located forward of the galley. The door was open. His mother sipped from a cup of coffee as she stood next to the galley sink.

"I'm glad you're going to Washington," she said.

"I haven't won yet."

"You will—everybody said your father would have won if he had run."

Michael looked out the door.

"How glad are you?" he asked.

"If you can help get the amount of research funding that you said Mr. Waverly discussed, you'll be more help to people than you ever could be as a doctor."

"That's not what I asked. I asked how glad are you?"

"You mean how do I like the idea of your leaving? I don't. I didn't like your leaving to spend the night at one of your friends' houses when you were a little boy.

I didn't like your going away to medical school. I'm possessive. But I'm proud of you."

"You know there's no reason for you not to go with me."

"We've already discussed that. I'll come and see you every so often. But this is where I live."

He came out of the head, drying his face with a towel. She handed him a white shirt.

As she walked with him toward the door leading to the walkway at the *Cassandra*'s side, he said, "I'll be flying here every weekend." He smiled. "To see my constituents."

Howard sat in his folding chair at the bow of the Hatteras. He wore his usual garb of shorts, leaving the vast majority of his wiry body exposed to the sun. His coloring stayed between dark brown and darker brown year round. He glanced over his shoulder as they stepped out of the salon to the rail.

"Going to rain," he said. He held his finger up into the air as if he were testing the wind.

The sky was perfectly clear, a bright sun beaming down and not a cloud in sight.

Michael said, "You better stick to engines instead of weather forecasting."

Howard stood and walked down the side of the Hatteras toward them. "No," he said, "I'm not wrong. Rain'll be in here day after tomorrow—though the TV hasn't figured that out yet." He nodded his greeting at Michael's mother. "Ma'am," he said. He glanced down at his shorts. "Excuse my lack of a shirt. Didn't know there was a lady in the neighborhood."

"Howard, this is my mother, Marjorie."

"Glad to meet you, ma'am. Again, excuse my baring my soul."

"I'm pleased to meet you, Mr. . . . . is Howard your first or last name?"

"Sadly my last name is Heartfelt. You don't think that didn't cause Daddy grief in the logging camps? I think my grandfather got it out of a romance novel when he came to this country. Least he could read English. Fact is, I can't pronounce his real last name anyway. Let me run in and get a shirt and we can talk."

"Oh, no, Mr. Howard," Marjorie said. "Michael's leaving right now—going to talk to a man about Michael running for Congress."

Howard's eyes narrowed a little. He looked at Michael. "Medical career crashed already? What did you do?"

"No, Mr. Howard," Marjorie said, "he just thinks he can help more people that way."

"As a politician?" Howard asked, his eyes narrowing again. "Just take me a second to get a shirt," he said, and disappeared inside the Hatteras.

Marjorie smiled. "Who is that? A regular chatterbox."

Michael had a thought. He glanced at the door where Howard had disappeared, and back at his mother.

"Are you going to stay here and fix me lunch?" he asked her.

"I wasn't planning on it."

"Why don't you? I've been berthed beside Howard since I moved the *Cassandra* here last month and haven't invited him over to eat a single time." He had drunk beers with Howard on the Hatteras, and had had Howard over as late as the last weekend to drink a beer on the trawler. But it wasn't *his* and Howard's socializing he had in mind now.

"I don't know," his mother said. "I have things to do at the house."

"Just this once—you know how I like your stuffed eggplant."

"Go to that trouble for lunch?"

"I have everything in the galley."

Marjorie looked back at the Hatteras. "Okay, if you

feel you owe him. He does look like he could stand a home-cooked meal."

Waverly's three-story brick and stucco home was twenty minutes away from the yacht harbor. Michael parked in the circular drive in front of the house. As he stepped from the Jeep, his attention was drawn to the street fronting the property as a man in a pickup truck honked his horn at a silver Expedition traveling too slowly in front of him.

Shannon ignored the man honking the horn behind her as she looked through Waverly's yard at the aging Jeep parked in the circular drive—and at Michael, his face turned in her direction. She stared at him. She knew who he was.

As Michael came up the wide, tiled steps at the front of the sprawling mansion, he was surprised to note that he was beginning to feel a pleasant sensation of antici-pation. When he had first decided to call Waverly to accept his offer, he had done so while feeling blue over his mother and Candice Schilling and Johnny Whitaker. He had been down and made the call because of every-one who had ever died because of the lack of intensified medical research. Now he had the same reasons in mind, but they felt different. If everything went as Wav-erly planned, Michael knew he could do more for med-icine as a congressman than a doctor, much, much more—and that did excite him. As he neared the front door, a butler in dark slacks and a red vest over a white shirt opened it. He had gray hair.

"Mr. Waverly is at the pool," he said.

It was beyond the glass doors at the rear of the spa-cious living room. Waverly, the stubble on his narrow face grown thicker in the last twenty-four hours, wore white slacks held up by a pair of gold-colored suspend-ers running down across a blue silk shirt. He stood, removed his sunglasses, and came around the side of a table next to the pool to shake hands.

"Dr. Sims, I very much appreciate your agreeing to work with me on my dream—our dream now."

The butler pulled a chair back for Michael, then hurried around the table to reseat Waverly.

A small glass bottle of nitroglycerin pills and a larger plastic one of Maalox stood on the table.

"I hope ham and scrambled eggs is suitable," Waverly said.

"Sounds good," Michael answered. The butler turned and walked toward the house.

Waverly lifted the bottle of Maalox and unscrewed the top. As he lifted the bottle to his mouth, Michael looked across the spreading grounds past the pool. Concrete and wrought-iron benches were strategically placed in small areas surrounded by neatly trimmed bushes. Starlings flew around a fountain full of water sparkling in the bright sunshine. A man with all of Waverly's money, Michael thought, and yet saddled with his health burdens. Waverly had said his dream was for others, but Michael couldn't help but believe the old man was hoping something in the research would happen quickly enough to help him, too.

Waverly wiped a white smear from his lips as he set the bottle of Maalox back on the table. "Well, Doctor, time is important," he said. "So let's get directly to the point." He crossed his thin legs. "First thing we do is announce your candidacy before anyone else decides to enter the race. And announce my backing. I have your statement already prepared. It will be on TV tonight and in the papers in the morning. When we finish our conversation here, I want you to go pay your respects to the Donnelly family—Lawrence's former wife and his daughter. My butler will provide you with the address."

An instant dislike of that idea passed across Michael. "Excuse me, Mr. Waverly, but—"

"No buts, Dr. Sims. I can imagine what you're think-ing. That with the tragedy just occurring, that your call-ing on the family to tell them you're running for the office might appear . . . unseemly. I respect that. But they'll understand, Dr. Sims. They're a political family. And, quite frankly, if the mother, or even the daughter, for God's sake, is thinking about running to fill his po-sition, your announcement—along with your explain-ing how I'm backing you—will put a halt to that. What *would* be unseemly, Dr. Sims, is for one of them to announce for the position and then be embarrassed by finding out—afterward—that I'm throwing my weight behind someone else." Waverly raised his finger in the air. "Trust me, Dr. Sims, I know politics."

Now Waverly clasped his hands in front of his chest. "After you pay your respects to the Donnellys, you will need to go to WLOX to tape the announcement of your candidacy. There will be a script already prepared, but I have no problem with you editing it into a form you feel best suits your manner of expressing yourself."

As Waverly paused, he smiled politely. "I know I'm overwhelming you, Dr. Sims, and I do apologize for coming at you so directly. But, again, I'm certain you would agree that if this race is worth running, it's worth going full steam ahead from the beginning."

Michael still felt a sensation of excitement at what he was about to embark on, but he also still didn't like the idea of having to visit the Donnelly home, and he wasn't certain at all that he would ever warm to Wav-erly with the man's aggressive personality. But he was keenly aware that Waverly knew what he was doing. One only had to watch election night results from var-ious parts of the country to know that. The Waverly organization had been linked to a half a dozen con-gressional and senatorial campaigns in the last election, and Michael couldn't remember any who had lost. No doubt he would have like-minded friends already in Washington when he arrived there.

The butler had come back outside the house with a tray. He set a plate of ham, scrambled eggs, grits, sliced tomatoes, and biscuits in front of Michael along with a cup of steaming coffee accompanied with small silver cream and sugar containers. He set a bowl of oatmeal and a glass of milk in front of Waverly.

"My stomach," Waverly said, nodding at the oatmeal. "Enjoy yourself while you're young. And, by the way, I have already dispatched a check to pay off your student loans." He smiled and raised the glass of milk into the air.

"To the dream," he said. "And to our long, long association."

△ CHAPTER TWENTY-TWO

The nearer Michael drew to Mrs. Donnelly's home, the slower he drove. He wasn't feeling any excited anticipation at the moment. In fact, quite the opposite. In medical school it hadn't been enjoyable working with the odors from some of the chemicals that preserved the cadavers. It seemed some of the smell stayed with him no matter how many times he washed his hands. But it was necessary to work with the cadavers. He could see how it was necessary to pay his respects to the Donnellys. But he felt cheap—he hadn't known the congressman personally and he didn't know either the wife or daughter. He knew the feeling would linger for a while—like the odor had.

Of course they wouldn't be aware that he hadn't known the congressman. Not with his father having been one of Donnelly's strongest supporters in his early years in Congress. And they would remember his mother, too. By inference they would not think it was out of place for him to be coming by to pay his respects. Still, he didn't like it. How in hell did he suddenly announce that he was running for the man's office so soon after he was found dead?

He parked in the drive of the sprawling stucco house, adjusted his tie at the entrance, and pushed the doorbell.

An attractive dark-haired woman in her fifties,

dressed in high heels and a beige linen dress opened the door.

"Mrs. Donnelly?"

"Yes."

"I'm Michael Sims."

He felt even cheaper than he'd thought he would. "You might remember my father—he had the same first name I do. He was Dr. Michael Sims."

A smile spread across the woman's face. "Remember? Of course," she said. "He handed my husband the first political contribution he ever received. He was a good friend of my husband and me."

She stepped back from the door. "Won't you come in?"

He walked past her into the house. He couldn't help but look toward the living room. The news reports said that was where the congressman had shot himself.

"I remember you, too, now," Mrs. Donnelly said.

"You do?"

"Yes. You're a doctor from Coastal Regional. I remember a feature they did about the hospital on WLOX. I caught your name then—the emergency department, right?"

He nodded.

"Yes," she said. "Shannon and I saw a reporter speaking with you and we wondered. I knew you were about the right age to be your father's son. So it's the second Dr. Sims now? Your father would be proud." She smiled pleasantly. "Would you care for a glass of tea?"

"No, thank you. I only wanted to stop in for a moment to say how sorry I am about the congressman's death."

"Thank you." Mrs. Donnelly glanced across her shoulder toward the center of the living room, then brought her gaze back to his. "I might like a glass of tea myself," she said. "Come on in here," she added, starting toward the kitchen door.

Seconds later, as she opened the refrigerator door, she looked back across her shoulder. "Are you sure you wouldn't care for something? We have Coke, too."

"No, thank you." There was a small TV on the counter next to the back wall. A soap opera played with the sound turned barely loud enough to hear.

Mrs. Donnelly filled a glass with tea from a pitcher and nodded toward the breakfast table.

After she settled into a seat, he pulled back a chair and sat down across from her. *How in the hell to start?* he thought. And then he decided simply to get it over with.

He phrased his words in a manner he hoped would deflect some of the hard feelings toward him, if there were going to be any. "Jonathan Waverly has asked me to run for Mr. Donnelly's seat. Before I accepted, I wanted your opinion." *Damn, I'm lying now—I've already accepted.*

Surprisingly, Mrs. Donnelly smiled softly. "Lawrence would like that," she said. "He thought a lot of your father, and you, too. I remember that now. He came home one day talking about you. It was when you were a cute little boy—I guess about three or four. He said you pronounced words starting with C's like they were T's. Said you were playing with a little toy castle and told him it was your tastle. I remember that because he bought Shannon a castle that Christmas. Said it looked like fun. Toy soldiers and all. I think he was trying to make a boy of her. Footballs, baseballs—that's the kind of things he always bought her. I had to buy her the dolls." She raised her gaze above him, a reflective expression on her face for a moment. "The old memories flooding back—I'm certainly glad you came by." She glanced toward her tea. "Are you sure you wouldn't care for something?"

"No, thank you. I've enjoyed speaking with you. I wish the circumstances could be different. I think I'll be going now if . . ."

"Mother."

The voice came from the living room.

"In here, Shannon. We have a visitor. The son of an old friend of your father's."

Shannon Donnelly appeared in the doorway leading from the living room. She wore a dark skirt cut just above her knees. A belt cinched her small waist. Her dark hair, resting against the shoulders of her blouse, framed a lightly tanned, oval-shaped face highlighted by deep green eyes. Michael had to make a small effort to keep from staring. He stood.

She was the one who kept staring, directly into his face.

"This is Dr. Michael Sims," her mother said. "Remember seeing him on TV? He's going to run for your father's seat."

When Shannon didn't speak, her mother said, "Honey, he came by to—"

"Have you paid your respects to Jonathan Waverly yet?" Shannon asked.

"Mr. Waverly is the one who asked him to run," her mother said.

Shannon kept staring.

"Shannon?" her mother said.

"Well, you've paid your respects, Dr. Sims," Shannon said. "I imagine you're leaving now."

"Shannon?" her mother repeated, her voice rising.

The cheap feeling was back. Michael turned toward Mrs. Donnelly. "I want to say again that I'm sorry about Congressman Donnelly's death. I do need to be going."

The woman smiled weakly and came to her feet.

Michael walked toward the living room. Shannon stepped aside and didn't look at him as he passed.

Her mother said, "Show Dr. Sims the way out."

"He'll find it himself," Shannon said.

"Shannon, what's wrong with you?"

Shannon came across the floor to the breakfast table.

Her mother looked past her to the living room. They heard the front door close.

"Shannon, what are—"

"Shhh," Shannon said, staring at the television on the counter.

Jonathan Waverly's shoulders and face filled the screen. He was clean-shaven. His narrow face had been powdered to keep his pale skin from reflecting the camera lights. He smiled pleasantly. But not too big a smile. He took a moment before he spoke. It was obvious he felt deeply about what he was going to say.

"First, let me state how saddened—no, sickened—I am about Congressman Donnelly's tragic death. I want to express my sympathy to Mrs. Mary Ann Donnelly and her daughter, Miss Shannon Donnelly—"

Shannon walked toward the breakfast table.

"—and also my sympathy to the hundreds of good friends Congressman Donnelly had, and still has. And then, my sympathies to the citizens—"

The channel changer lay at an end of the table and Shannon lifted it into her hands.

"—of this district. My sympathies to the citizens of this country whom he represented so well—especially those hundreds of thousands suffering from diseases that should not still affect . . ."

Shannon looked at her mother, and thought how the kitchen had become her real home, the rest of the house reachable only by walking through the cold, empty living room highlighted by the absence of the easy chair and throw rug.

She looked back at Waverly's face, and pressed the button on the channel changer, cutting the television off.

"You bastard," she said.

Michael thumped his fingers on the steering wheel as he guided the Jeep out of the drive onto the street in front of Mrs. Donnelly's house.

He felt cheap.

Irritated.

With the daughter.

With himself.

With Waverly.

"Son-of-a-damn . . ." He shook his head and turned in the direction of the hospital.

Shannon spoke into the telephone in the kitchen. "James, do you know Dr. Michael Sims?"

"I know *of* him," the sheriff said. "I knew his father personally."

"Will you do me a favor?"

"Yes, certainly."

"Will you run a check on him for me?"

"You mean a criminal check?"

"Yes. And anything else you can find out about him. I, uh . . . I mean everything. I would like to know his family background too—his father and mother, back as far as you can get. It's important to me. I'll owe you."

Johnny heard the soft sound. Soft, but metallic-sounding. He heard it again, barely perceptible. He quit breathing so he could hear better.

Just the faintest sound of metal scraping against metal.

Then a sudden loud scream caused him to flinch. The cages bounced against each other. The monkeys screamed at the top of their lungs. They were fighting. Their cages had swung together from their motions and they were trying to get through the wire to each other, each head trying to attack its former body.

The light came on.

Johnny shut his eyes against the blinding glare.

Dr. Lobb, the syringe with the long needle in his hands, walked toward the bed.

"No, you son-of-a-bitch, get away from me!"

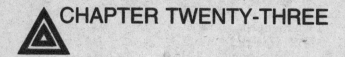

CHAPTER TWENTY-THREE

The *Sun Herald* announced Michael's candidacy on the front page of the second section. Many of the doctors and other staff had read it. A few were curious about why he was leaving the medical profession. He told them it was only temporary. Most wished him well.

In the emergency department, he straightened from examining a little girl who sat on a stool in front of him. Her mother looked at him.

"She could have asthma," he said. "But I don't think so. Even if she does, many children eventually grow out of it. You're moving to Pensacola?"

The woman nodded.

"I'm going to write in the chart that I treated her for a cough. If I put down the possibility of asthma and later an insurance company finds the notation in her records—even if she doesn't have asthma or has grown out of it—she'll have a hard time getting medical insurance at a normal rate in the future. If her cough comes back—becomes chronic—when you see a doctor in Pensacola, you need to tell him there's the possibility of asthma. But I think she's going to be fine."

The woman, a petite blonde with long hair hanging past the shoulders of a noticeably faded blouse, smiled at him. "Thank you, Doctor."

He wondered if she even had insurance. Her skirt

was also faded from so many washings—and they had come into the emergency department in the middle of the day rather than go see a doctor at his office. He hoped maybe when he got to Congress he could do something about people in that kind of situation, too. He looked back at the little girl. When she had walked into the department beside her mother, he had thought of how much she reminded him of Candice. Especially her smile. He patted her on the shoulder. She rose from the stool and walked to her mother.

"If you'll just give me a minute," he said, "I'll write up her discharge papers and you can get on out of here."

"Thank you, Doctor," the woman said again.

As Michael walked toward the counter, Olga Lindestrom approached him. "I hate that we're going to lose you," she said as she stopped in front of him. "But maybe you can help us more as a Congressman. We so badly need medical care that everyone can afford—and if anyone can help to persuade politicians in Washington of that, I'd put my money on you." She looked toward the blonde and her child. Then her gaze came back to his. She patted him on the shoulder.

"Good luck, Doctor."

Shannon listened over her speakerphone as Sheriff Everette summarized the results of his department's hastily done background check on Dr. Michael Sims and his family.

"Basically it's your average Joe family, maybe slightly above average financially until the old man died. He was a throwback to the old-fashioned general practitioner; had his own one-doctor office in Gulfport. Died with a lot of patients who would go to the wall for him, but a lot who hadn't paid their bills either. Turned out he had zilch to leave to his wife and son. She hadn't worked out of the home a day in her life. She opened a little pottery place and made ends meet.

Michael graduated fourth in his medical school class and was chief resident in emergency medicine in his last year at the medical center. Moved back here, and been working at Coastal Regional for a little over a year. No bad marks on his record of any kind."

Shannon bit absent-mindedly at her thumbnail as she continued to listen.

"As far as the politics, the old man was drafted into being Republican county chairman when nobody else would have the position. I can remember those days: Sometimes during a primary election you couldn't find anybody at the Republican polls but the poll watchers. As the party grew in the state, his power did, too. His involvement pretty much ended when Jonathan Waverly moved here from Los Angeles and more or less took over your father's campaigns—but you and your mother would know more about that than the people my deputies spoke with. In other words, the whole family, the young Dr. Sims included, is about as clean as they come—at least on the record."

Shannon removed her thumbnail from her mouth.

"Thanks," she said, "I owe you one."

She cut off the speakerphone.

Carol stood in the office doorway. "If you ask me, Shannon, if Waverly took the congressman away from Dr. Sims's father, then Sims and Waverly wouldn't exactly be bosom buddies. But you didn't ask me."

Shannon nodded. "Stands to reason, doesn't it?"

"By the way, Judge Cox moved Ronnie Packard's case back for you indefinitely—he said you should call him when you're ready. He said to tell you how sorry he was about your father."

Off to Shannon's side, the smoke detector hanging on the wall close to the fireplace chirped.

Carol stared at it. "That thing eats batteries—I just put new ones in it a couple of months ago."

*   *   *

Inside his office, Sheriff James Everette, leaning back in his chair, had gazed idly up into the air after finishing the conversation with Shannon. Now he looked at his chief deputy, Dennis Allen, sitting in a straight chair at the other side of the desk.

"Dennis, that wasn't for a case she's been hired on. It's about her father. How does knowing about Dr. Sims have anything to do with the congressman?"

Allen, a tall, raw-boned man of twenty years' service, pushed a cut of chewing tobacco into his mouth and moved it to the inside of his cheek before he spoke.

"She's heard something. Or imagined something. Bottom line is she doesn't want to accept the fact her father could kill himself."

"There would be hell to pay if we said it's suicide," Everette mused, "and she comes up with something showing it isn't."

"Come on, Sheriff."

"Dennis, what would you say is the strongest case we ever had against a murderer?"

"Damn, there've been a load of 'em."

"Gerald Clayton," Everette said. "His mother was beaten to death. He was standing there scratched up. Everybody in town knew he was a crackhead; she had called us on his stealing from her before. We knew right then at the scene that the skin she had under her fingernails was going to be his. It was. He tried to say his mother scratched him when he tried to lift her from the floor after he found her like that. You remember that, too, don't you? When Shannon had the body exhumed though, there was more skin under the woman's nails than just that one sample. DNA didn't match. Semen on her clothes didn't match either."

Dennis shook his head. "I'm still not certain he wasn't in on it."

"I am—he wasn't. But that isn't the point. The point is that when you and I first saw the scene, we would have bet our lives that we knew exactly what happened.

It isn't emotion on Shannon's part anymore—if it's ever been. I'm telling you, I know her. She's not the type to give in to emotion—she's tough. Hell, I coached her in youth-league softball. She was a little tiny thing then, but a catcher didn't want to get in her way when she was coming toward home plate. And when she makes up her mind about something, she'll hang on to it like a snapping turtle. This crap about her telling us she has an important case . . . When she was a little girl and wanted something, she could look up at you with those big green eyes and tell you anything and you'd believe it. She has some serious reason to be doubting it's a suicide—at least what she thinks is a serious reason. What I want to know is where Dr. Sims fits in in her mind."

Everette paused as he sat up in his chair and stretched his arms over his head. "I'm going to wait until after the funeral, give her time to collect her thoughts. Then I think it'll be about time for me to go speak with her one-on-one. Meanwhile, you see if you can do a little more checking on Dr. Sims."

"What else is there to check?"

"You'll think of something."

▲ CHAPTER TWENTY-FOUR

Congressman Donnelly's funeral came sooner than Michael would have liked: the very next day. Yet no matter how long it might have been put off, he wouldn't have liked having to be there any better. He stood in the large crowd of dignitaries, friends, spectators, and news media surrounding the grave. When he had attended the services at the church, he had felt inconspicuous in the overflow of people having to stand against the wall behind the pews. But as he had driven toward the cemetery, the cheap feeling had become nearly overpowering. He had slowed his Jeep until it was at a crawl, nearly stopping it completely. Dressed in a dark suit and appropriate black tie, he had felt a mixture of a fool and a con man. It was all he could do not to turn around and drive back to the hospital—and call Waverly to tell him there was no way in hell he was running for Congress. That's what he had wanted to do. But he hadn't. He raised his head as the minister finished his sermon and closed his Bible.

He noticed Sheriff Everette glance in his direction again. He had done that several times. He wondered if the sheriff was a close friend of the family and felt the same way Shannon did about his announcing for her father's seat so soon after his death. He looked back to the grave. Mrs. Donnelly laid a rose on the coffin. She was dressed in black. Shannon laid a rose beside her mother's. She wore a dark blue dress. The Senate Majority Leader, his trademark red bow tie out of place among the somber dark ties most of the mourners were wearing, stepped close to speak with them. Television cameras from national networks to individual stations in and outside the state focused on the conversation. Some in the crowd watched the reporters and cameramen jostling for position, but most moved toward the exits. It wasn't too soon for Michael. He glanced in Everette's direction, then back at Shannon—she had stepped away from her mother and the majority leader and now stood in front of a thin, gray-haired man with a narrow face. He started toward his Jeep.

Shannon glanced in Michael's direction, then faced back to Robert Samples. He had just explained to her that a fax containing the Englands' phone records should be arriving at her law office at any moment, if it hadn't already. But she knew it hadn't. She had her beeper in one of the big side pockets of her dress and had told Carol to call if the fax came in.

"Thank you," she said. "I really appreciate all the help you've been."

Samples brushed his hair back from his forehead. "You ready to tell me what you're thinking?" he asked.

"Let me have a little while longer."

Samples glanced toward the sheriff.

"And please don't say anything to him," she said. "I really just need a little bit longer before I have to talk to anybody."

Samples nodded.

"You'll be the first to know if I do come up with anything," she added. ". . . If I do."

He nodded again.

"Thank you for coming," she said, and glanced at Michael as he walked toward his Jeep. He stopped to speak with a couple of older men. She recognized one as the hospital administrator.

"I wish there hadn't been a reason for coming," Samples said.

She squeezed his arm gently and started to turn in Michael's direction.

"The fax might be at your office by now," Samples reminded her.

"I want to see it as quickly as I can," she said. "But I have an opportunity right now to set something up—and I can't let it pass."

She turned toward Michael, leaving Samples to wonder what she meant.

As Clark and Dr. Reid walked away from him, Michael looked toward the delegation attending the services from the Waverly Corporation. There were three of them, including the national vice president of the organization. Despite how close Congressman Donnelly had been to the corporation, they had remained off to the side from the rest of the crowd during the services, and not even spoken with Shannon or her mother. Then he saw Shannon coming his way.

"Dr. Sims," she said.

He didn't know if he was prepared or not. After the way she had acted at her mother's, he had thought about her confronting him at the cemetery.

She continued across the grass.

The majority leader came up behind her and said something, and she turned back to him. She looked across her shoulder.

"Dr. Sims, could you wait a moment, please?"

Carol heard the fax machine when it rang. It was the one in Shannon's office. She hurried up the hallway.

A sheet of the thin paper slid slowly out of the back of the machine. It contained the record of long distance calls made from the Englands' home. The machine stopped after just one page.

There was only a single long distance call over the

entire several-day period covered by the records, the call Shannon was looking for—to her father in Washington. But it had been made only minutes before he had in turn called her. So whatever the Englands had told him when they called obviously hadn't started him drinking—the alcohol had already taken effect by the time Shannon had spoken with him.

Carol's gaze moved to a list of collect calls made to the Englands' number, a line of eight of them, all from a single Biloxi number. And not only all made the same Monday night in question, but all of them within an hour of when the Englands had called him, and he had called them back. Carol reached for the telephone on Shannon's desk.

Seconds later, she had punched in the number and listened to it ring.

It rang three times, four times, a fifth time, and finally a sixth time before she replaced the receiver and looked back at the fax.

Eight collect calls to the Englands with the first one made at eleven fifty-seven and continuing up through and after the call Shannon's father had made to her at twenty minutes after twelve. On Shannon's desk, the thin copies of the calls from her father's apartment lay face up. He had been speaking to someone at the center at the same time the last collect call was being made to the Englands.

Carol punched in the number again.

It rang several times without anyone answering. She kept waiting.

Then she heard the receiver being lifted on the other end of the line. A female voice said, "Hello."

"Who is this?" Carol asked.

"Who are you calling?"

"I, uh, I think I might have the wrong number."

"I think you probably do, ma'am. This is a pay telephone at Coastal Regional Hospital."

*   *   *

Michael waited as the majority leader turned back toward the grave and Shannon's mother still standing there, and Shannon came across the grass.

She stopped in front of him. Michael forced a polite smile. To his surprise, she smiled back at him.

"Dr. Sims, I would like to apologize for how I acted when you were at my mother's. Your deciding to run for his seat so soon . . . in my frame of mind it somehow just caught me the wrong way. But you were doing the smart thing."

Michael felt a greater surprise, and a measure of relief, pass over him. "You don't know how badly I felt about it myself," he said. "I had been approached by . . . by several people. I was trying to make up my mind whether to . . ." Lying again. "I wanted to know what you and your mother thought." That was true.

"Your getting out there first will discourage some of the others from announcing—especially with you having Mr. Waverly's support."

Waverly had said her family understood politics.

"There is one thing I would like, Dr. Sims. I don't know if you're aware of it, but my father was chairman of the health committee in the House."

He hadn't known that. But he nodded.

"I'm certain you know that Mr. Waverly was his biggest supporter."

He nodded again.

"Daddy spoke all the time about the medical research the Waverly Corporation did. It was almost like he was part of it. I have decided that I would like to see the center for myself. Somehow, I think it would make me feel better—something that Daddy cared so much about. With your having Mr. Waverly's support, I thought maybe you could arrange a tour. Of course, I will understand if you don't wish to go to the trouble."

*   *   *

Michael used the cellular telephone from the glove compartment in his Jeep to telephone the center. He noticed Shannon staring at his scrubs folded on the back seat. The receptionist connected him to Dr. Lobb.

He got a surprise after telling Lobb of Shannon's request. "Dr. Sims, I'm sorry, but we have proprietary information here. Not to mention that the patients are not served well by strangers coming in among them."

"But Mr. Waverly brought me in."

"You're one of us now."

"Dr. Lobb, when I came there neither you nor the patients had ever seen me before." Michael didn't realize why he suddenly felt so irritated, and he didn't care either. "I'm being asked to do several things I'm not particularly happy with—I thought maybe I could get something done for me in return."

"I'm sorry, Dr. Sims—it's our policy."

Michael clicked the disconnect button.

"Maybe if you called Mr. Waverly direct," Shannon said in a soft voice. ". . . If it's not too much trouble."

Before he could respond, she reached into one of her dress's big side pockets and lifted out a beeper. It hadn't rung. She obviously had it set where it vibrated, for she now looked at the number printed at its top.

"Can you excuse me for just a moment?" she said, and stepped away from him, opening her purse and lifting out a cellular telephone as she did.

As she punched the number into it, she took a couple of steps farther away from him, then lifted it to her ear.

"Carol," he heard her say, and then she turned her back to him. He lifted his phone and pushed in Waverly's home number.

Carol, holding the telephone receiver to her ear, stood next to the fax machine in Shannon's office.

"Shannon, Joe England didn't call your father the night he called you, but I'll bet you lunch at the Blow

Fly Inn his wife did. Samples came through. I've got their phone records."

Shannon spoke in a low voice. "What do you mean you bet his wife did?"

"There are eight collect calls to the Englands' house around the same time your father was making his calls to you and the Englands and the center. All the calls were from the same number. I called it. A nurse picked up. At a pay telephone on the third floor at Coastal Regional. I called Mr. McAffey. He said Joe England was still in the hospital with his bad back Monday night; he wasn't released until the next morning. Guess what floor he was on? That's right, girl, the third. He kept calling his wife, she called your father—and not earlier in the day, but that night, right before he called you."

"England was calling from the hospital?" Shannon asked, her voice still low.

"Every few minutes starting around eleven that night. He was still calling his house when your father was speaking to you and the center."

"England saw something at the hospital rather than out at the center?"

"If there was anything to see. He certainly got busy calling his wife about something. She called your father—and I don't know many people who would be brazen enough to call a U.S. congressman at midnight for small talk. It was bound to be something they thought important—and I'd be willing to bet that it came from what England told her."

"I'll be at the office in a minute," Shannon said, and disconnected the phone.

Michael noticed the brief questioning look that crossed Shannon's face when she turned toward him.

"I tried Waverly," he said. "He's not at the center or his office. They said they would have him call me when they located him."

Shannon took a moment before responding. "Yes,"

she said, "I'd appreciate that." Her mind seemed to have wandered off, and then she looked directly into his eyes. "How long have you known Waverly?"

"I met him day before yesterday."

"For the first time?" She had a questioning look on her face, like she didn't believe him.

"Yes."

"Why does a doctor want to be a politician?"

"I didn't."

"What do you mean, you didn't?" Her tone was almost demanding.

When he didn't answer she said, "Oh, I'm sorry. You'll have to excuse me. It's just . . ." She shrugged. "I'm sorry."

He realized how he would feel if he were burying his father. He nodded.

"What *did* you mean you didn't want to be a politician?" Her tone was soft this time.

"Mr. Waverly approached me. He wants someone in the Congress who understands the need for medical research. I thought about it, and decided I might be able to do more good there than as a doctor."

"Why you?"

"That's what I asked him."

"How did you get your money to go to college?"

He almost had to smile at the question. "Where did you get yours, Miss Donnelly?"

She didn't apologize this time.

"How well do you know Waverly?" he asked.

"Not very well. Why?"

"I thought you would know him well since he was such a big supporter of your father."

"I don't."

"In a way I find him arrogant. In another way I consider him one of the most magnanimous people I've ever met. With all his money he could be enjoying what time he has left—and yet he has this burning ambition to help others. I was wondering what you thought of him."

She was staring again and, again, seemed to be thinking of something other than their conversation.

Then her mother and the majority leader came toward her.

"Shannon."

At her mother's voice, she glanced across her shoulder, then back at him. "I *am* sorry for the way I acted, Dr. Sims," she said, and turned and walked toward her mother and the majority leader.

Her voice had been soft again, and there had been a definite genuineness in her words. *Damn,* he thought. *She's almost demanding one minute, friendly the next; her personality goes back and forth like a tennis ball.* He watched her walking away from him, then glanced into the sky and noted that it was starting to be spotted with clouds moving in from the Gulf. Howard was going to be right about the rain, he thought, and didn't have the slightest idea why that had popped into his mind.

Off to his side, he noticed the delegation from the Waverly Corporation staring at him.

"You see," Mr. Whitaker said, "we buried our son today."

"And you haven't seen your wife since?" the officer at the Biloxi City Police Department asked over the phone.

"She wanted to stay at the grave alone for a while—she insisted. I waited an hour and went back there—and she was gone. She didn't have a car or anything."

CHAPTER TWENTY-FIVE

When Shannon walked inside her office, Carol handed her the fax. She looked at the long list of collect calls from the hospital to the England house, and the call from the house to her father's apartment in Washington.

"From the third floor?" she asked.

Carol nodded. "The same floor Joe England was on."

"Why didn't England call Daddy himself rather than relaying something through his wife?"

"You want me to make the kind of guess you would?"

"What?"

"He didn't want to leave any record on a hospital telephone of him calling your father—if he saw something there that upset him . . . or scared him."

"Daddy was already drinking by the time England called him."

"So, Shannon, he was more depressed about his health than he let on to you. How would your mind be running if you were told you had cancer? He took a few drinks to try to get to sleep. And the calls started. And Joe England went in to work the very next day—and died coming home." As Carol paused, she held her hands out to her sides. "Am I going to have to convince you of the merits of your own argument?"

Shannon glanced down the hallway toward her office door. "Carol, Dr. Sims has a cellular phone. See if you can get the number. If you can't, then get me the number of the emergency department at Coastal Regional. He might have been going there—he had a scrub suit in the back of his Jeep. I need to speak with him."

"You're thinking he's okay now?"

"Hell, I don't know. But I don't have any choice. I'm going to need someone to guide me around the hospital."

"I'm surprised you hadn't already asked him to show you around the center."

"I tried."

"She was speaking with Sims at the services," Dr. Lobb said. He scratched his beard, partly out of habit, and partly from nerves. "He tried to bring her out here—said she wanted to get a feel for the center. I'm thinking like Murphy now. She's not going to stop. And now she's making me wonder about Sims—maybe we should make sure."

He was speaking over the telephone.

In Biloxi, Jonathan Waverly held the telephone receiver close to his ear as he listened. His breathing began to grow heavy.

"Go ahead," he said. "Both of them—where there is no doubt."

Shannon finished separating the last of the sheets she considered most important from the hearing files, and gathered them up, slipping them into a folder.

"Going to get him to read all that?" Carol asked.

"I'm going to try. I need him."

"No pun intended," Carol said and grinned.

"Excuse me?"

"I saw him on TV once when they were doing a feature on the hospital. He wouldn't be hard to need.

Reminds me a lot of Bobo, except he doesn't have Bobo's receding hairline."

"Carol, did you get his cellular number?"

"Couldn't."

"What about the emergency department number?"

"It's on my desk."

"Do you mind if I see it?"

"Well, if you put it that way." Carol said, moving out into the hallway. "And a doctor, too," she said, looking back across her shoulder and speaking loudly enough for Shannon to hear. "Marry somebody like that and I wouldn't have to keep working for an attorney who was a tyrant."

She raised her voice a little more as she continued down the hall toward her desk. "And, by the way, remember I'm going out of town for the weekend, so I won't be here for you to kick around tomorrow. Richard Nixon said something like that. I think."

In her office, Shannon rested her fingers against her mouth, leaned back in the chair, and stared at the ceiling.

Daddy, don't let him be in on it with them.

The report from the Regional Organized Crime Information Center came slowly from the fax machine.

A report from the Mississippi Attorney General's Office already lay on Harrison County Chief Deputy Dennis Allen's desk. He used his tongue to move a chew of tobacco to the inside of his cheek before adding to what he had just said to the chief of the campus police at Ole Miss.

"S-I-M-S. That's right, Michael Sims. He graduated from there about eight or nine years ago. We want to know if your records show him getting into any trouble that the state records might not show."

As Dennis waited for the officer to check his computer database, he spat a stream of brown juice into a Dixie cup, then looked at Sheriff Everette. "So maybe we're going to find out Sims had too much to drink at a fraternity party—who cares?"

"I'm going to give Shannon all I can find," Everette said. "I'd want somebody to if she were my daughter. And I need a reason to go and talk to her anyway. This keeps going on about her father. What Shannon's reason is, I don't know—but I'm going to find out."

△ CHAPTER TWENTY-SIX

Howard, standing inside the Hatteras, watched the man come down from the parking area onto the wooden walkway between the *Howard* and the *Cassandra*. He was a slim, blond young man, maybe in his mid-thirties. He was dressed in jeans and a white dress shirt open at the neck. There was something in how he glanced at the Hatteras and Michael's Gulfstar, then looked across his shoulders up and down the lines of boats berthed to each side of the two yachts. To get to the walkway, he had stepped over the gate clearly marked BOAT OWNERS ONLY BEYOND THIS POINT.

Now he leaned forward, trying to see inside the Hatteras, and Howard stepped back where he couldn't be seen. The man looked through the big windows at the side of the *Cassandra*'s salon, and then turned and walked back to the front of the walkway. He glanced toward the restaurant, a hundred feet across the paved area leading away from the boats.

When he came back down the walkway this time, he did so with quick steps, and, without stopping, hurried across the *Cassandra*'s gangplank to the salon and slid the door back.

He knelt on one knee and leaned down, reaching into the trawler and running his hand around the base of the door.

As quickly as he had moved aboard, he stood, slid the door shut and hurried back across the gangplank to the walkway.

Howard walked to the Hatteras's interior control station, opened a panel to the side of the steering wheel, and lifted out a revolver with a long barrel.

When he stepped outside onto the Hatteras's deck, the pistol hidden in his hand behind his hips, the young man, nearing the gate leading to the paved area, glanced in his direction. The man smiled feebly, hesitated a moment, then continued toward the gate.

Howard stuck his forefinger and index fingers inside the corners of his mouth and whistled shrilly.

The man jerked around—to see Howard pointing the pistol in his direction.

The man took a step backward.

Howard said, "If you run I'll have to fire a couple of warning shots. I'll have to fire them into your legs to make sure the slugs don't bounce off something and ricochet into one of these pretty boats. I like to fire warning shots. Now you stay right there until I call the police."

Howard looked back across his shoulder. "Marjorie, bring me my cellular phone." The man turned and jumped the gate.

"*Damn it!*" Howard shouted, "*Stop!*"

The man ran across the pavement, dashing past an older couple coming out of the restaurant toward their car.

"*I'm going to shoot!*" Howard yelled as loud as he could.

The couple looked toward him. The woman screamed.

Her husband grabbed her around her shoulders and dragged her to the ground. The fleeing man disappeared around the side of the restaurant.

Marjorie stepped out onto the deck. "What were you yelling about?" she asked.

When Howard looked at her, she held a plate up in front of her and smiled.

"Finger sandwiches are ready."

Despite it only being mid-afternoon, Daryl yawned as he came across the emergency department floor. His eyes were tinged red and even his hair seemed to hang more limply than normal across his forehead. Michael, dressed in his green scrubs now and filling out a chart on the counter in front of the nurses' station, glanced at him and smiled. "I hope I don't look as bad as you do."

"Thanks, buddy," Daryl said. He raised his hand to cover another yawn. "Going from night shift to day kills me."

"More like too much prowling last night."

Daryl grinned. "She was worth it."

Then his expression grew more serious. "I keep wondering who I'm going to get to go chick-hunting with me when you're gone," he said.

"You'll manage."

"When are you going to become a full-time campaigner?"

"Clark asked me to give him a week to work out the department schedule."

"Yeah, I heard he's been all over the hospital, trying to collar someone to volunteer a few days a month to cover for you until he can hire somebody else. Like everybody here hasn't already got more to do than they can handle. You're not going to be voted doctor of the year by the staff, I can tell you. You better win the race. If I was you, I wouldn't want to come back here."

Michael turned his attention back to the chart.

"Misspelled that word," Daryl said.

"Which word?"

Daryl pressed his finger under the word *succinylcholine* on the chart.

"Did not misspell it, Daryl."

"You certain?"

"Positive."

"Hmmm, I thought it had an E instead of an I in *succinyl*."

"Doesn't."

"Okay, don't take it personally, Mr. Spelling Champion."

"Dr. Sims, telephone," a nurse down the counter said. She held the receiver out as he walked toward her.

"Thank you," he said as he took it into his hand. "Hello."

"Dr. Sims, this is Shannon Donnelly. I'm sorry to be bothering you at the hospital, but I'd like to speak with you if you have time."

Is she going to be up or down this time? "Sure, go ahead."

"Dr. Sims, I need to speak to you in person. If I come to the hospital, could you give me a few minutes?"

Come to the hospital. What for? But what difference did it make?

"Come around to the emergency department entrance."

He replaced the receiver.

"Who was that?" Daryl asked.

"A crazy woman."

"Damn, Michael, how do you do it? I've always wanted one of those. Man, I'm going to miss you—it's going to be like my training shuts down."

Howard held up the flat, disc-shaped piece of metal about the size of a silver dollar. It had tiny, almost imperceptible holes covering one of its sides.

"My expertise is motors," he said, "but I think you're going to find this is some kind of listening device."

The police officer used a handkerchief to take the disc into his hands. "Mr. Howard, it would have been better if you hadn't handled this before we got here."

"Little late to be telling me that now, isn't it? And Howard's my first name, not my last."

The cop stared at him for a moment, then pulled a notepad from his pocket. "Can you give me a description?"

"Reason he's not lying out there on the pavement for you to see for yourself is because of liability purposes."

"Excuse me?"

"Didn't shoot him because I'd get sued. He might end up with what little money I got left."

The officer looked at Howard's gleaming white yacht and back to his face.

"The description now, please, Mr. . . ."

"Howard will do."

Marjorie stared down the walkway toward Michael's trawler. "This scares me to death," she said.

"Appears to me to be like Watergate," Howard said. "Bugging the enemy. *Politics*." He nodded his head at the thought.

Several miles east of the marina, Carol locked the front door to the Donnelly law firm and walked toward a yellow pickup driven by a man in his forties with a receding hairline.

After she climbed inside the truck's cab, she leaned across the seat and kissed him on the cheek.

"Gulf Shores, here we come," she said, and then immediately changed her expression. "You know, I feel so sorry for Shannon. Worry a little about her, too. She could be getting in over her head with what she's doing."

Then she smiled again, and reached to the top of Bobo's head to tousle what little hair he had there.

"What are we waiting for?" she said.

As they drove out into the narrow street in front of the office, Bobo said, "Now, what's this about Shannon?"

Carol began the story.

After the pickup disappeared from sight, the same young man who had tried to plant the listening device on the *Cassandra* came across the pavement, paused a moment looking in the direction the receptionist had driven, and walked at an angle across the firm's small parking lot to disappear around the corner of the building.

Seconds later he worked a small, wirelike instrument inside the lock at the building's back door, pushed it open, and walked inside, closing the door behind him.

In less than a minute, he came back outside, closed the door, and hurried down the street toward an old car parked off to the side of the blacktop.

Several miles in another direction, at the complex where Shannon Donnelly lived, Murphy, his wide, slumping shoulders covered in a light jacket, stepped outside her apartment and closed the door behind him. His head came around quickly when a young couple he hadn't noticed when he had peered through the apartment window before stepping outside walked past him.

They smiled politely and continued toward the steps leading down to the building's first floor.

He stared after them.

In the doctors' parking lot at Coastal Regional Hospital, a stocky man in his forties straightened from where he had been leaning over into the front seat of Michael's Jeep.

He looked up and down the line of much nicer vehicles owned by the other doctors, then walked toward his car.

▲ CHAPTER TWENTY-SEVEN

The glass doors at the emergency department entrance slid open when Shannon came toward them. She had changed out of what she had worn to the funeral services and was now wearing a black knee-length skirt and white linen blouse. Michael slipped from a stool against the nurses' station and walked to meet her.

Behind him, Daryl stared at Shannon's tight figure and face and muttered, "Damn."

She stopped just inside the doors. Michael noted the manila folder she held at her side. "About the only privacy we can get around here is standing outside," he said.

As they moved back through the doors, Daryl looked after them for a moment, then turned his face across the counter toward a young nurse filling out a chart inside the station. "Where can we go and talk privately?" he asked in a low voice.

The brunette showed her wedding ring. "All the time you've been here and you haven't noticed?" she asked.

"I've noticed," he said. "I've just reached the point where I don't care."

"Have you ever heard of Zack Hastings?" she asked.

He shook his head no.

The nurse said, "He's a pro boxer—moving up

pretty quickly in the welterweight ranks. He's my husband. You still want to talk privately?"

Daryl theatrically ran his eyes up and down the woman's surgical scrubs.

"Might be worth it," he said.

The nurse smiled and turned her attention back to the chart.

Standing outside the hospital next to the emergency department, Shannon held the folder in front of her waist, her fingers nervously moving against it.

"Dr. Sims," she started, "I . . . I, uh . . ." She took a deep breath. "Dr. Sims, my father didn't commit suicide. He was murdered."

At his questioning look, she added, "No, I'm not reacting on emotion. I know anybody can become depressed to the point they're no longer themselves, but I spoke on the phone with him nearly every week. I know he wasn't down."

She quit moving her fingers. "Until last week," she said. "He called me upset about something. Not depressed, but something was bothering him. When things upset him he'd often call me. He said there was an old problem that might be recurring that could cause him a lot of trouble. That bothered me. But it didn't bother me as much as you might imagine. Daddy always blew things out of proportion when he was worried. He was . . . he was drinking. After he told me he was worried about the problem, he started being evasive—not making a lot of sense. I thought it was the liquor." The breeze coming off the nearby gulf whipped a strand of her dark hair across her face, and she pushed it back out of her eyes.

"I told him to call me back the next day. I didn't exactly hang up on him, but I more or less made him hang up. He didn't call me back." She looked at the emergency department doors sliding open, and waited for a young orderly to pass by on the way to the parking lot.

"Daddy never flew into here or New Orleans that he didn't call me to pick him up at the airport. He didn't this time. His staff didn't even know he had left Washington. What he did or who he went to see when he got here—if he saw anybody—I don't know. Then he came to my mother's house. He hadn't been there since they were divorced. And somebody murdered him there."

She was staring into his eyes. He didn't know why she was telling him this. What was the point in his knowing what she thought? Her gaze seemed almost penetrating, as if she were trying to stare inside him rather than at him. The glass doors to their side slid open again. A young, female nurse with dark hair stepped out onto the sidewalk. "Dr. Sims, a gunshot victim coming in—wound to the lower stomach."

He nodded at the woman and looked back at Shannon. "Why are you telling me this?"

"Because I need you to help me."

"I don't understand."

"I told you Daddy said he was worried about an old problem that could cause him trouble. But nothing that anybody could do would cause trouble except for Jonathan Waverly. Daddy was so closely tied to him in the public's mind that if Waverly did something illegal, that could create a problem for him."

Waverly? Involved in something illegal? Michael didn't know whether he should look serious or smile. "Illegal? For what motive? What could Waverly want that he doesn't already have?" From up the highway, the sound of a siren traveled to them.

"I don't know. Maybe it's not specifically him, but somebody else from the center. His corporation got in trouble years ago for experimenting with unauthorized spinal tissue. I thought they might be doing it again—doing something again—because that's the only thing I could think of that would be an old problem coming back. And the ones who I think told Daddy there was something going on were also involved with the center. That made me even more certain the center had something to do with whatever was being done wrong—"

He knew now why she had been so anxious to tour the center.

"—but now I have reason to believe it might be something here at . . ." As Shannon paused, she took a deep breath. ". . . At the hospital."

If she hadn't hesitated, he wouldn't have been able to keep from smiling. But she had hesitated. She knew how crazy she was going to sound to him. And she had said it anyway. "Here, huh?"

She nodded. "And I need you to help me find out what."

The wailing of the siren grew louder. Michael glanced up the highway, and back at Shannon. "You said you know who told your father? Why don't you simply go to the police and tell them who it is so they can talk to them?"

"Because they're dead. They died in a car accident within thirty-six hours of calling him."

The way she pointedly included *within thirty-six hours* in her statement left no doubt but that she didn't think it was an accident.

"He came here as soon as he knew they had been killed. And then he was killed. I just found out that the husband was here in the hospital with a bad back the night his wife called Daddy. Her husband called her several times from here and she called Daddy and he called her back and then she talked to her husband again. It was midnight, Doctor. Doesn't it seem unusual for everybody to be calling back and forth at that time of night?"

Somebody killed in a car accident she obviously didn't think was an accident? Her father murdered? Phone calls going back and forth? Something illegal? She was desperately trying to convince him, and going in every direction at the same time. The siren wailed loudly. He could see the ambulance's flashing red lights now, then the blocky vehicle itself as the ambulance swerved around a large transport truck and raced up the highway toward the hospital. A police car sped along behind it.

Was she *really* crazy? "Is the reason you haven't gone to the police because you think they're involved in this?"

She frowned. "Don't treat me like *I* am crazy, Doctor. Of course I don't think they're involved. Sheriff Everette is a friend of the family. He would do all the investigating he could if he thought Daddy had been murdered. But all I have now is a series of phone calls and my idea of what they mean. Look at me now, trying to talk you into believing me—and I can tell I'm not getting anywhere."

"How do you know this woman called your father if she's dead?"

"I was able to get her telephone records." She held the folder out toward him. "I'll tell you everything I know, but I want you to read through these papers first. I picked out the ones that summarized each thing that was important in the hearings. Then I want you to tell me what I should look for."

"Look for?"

She nodded. "And I want to see the hospital records."

"For what?"

"To see if anybody was on a life-support system the night the Englands called my father."

"A life-support system?"

"That's what the person was on who they stole the tissue from the last time."

She moved the folder toward him again. "Will you please read these?"

To their side the glass doors opened and the young nurse and an orderly walked out onto the sidewalk.

"Dr. Sims, he was my father."

The front of the ambulance suddenly nosed lower to the pavement as the driver braked it abruptly. Its tires screeched as it turned sharply into the hospital drive.

"Please, Dr. Sims."

Daryl stepped outside the doors and walked to them, holding out a sterile packet of latex gloves.

Michael took them and stared back into Shannon's eyes. "You think three people have been murdered. That somebody out at the center, or somebody here, is a killer. And you walk around telling everybody you're investigating it yourself?"

"I'm not telling anybody but you, Doctor." She shook her head. "I don't have any choice but to investigate it myself until I come up with something more substantial."

"You're telling me," he said.

The ambulance came to a rocking stop in front of them. "Michael," Daryl called. The driver hurried out his door toward the rear of the vehicle. He threw its doors open as the orderly joined him and they reached for the stretcher, pulling it toward them. A paramedic came outside with the stretcher, leaning over it, pumping with the flats of his hands against the chest of the stocky man lying there, his shirt open and three EKG electrodes dotting his chest. The nurse grabbed a side of the stretcher and helped propel it toward the doorway, using her free hand to squeeze an Ambu bag connected by a strawlike endotracheal tube running down inside the man's mouth, forcing oxygen into his lungs.

"Don't leave," Michael said to Shannon, still wondering if she was crazy, not certain why he was asking her to stay.

Then, slipping on the gloves Daryl had handed him, he hurried after the stretcher through the open glass doors.

CHAPTER TWENTY-EIGHT

Marjorie laid the cellular telephone back on the endtable next to the couch in the Hatteras's spacious salon. She looked at Howard.

"Michael's still tied up," she said. "He can't come to the phone." She glanced through the window toward the Gulfstar. "This just scares me so bad."

"I wouldn't worry about it, Marj. I gotta figure it's politics. Like when Nixon had those Democrats bugged during the campaign. That's what I told the officers."

"You think so?" Marjorie asked. "I don't. But I can't think so well, can I?"

"You can cook real good, though."

She looked at Howard, and shook her head, but didn't say anything.

"Don't worry so much, Marjorie." Howard walked across the thick carpet to her.

He patted her on the back. "If I'd shot him, I'd've made the news everywhere. Might have got a book deal out of it, if it is another Watergate. That would be worth some money."

Marjorie started crying.

"Marj, what's wrong?"

She shook her head in dismay, the tears starting to roll down her cheeks. "I looked at my watch to see what time it was, and I wasn't wearing it. I didn't remember I hadn't put it on. Now I don't remember if I left it at home or had it on Michael's boat."

"And you're crying about that?"

"My mind's no good."

"No good? Of course it is."

Marjorie shook her head, crying harder. "No, it isn't. It really isn't."

Howard stepped closer to her and placed his hands gently at the sides of her shoulders.

"Marj, what is it?"

She kept shaking her head, kept crying.

"Marj, tell me about it."

Shannon watched as the stocky man's body, a sheet covering his face, was rolled on a stretcher out of the rear of the emergency department toward the hospital morgue. The police officers who had arrived with the man followed the stretcher out of sight. She clasped the folder closely to her chest.

Michael and Daryl, finished washing their arms and hands, walked across the floor to her.

"Shannon, this is Daryl."

Daryl smiled. "If you ever need somebody to talk to," he said, "and Michael's not around, I'm always available."

Shannon forced a feeble smile.

Michael said, "We have some paperwork to fill out," and caught Daryl's shoulders, guiding him toward the nurses' station. "It'll only be a few minutes more."

She looked in the direction the orderlies had rolled the stretcher. She felt queasy. A shooting death struck too close to home. She took a deep breath in through her nose to relieve the feeling, but the air smelled of antiseptic—and of the same foul odor of blood she had experienced when she had walked ahead of Sheriff Everette into her mother's living room.

Clasping the folder to her chest, she walked toward the glass doors. A tall, black male nurse in a scrub suit started to step through them ahead of her, then nodded her in front of him.

"Thank you," she said.

He smiled politely and walked past her toward the parking lot. She stopped on the sidewalk outside the entrance.

The smell of salt on the breeze coming in off the Gulf was refreshing, driving the odor of the hospital from her mind. The sun was hot, but she much preferred it over being inside. She was looking toward the doctors' parking area when a sheriff's department cruiser stopped there.

Everette and his chief deputy, Dennis Allen, stepped from the car. Allen hooked his forefinger into his mouth, pulled out a wad of wet tobacco, and flicked it out to his side.

They saw her at the same time. Allen said something to the sheriff and Everette nodded.

They came across the pavement and stopped in front of her.

"Shannon," the sheriff said. Allen nodded his greeting.

"James," Shannon said. "Dennis." She tightened her arms around the folder.

Everette looked past her to the glass doors. "Dr. Sims in?"

She nodded.

"You're here to see him?" Everette asked.

She nodded again.

"About your case?"

"Yes."

"Important case?"

"Very important. I appreciate the help you've been."

"Yeah, Shannon. I have to speak to him for a minute, myself. Then I would like to see if I can speak with you. If you don't mind."

"What do you want with him?"

"Somebody tried to bug his trawler."

* * *

"Damn good-looking," Daryl said. "Dresses like she has money, too."

Michael continued filling in the chart open on the counter before him. "I'm not certain she's not crazy."

"Who cares? Where did you meet her?"

"She's Congressman Donnelly's daughter."

Daryl looked toward the emergency department doors.

"And," Michael added, "according to which way the coin lands when you flip it, she really is crazy, or a damn gutsy woman."

"Gutsy?" Daryl asked.

Michael laid the ink pen by the chart and rubbed the back of his neck. "Yeah, gutsy, or a wacko," he said, glancing toward the doors.

Sheriff Everette and a deputy walked toward him. Shannon followed close behind them.

"Dr. Sims," Everette said.

"Sheriff."

Everette looked toward the deputy. "This is Dennis Allen."

Michael nodded and glanced across his shoulder toward Daryl. "This is Dr. Stillman."

Daryl nodded his greeting.

"Had a little problem out at your boat," Everette said.

Michael thought of his mother. "What?"

"Somebody put a listening device in your salon. The fellow on the yacht next door ran him off and found it."

"A listening device?"

"That's right," the deputy said. "A bug."

Michael looked at Shannon, standing off to the side behind the sheriff.

"I don't guess you have any idea why?" Everette asked.

"What you're saying is not even registering, Sheriff—

why is right. A listening device?" He glanced at Daryl. For once Daryl was at a loss for words. He wasn't even staring at Shannon.

"There's some crazy things go on in this world," Everette said. "But most of them make sense after you get to the bottom of it. I wish you'd think about it some. You have any lawsuits pending against you?"

Michael shook his head.

Everette glanced toward the orderlies cleaning up the last traces of blood from the trauma area.

"Any reason to think someone might be getting ready to hit you with a malpractice suit?"

"No."

"Maybe Johnny Whitaker's mother," Daryl said.

"Who?" Everette questioned.

"A teenager named Johnny Whitaker died here after coming through the department. The mother lost it, saying Michael promised her the boy was going to be alright. She really went nuts," Daryl added. "She said she was going to get Michael."

"Admissions will have her address and number?" Everette asked.

Daryl nodded.

"The man who ran the guy off told the Gulfport officers he thought it had to do with you announcing for the congressional seat," Everette said to Michael. "Now that doesn't make any sense to you, does it?"

Michael looked at Shannon again. She was expressionless, but staring at him. "No, it doesn't," he said.

"Could have been a private detective got your boat mixed up with somebody else's he was supposed to bug," Everette said. "We got two of the boats out there tied up in divorces now. Anyhow, I wanted to let you know what happened—just in case."

"Just in case what?" Daryl questioned across Michael's shoulder.

Everette shrugged. "Just in case." He turned toward

Shannon. "You think you might get a minute to come by the office today or tomorrow?"

When Shannon didn't immediately answer, Everette said, "Or I can come by your office. We need to have that talk."

"I'm tied up the rest of today," Shannon said. "I'll call you tomorrow."

"Fine. Tell your mother I said hello." Everette looked across his shoulder. "Nice meeting you, Dr. Stillman."

"Yeah," Daryl said.

As the sheriff and the deputy walked toward the exit, Shannon stepped closer to the counter.

"It's because you asked if I could come out to the center," she said.

She held the folder toward him.

Allen stuffed a cut of tobacco inside his mouth as he walked from the emergency department. He glanced back over his shoulder toward the sliding glass doors. "What's she up to now?" he asked.

Everette shook his head. "I'm going to find out tomorrow."

"And what's the deal with the doctor?" Allen asked. "She's worrying our asses off wondering if he's a crook one minute . . . now she's talking to him."

"I'm going to find that out, too," Everette said.

Papers from the manila folder were spread out on the counter fronting the nurses' station. The nurse Daryl had teased earlier glanced at them as she carried a box of bandages across the floor. Michael turned through three pages stapled together, scanning the information they contained. Daryl idly looked at a page he had picked up from among those already read and laid aside. A corner of his mouth lifted in a one-sided smile.

"Living tissue," he said. "Not exactly an educated statement by the old . . ." He quickly looked at Shannon, who was standing beside him. "Sorry," he said.

She kept staring at Michael. "Well?" she asked.

He shook his head. "I couldn't tell the difference in fresh tissue and old tissue a few days after it was taken—nobody could."

"There's not any way?"

"Unless they didn't preserve it after they took it. But that wouldn't be the case—it would deteriorate. It wouldn't be any good to them then whatever they would be studying." He laid the stapled sheets back on the counter.

"So what do you think, Doctor?" She had kept peppering him with all she could think of while he skimmed through the files—all she knew, and all she had guessed at.

"Frankly, I don't see anything to glue what you're saying together. Until now you have only coincidences. One after another, I'll admit, but still only coincidence. The Englands called your father. He was upset because of an old problem resurfacing. And they died soon after they told him—if they told him anything and weren't calling for some other reason."

"At midnight?" Shannon questioned. "And he was murdered as soon as he got here—after finding out they were dead. And your boat gets bugged—after you ask to take me out to the center."

"Michael," Daryl said. "That's a lot."

"That's why it's called coincidence, Daryl."

Shannon lowered her gaze to the papers. She looked dejected.

Mary Liz, her blond hair in a ponytail, stepped up to the other side of the counter. "Doctors, we have a twenty-five-year-old stripper coming in with contusions and a broken leg—fell off a stage."

"Sounds like my kind of woman," Daryl said. "Those contusions will no doubt have to be examined carefully."

Mary Liz frowned and, shaking her head, turned toward the opening in the counter leading out onto the floor.

Normally Daryl would have another remark to make, if for no other reason than to further irritate her, but this time he didn't say anything else. He turned his gaze back to the papers scattered around the folder.

"It *is* a lot of coincidence," he said.

Shannon began gathering up the papers, slipping them into the folder. Her face still showed her disappointment.

Coincidence or not, Michael couldn't help feeling sorry for her. There was something else, too. He was about to campaign for Congress with Waverly's support. If there was any chance Waverly really could be involved in something . . .

"It would be no problem to see if anyone was on life support when England was here," he said.

◣ CHAPTER TWENTY-NINE

"Two, seven, eight, four, six, five, three, nine," Marjorie said. She stood at the bow rail of the Hatteras, backed into its berth next to Michael's trawler.

"See," Howard said, "phone numbers are seven digits because studies have shown that most people have a hard time remembering any more than that, and you just remembered eight. Now add a six and a four to those you just said."

"Okay," Marjorie said. "But first you say them all in a row for me again."

"No, you remember them and add the six and the four."

"Howard, I—"

"Concentrate, Marj. You can do it. Unless you start thinking you can't."

"Two, seven, eight," Marjorie started.

Howard nodded.

"Four, six . . ."

"Come on, Marj."

She tightened her eyes and thought. ". . . Five, four, nine, and a six and a four."

A broad grin spread across Howard's face. "That's my girl," he said, clapping his hands. He narrowed his eyes in thought. "You might have got one wrong."

Marjorie frowned.

"But I'm not sure," Howard said, "so how am I thinking any better than you, if I'm not sure?"

Marjorie smiled.

She looked toward the Gulfstar. "That still worries me."

"Politics," Howard said.

"Now add a six and a one," he added.

"Howard, you're going to have to tell them to me all in a row again."

"I can't," he said. "I forgot."

They both laughed.

Shannon looked at the pay telephone in the visitors' waiting area on the third floor. It was the floor that Joe England had been on—in a room a half dozen doors down from the waiting room. There had been nobody on life support in over a month at the hospital, either on the floors or in the ICU. Shannon turned from the doorway. Her head slightly down, staring at the floor in front of her, she walked toward the elevators. Michael walked beside her.

Now she raised her face and looked at him. "It wouldn't have had to be somebody on life support," she said. "It could have been just someone who died when England was here. That makes more sense anyway. Somebody died, and somebody was taking a tissue sample, he saw something—glanced in a room or something."

"Like they forgot to shut the door while they were operating on a spinal cord?" he asked.

"We don't know what he might have seen, Michael." She turned into the alcove toward the elevators, but passed by them without stopping and walked to a window a few feet away. The bright sunlight shining in through the glass outlined her slim figure. He stopped beside her.

"They could have used a truck," she muttered in a

voice almost too low to hear. She was looking down toward the ground.

Below them, the aging panel truck used by the hospital maintenance crew was parked on the pavement next to a flower bed. Its wide rear door stood open.

"Some kind of truck," she said, still in a low voice. "Some kind of vehicle." She turned toward him and her voice was stronger again. "Maybe that's it. England wouldn't have seen somebody doing an autopsy or taking tissue from a spinal cord and thought anything about it. He wouldn't any more know the difference in what was normal procedure here than a New Yorker would know the difference between a magnolia bud and a cotton boll."

Michael smiled a little.

"He had to see something really unusual to recognize something was wrong," she said. "Something that any layman would know was unusual—something that would be instantly recognized as not normal hospital procedure."

Michael glanced at his watch. "I'm going to have to get back to the department."

She stared down at the truck again, then back to him. "Michael, that something unusual that England saw could be somebody taking a body away. It might be crazy. Most of the things that have passed through my mind since Daddy was killed *are* crazy. But can't we at least see if somebody died while he was here?"

Minutes later, Michael ran his finger down the admissions and discharges printed out on a long sheet for them by a gray-haired lady in the administrative office. As his finger reached the bottom of the list, he looked at Shannon. "England was here six days. Two people expired during that period."

Before she could ask, he said, "When somebody dies they're taken downstairs to the morgue and the funeral home or the coroner is called. There's either somebody from the hospital in there, or it's kept locked until a hearse comes for the body."

"Like somebody couldn't find a way to get in there?"

"Shannon, no one would be crazy enough to be standing in the morgue removing spinal cord tissue where anybody could walk in and catch them."

"Couldn't England have seen somebody taking a body away—maybe knew something was wrong?"

"First, how would a hearse coming for a body seem unusual? Second, both patients died the last night he was here. Their bodies weren't moved until the next day—after he was discharged."

She looked at the sheet. "It says that?"

He nodded. "There weren't *any* bodies moved while he was here—in any kind of vehicle."

She raised her gaze to his. "Michael, people make mistakes. There could be a mistake in the dates. If the date was only one day off. Just one day, Michael, think about that. Whoever filled out those records could have been off just one day. The bodies could have been moved the day before. While England was still here. It could be something to do with that, with something about them being moved."

"You said he didn't call his wife until late at night. They move bodies during regular hospital hours."

She glanced at the sheet again. "It says that, too?"

"No, Shannon, it—"

"What about the family asking for the body right after someone died? I know the hospital would let them take it no matter what time it was. It would be, uh . . . religious discrimination . . . not to let them."

Michael shook his head in amusement, and a little bit in exasperation. "Okay," he said. "This last thing."

He looked across the counter at the woman who had printed the sheet for them. "Patricia, I need one more favor."

The individual admissions charts would list the patients' closest relatives, and those relatives' telephone numbers.

It only took a couple of minutes for the woman to find the records. Michael carried two folders with him as he walked down the counter to a telephone placed close to the wall.

One of the two deaths had been the result of injuries suffered in an MVC, a twenty-six-year-old male brought in through the emergency department, rushed into surgery, then admitted to the ICU. He lingered there for thirty-six hours before expiring of heart failure at eleven fifty-seven the last night that England was in the hospital. His admissions information had been filled out by his wife. Her name was Mitsi Showers. Her occupation was listed as a cosmetics saleswoman and her telephone number at work and at home were the same. Michael punched in the number. When the woman's telephone started ringing, he held the receiver out to Shannon.

"Your ball game," he said. "I'm not going to ask a widow what she did with her husband's body."

Shannon frowned but took the receiver and lifted it to her ear.

A moment later she said, "Is this Mrs. Showers? . . . Mrs. Showers, this is the Coastal Regional Hospital. I'm, uh . . . I'm Dr. Sherry Armstrong."

Michael narrowed his eyes at her.

"Mrs. Showers, I'm sorry to bother you, but I need some information, if you wouldn't mind. Yes. Your husband . . ." She held her hand out to her side for Michael to tell her the name. He looked back at the chart.

She frowned when he didn't immediately reply. "Mrs. Showers, what was the date of your husband's death . . . Yes, the date of death. We have to verify the hospital records with the next of kin—a health department rule."

Michael shook his head in exasperation.

Shannon turned her back on him. "Yes, thank you. And, uh, when was he moved from the hospital morgue?"

She nodded and said, "Yes, ma'am, thank you. Oh, also, what funeral home was he taken to?"

A second later she repeated, "Yes, what funeral home?"

"Yes, Mrs. Showers, thank you. Uh, Mrs. Showers . . . was it a closed-casket burial? Yes, Mrs. Showers. Thank you. I apologize for bothering you. You've been very helpful. Good-bye." She replaced the receiver on its cradle.

"The date in the record is correct," she said. "He died during the night. They didn't move him until the next day. It wasn't a closed-casket funeral."

"A closed-casket funeral?"

"I started wondering if maybe one of them had a closed-casket funeral—no one would know if a body was in the casket or not."

"In it?" He shook his head and looked at the chart of the other patient who had died while England was at the hospital—a forty-one-year-old female who had suffered a massive stroke and died only a few hours after being admitted to the ICU at four P.M. England's last day there. Michael punched in the number and handed Shannon the receiver.

"Her husband is Clyde. This is his telephone at work."

Patricia and one of her co-workers stared at them from down the counter.

"Hello, yes," Shannon said. "I'm calling for a Mr. Clyde . . ."

"Paschal," Michael said.

"A Mr. Clyde Paschal, please . . . Yes, I'm Dr. Sherry Armstrong at Coastal Regional Hospital. I need to verify some information with him."

It took a few seconds for the man to answer. "Yes, Mr. Paschal. I apologize for bothering you at your office, but I'm having to fill out some information here. I need to verify the date of your wife's death. Health department rules."

Her eyes suddenly narrowed. "Oh, no, sir. I certainly don't mean to be inconsiderate, but I . . . Yes, sir, the health department . . . the state health department . . . Thank you. That matches our date. Sir, one more thing: Was it a closed-casket funeral? Thank you. I . . . oh, and the funeral home she was . . ." Shannon's eyes blinked at the man's slamming the telephone down. Michael even heard the bang of the receiver.

"Well?" he asked.

"The dates are the same as in the records."

He smiled. "Armstrong? For the health department?"

She ignored him and looked at the charts lying next to the telephone.

"There has to be something," she said. She leaned closer to the charts. Her eyes narrowed. "It says here that Showers' room was on the third floor."

He nodded.

When he did no more than that, not saying anything, she took a deep breath and shook her head. "I know, there's only three floors. One chance in three—coincidence."

He nodded again.

She sighed wearily. "I've been beating my head against the wall ever since the night Daddy died. I've been imagining everything possible. I know most of it—I hope not all of it—is wrong. I need somebody to talk to who can help me to sort out everything that's going through my mind. Is there any way at all you could get off work early, maybe go with me to my apartment where I can set and think—have you to bounce my questions off of?"

He stared at her for a moment. He couldn't help but notice the deep shade of green in her eyes—and that helped him with his decision. Hell, maybe he was as bad as Daryl.

"I have a couple guys who owe me favors," he said. "It'll only take me a little while to get one of them down here to relieve me."

◬ CHAPTER THIRTY

Dr. Lobb looked at his watch as he came out of his room into the detention area. "If we're going ahead we need Murphy to be on his way," he said.

Waverly, standing a few feet from the cells, nodded without looking back at Lobb. As the short doctor walked toward the steel door leading from the area, Waverly kept his gaze fixed on Blue's face—on his son's face. Blue's expression hadn't changed; his eyes showed no obvious recognition. They never did. Waverly wondered if the poor, hulking brute he looked at had even the faintest idea he was staring at his father. There had been a time when Blue knew.

First there had been the stupid whore who had gotten pregnant, and then announced the pregnancy with a smile on her face. *Like she actually thought she could make me care for her because of that?* Waverly thought.

And then the drugs, and whatever else she had done to her body during the pregnancy. Blue had been born insane.

Not noticeably at first, except maybe for his inability to speak. This foreshadowed a much more serious problem that was to emerge first in extreme temper tantrums he started exhibiting before he was even a year old.

Waverly remembered banishing both of them. The whore had been lucky that banishment was all he had done to her for trying to use a child to stay close to him.

He had forgotten about them. Then Blue had penned a letter in a nearly illegible scribble one day asking if he could come and live with him.

Waverly remembered the strange, warm, almost fatherly feeling that had swept over him as he read the letter, remembered even entertaining the thought that he would let Blue come back to Los Angeles, find him something to do without anyone ever knowing he was his son. He even called the whore; the first time since she had left the city that he had spoken with her. "Yeah, Jonathan," she had said. "Take him back; take the crazy bastard back and good riddance to both of you." Her reference was to Blue's unmanageable personality, and a long line of recorded run-ins with the police.

Then, only days later, with Waverly's mind not yet made up as to what he was going to do, there was the car accident and the killing of the officer. The damage to his brain had erased whatever sanity Blue had left—and all knowledge of who had been his father.

For a while, given this sudden opportunity, Waverly remembered thinking that maybe he had a chance to remold Blue in a different image under another name—to work to cure Blue's insanity. If he succeeded, then the "insane" patient could die—and a new son, not knowing he was a son—could become a confidant.

But there had been no cure. The muscle control lost after the accident had come back relatively well under the influence of the injections, therapy, and nerve implants. But the mind had remained hopeless.

And now it was nearing the time to end what had been a tragedy from the beginning. There was no way he could take Blue with him when he left. No purpose in it. Nothing any longer to learn from the nerve study Blue had afforded him. Really no purpose in a son of his suffering any longer.

Waverly knew that fact in his heart and in his mind.

He realized it would be hard—that was obvious from the two times he had hesitated in the past. But it was for Blue's own good. A son long-suffering, finally at peace. One who, even if unknowingly, had nevertheless contributed greatly to scientific advancement in allowing his body to be used in the experimentations. One, Waverly knew, who had allowed him—an old, frail man—to be poised at the point of the complete rehabilitation he was about to take. Despite Blue's handicaps, it could be truthfully said that he had done more for his father than almost any man in history before him, and that thought caused a tender sensation to pass through Waverly once again. He smiled softly at Blue, who, still clasping the bars of his cell with his big hands, stared back at him.

"There has to be something," Shannon said for the tenth time.

"What else?" Michael answered.

"I don't know, but there has to be something—they killed my father and I know they did."

They were in her second-floor apartment in a small complex bordering Highway 90 in Biloxi. Michael glanced through the glass doors leading to the balcony. Beyond the glass, the waters of the Mississippi Sound had begun to darken in the fading sunlight. He could barely see the dim outlines of the barrier islands cloaked in haze in the distance. He looked back at the open folder and the papers spread out across the coffee table. Shannon sat on the couch, going through them for the third time in the last thirty minutes.

"Something," she mumbled to herself. "Something I'm missing." She raised her face toward his. "It was a pathologist who stole the tissue in Los Angeles. He got the family to let him in the room right after they turned off the life-support system. When the body was taken to the funeral home is when the incision was noticed. It wouldn't have to be a very big incision, would it? It *could* go unnoticed. How long would it take?"

"If somebody only wanted a gross sample, just seconds."

"Any doctor could do it, couldn't they?"

"It wouldn't necessarily take a doctor."

"You said a body is kept in the hospital morgue until a hearse comes for it. Who did you say was in charge of the morgue?"

"Shannon, the pathologist in charge of the morgue taught me in medical school before he took the job here. There's no way he's involved in anything."

"You don't know all the doctors. You don't know what one of them might do."

He shook his head. "I've already told you, Shannon, no doctor, or anybody else, would be stupid enough to be in the morgue removing tissue where somebody could come in and see them."

"How can you be so certain?"

He didn't say anything for a moment, then he shook his head again, this time partly in exasperation, and moved to the telephone on the table next to the couch.

"Don't ever tell anyone how crazy I am," he said, lifting the receiver.

"Who are you calling?"

"Dr. Bacon, the pathologist at the hospital—he's in charge of the morgue."

Dr. Bacon had to be paged. It took a full five minutes before his voice came across the line. "Dr. Sims?"

"Yes, sir. I wonder if you could do me a favor. An MVC victim, a Mr. Bobby Showers, expired at the hospital a little over a week ago. That same day, a stroke victim, a Mrs. Fayrene Paschal, expired. I was wondering if you personally signed their bodies out to the funeral homes, or if there was any reason you might have been away from the hospital at the time—like maybe on vacation or something?"

"Vacation?" the aging doctor said in a voice so loud

Michael moved the receiver away from his ear. "Hell, Michael, I haven't had a vacation since before I had you in class at UMC. Vacation? Hell, how can anybody afford something like that anymore? I've got kids from both my first and second wives in graduate school now. You know what that's costing me?"

"Yes, sir, I—"

"Yes, Michael, I remember the deaths specifically. I signed them both out to the funeral homes. I remember the young man in particular. Way too young. About the age of my oldest son—by my first wife. Damn shame."

The ages of Candice and Johnny Whitaker passed through Michael's mind. "Thank you, sir."

"Any particular reason for wanting this information?"

"Just talk in the emergency department."

"Talk in the department? Damn, I wish I had the time for idle chatter. Well, hope you win the election."

"Yes, sir. Thank you." Michael replaced the receiver. He faced Shannon.

"He remembers signing out both bodies."

"Then they removed the tissue at the funeral home," she said. "But what did England see here?"

He waited a moment before he answered her. "Shannon, there comes a time when you have to say that what you're thinking—guessing at—is simply not possible. There are no mistakes, or vacations taken by Dr. Bacon where somebody else would have been in charge of the morgue . . . or anything else. I know how everything looks to you. Hell, it *is* a lot of coincidence. But there's a point where you simply have to let what you see and hear win out."

"I had a client not long after I graduated from law school," Shannon came back in a low voice. "They found him standing over his mother with blood all over his clothes. He was a crackhead and on about everything else you can think of. He had stolen from her before. He had threatened her. He had her skin under his fingernails. Thank God for his sake I didn't simply let what I saw and heard stop me from helping him. I wouldn't let it stop me after I reached the point of believing what he said. He was innocent, and I eventually proved it. And I believe now. I believe Daddy and the Englands were murdered. I know my father was murdered. And I'm not going to stop until I prove it. I simply have to find what it is we're missing—what we're overlooking. Why are you here if you don't think I might be right?"

"Partly because you asked me—and I could tell how sincere you were in what you're thinking. And partly because you said Waverly might be involved and I'm going to be associated with him." As he paused, he smiled. "And partly because you were lucky enough my boat was bugged—and that threw me off a little bit, made me wonder."

Despite his smile, her expression didn't change. She looked back down at the papers. The framed photographs of her father and mother sat where she had slid them to the side of the table before she opened the folder. "Your father was a nice-looking man and your mother is very beautiful."

Her eyes came up toward his. "Thank you. She's angry with me right now because of how I treated you at the house."

She smiled. It was the first smile he had seen on her face. But then it faded quickly as she dropped her gaze back to the table, lifted a thin stack of the papers, and began to sort through them again.

"Why did you assume Waverly in particular was involved in this?"

She looked up at him again. "The files only implicated the pathologist in Los Angeles. But there was testimony that there were others at the center who should have known what he was doing. Four other people in the laboratory with him, Michael. Working on a project together. A whole department. You don't think Waverly knew what they were doing?"

"Your father didn't think so."

"Because they were trying to earn the bonus Waverly had offered if anybody made a breakthrough."

He nodded. "A million dollars."

"You haven't studied these files like I have," she said. "Nobody else at the center who was questioned knew anything about any bonus but those four. So maybe there wasn't any bonus. Maybe the only million that was offered was for each of them to *say* they were off on their own rogue research?"

"The pathologist lost his license."

"Okay, Michael, what about ten million dollars for him, twenty? You think that much money would be sufficient compensation for him to give up his license and keep his mouth shut? Whatever any of them asked for they would have gotten—Waverly would miss twenty million dollars about as much as I would a hundred."

He looked back out the window, beyond the shallow water markers in the sound. A long, custom-built yacht, its running lights already turned on and dimly glowing red, green, and white in the fading twilight, moved slowly in the direction of New Orleans.

"A funeral home would be the best place to remove the tissue without anyone knowing," Shannon said. "But what does that leave England seeing at the hospital?"

Before he could respond she suddenly said, "I haven't eaten all day. I didn't think I could. But right in the middle of being sick to my stomach about how this is going, I'm hungry. I'm going to fix something. How does shrimp pasta sound to you?" She smiled for the second time. "Or would you rather have a ham and cheese sandwich?"

He returned the smile. "Given the choice of the former over the latter . . ." he said, and spread his hands.

The smile stayed on her face this time as she moved toward the kitchen.

Dr. Lobb stepped inside the surveillance room near the front offices of the robotics plant. Murphy, his big frame leaning forward in a straight chair, turned up the volume on a speaker.

The sound of plates being moved was clear. Shannon could be heard asking Michael to hand her a colander out of the top kitchen cabinet above the sink. She asked him if he wanted a beer.

The sound of the refrigerator door opening and closing was clear.

Even the sound of pressure being released in the bottle of beer as Michael twisted its top loose was audible.

"They can't fart without me knowing it now," Murphy said.

Dr. Lobb glanced at his watch. "I thought you had business to take care of."

"Hell, doc, don't you want to wait until it's good and dark?"

Lobb turned and walked from the room without commenting.

Murphy, a frown across his face, stared at the door closing, then came to his feet.

Waverly watched the stocky black orderly lift a paper plate of food and paper cup of water off a tray and slide them through the narrow opening in the bars at the bottom of Blue's cell. When he was done, the man turned and walked away from the detention area, closing the steel door behind him.

Then Waverly, carrying a tray of his own, smiled softly at his son and walked to the door at the very rear of the area. The paper plate contained spaghetti, reinforced with vitamins and minerals, a slice of enriched brown bread, and a half dozen Oreo cookies mounded in a small pile. The cup contained Diet Coke.

When he stopped in front of the door, he slid a small device that looked much like a garage-door opener from his pocket, started to push the button at its center, then thought better of it. He grinned, knocked on the door, waited a moment, then pushed the button—and the door swung open.

▲ CHAPTER THIRTY-ONE

Michael lifted a bite of shrimp to his mouth. Shannon twisted a strand of fettuccine around her fork.

"Why a one-woman law practice?" he asked.

"I couldn't see myself working at a big firm as a gopher for a bunch of gray-haired old men for the next however many years."

"This is good," he said, nodding toward his plate.

"Thank you."

A heavy cloud line was moving in from the Gulf toward the barrier islands. He shook his head. "There's this old guy who's berthed next to me. He predicted two days ago it was going to rain today. He's full of bull, but he's a helluvan interesting—"

"Michael," she said, "I . . . excuse me for interrupting, but I've thought and I've thought, and there's only one thing left that I can think of that we can do. I know you're sick of this. But I want you to help me find out. If . . ."

As Shannon stopped speaking, she narrowed her eyes at whatever passed through her mind.

He waited for her to continue.

But she didn't. She stood, and walked to the kitchen counter. A ballpoint pen lay there, and she lifted it and wrote something on a pad that had lain beside it. When she faced him, she held up the pad so he could see what she had written. She had printed the words in big block letters.

DON'T SAY ANYTHING

She lifted her finger to her lips in a further sign for silence.

"Michael, I feel nauseated," she said. "I hope the shrimp wasn't too old." She motioned with a sideways movement of her head for him to follow her, and started for the living room. "I need some fresh air."

He knew what was going through her mind now, and didn't speak until they stepped out onto the walkway in front of the apartment.

"They tried to bug my boat."

She nodded. "And maybe my apartment, and God knows where else."

"I can't see why you won't go to the police. You said the sheriff was a family friend—tell him what you think, and why. Let him try for a while." He looked at the closed door behind her. "And if you are being bugged, what's next?" he added.

"You mean like the fair damsel in distress? I might get hurt if I keep this up? Michael, I'm a criminal attorney, remember? It's not like these kinds of people are something I'm unfamiliar with. They're *not* fools. People don't keep killing simply for the sake of killing. I don't know anything. I'm not any danger to them until I do. When I know something, I'll run to the police so fast it'll make your head swim. But I'm not going to now. If there was tissue stolen at—"

Shannon stopped speaking as a young couple came up the steps and walked past them on the way to their apartment.

When the couple was far enough away not to overhear her, she continued. "If there was tissue stolen at the hospital, it had to be from one of the two people who died there while England was there—either Fayrene Paschal or Bobby Showers. If there was, then there has to be some doctor at the hospital who is responsible—*somebody* who's responsible. I want to know the background on everybody there. I want to see the hospital personnel files."

"What could they possibly tell you?"

"I don't know. Maybe somebody who's been involved in nerve research somewhere before. Maybe we would notice something I haven't thought of."

"In addition to that being about a one in a hundred billion, there's no way in hell that Clark would let us go through the personnel records, anyway."

"Of course he won't allow it. That's why I want to go see them tonight. Right now. When nobody knows we're looking at them."

"You have to be kidding."

Murphy stood on the pavement under the wide overhang spreading out across the entrance to the Gulfport Grand Casino. To his left, the casino's accompanying, brightly lit hotel rose eighteen stories toward the cloudy sky. In front of him, dozens of gamblers walked to and from the parking lots or waited on a valet to bring their cars to them. He watched a young, slim man, who appeared to be in his mid-twenties. The youth hadn't walked to a car or handed a ticket to a valet. He was waiting for one of the casino's shuttle buses now slowing as it came around the wide, curving drive toward the entrance.

When he stepped up into the sleek shuttle, Murphy followed him aboard. He took a seat directly behind the young man.

The youth wore jeans and a short-sleeve white shirt. Murphy had decided on him partly due to his having been alone in the casino. A young person out by himself for a night of enjoyment was more likely than not to be a loner—and wouldn't have that many people who would miss him.

*   *   *

A few minutes later, the youth stepped off the shuttle in front of an aging motel built long before the gambling boom came to the Mississippi Coast. Murphy had the shuttle driver stop a hundred feet farther along the highway and let him off.

He came quickly back down the side of the pavement.

The young man entered one of the middle rooms in the one-story line of structures running back into the darkness. Murphy looked to his left and right, then slipped a ski mask on over his head and knocked on the door.

It opened.

The nice-looking youth, his eyes widening at the sight of Murphy's leveled automatic, stepped backward in shock.

Murphy quickly came inside and closed the door. "Turn around," he said, reaching for the syringe in his pocket.

The boy must have thought he was going to die, for suddenly he screamed at the top of his lungs and stepped forward in the face of the pistol and swung at Murphy's face.

Murphy hit the boy once, and his legs buckled and he fell backward to the floor, crumpling over onto his side.

Somebody pounded loudly on the wall from the next room.

A shout followed. "What's going on in there?"

"Shut your damn mouth and mind your own business!" Murphy yelled back at the wall.

He looked down at the boy. Then he shook his head and hurried to the window at the back of the room, sliding it open.

As he climbed outside, the telephone next to the narrow bed in the room started ringing.

*   *   *

In the motel office, the night clerk, alerted by a guest's calling about a scream in the next room, let the room's phone ring three more times, then disconnected the line and called 911.

Murphy hurried through the darkness at the rear of the units, passing alongside a line of tall bushes that followed the motel's property line; a thin branch slapped him a stinging blow in the face, and he cursed and threw it back out of the way.

A hundred feet farther and he cut through the bushes and broke out into the open, illuminated by the glow of lights from a neighboring motel. He came to a walk, perspiration dotting his wide forehead as he glanced back over his shoulder occasionally. When he heard the first siren, he increased his pace once more.

The first police car arrived at the motel in only three minutes. The door to the room stood open. The shaken youth sat on the side of his bed holding a wet washcloth to his swollen jaw.

Two police officers stood in front of him. "You can't give us a better description?" one asked.

"No, sir—just that he was a big son-of-a-bitch."

Tiny drops of blood fell unseen in the darkness to splash silently on the concrete floor. Johnny lay in an exhausted state halfway between sleep and consciousness, unable to fall fully asleep because his arms were pulled uncomfortably down to the sides of the bed and the straps were cutting into his raw wrists. The pain that had begun soon after Dr. Lobb had injected the yellow-colored milky fluid into his neck was growing worse, starting to send tingling shocks down his spinal cord.

The monkeys screeched when the bright light flashed on.

Johnny jerked and started to sit up, but the strap

across his chest stopped him, and the pain from the restricting straps pulled on his wrists, causing him to cry out.

Jonathan Waverly walked toward him, smiling pleasantly when he stopped beside the bed.

"Please," Johnny said to this new man. "Please let me go home. Please."

As Waverly continued to smile, Johnny said, "I'll do anything." A tear formed at the corner of his eye. "Please, mister. I won't tell anybody what happened. About anything." He gestured toward the monkeys with his chin. "About them."

"What about them?"

Johnny shook his head back and forth. "Please."

"What about them, Johnny?"

"Their heads have been cut off," the teenager said in a low voice.

"But they're alive," Waverly said.

Johnny nodded.

"That's what I want to speak to you about," Waverly said. "You're going to be perfectly all right."

The tear rolled down Johnny's cheek. Another one formed in its place. "You're . . . you're not going to do that to me?"

"You're going to be my . . ." Waverly searched for the proper word. "My pathfinder."

"Wh-what's that?" Johnny asked in a quivering voice.

"My point man, Johnny. If you don't understand yet by looking at me, how I look, how old and sick I am . . . It is I that is going to have my head cut off."

Johnny's eyes narrowed in confusion, then suddenly widened in shock. He turned his eyes toward the monkey, and shook his head. "No," he said. "*Nooo!* You're going to take my head. *No!*" He pulled at the straps binding his wrists. "*Nooo!*"

"Johnny, Johnny," Waverly said, "I told you that you were going to be perfectly all right."

"Nooo!"

"*Johnny, stop that!*" Waverly snapped, the sudden sharp coldness in his voice causing the teenager to quit fighting against the straps.

"That's better," Waverly said, his voice soft once more. "Now listen to me closely. I'm going to explain everything. I'm going to be perfectly honest. And if you'll listen closely, I think this will give you some measure of comfort. The injection Dr. Lobb gave you was a combination of fetal tissue and a growth hormone. I know it causes some pain, but not unbearable pain. I made certain of that when we formulated the mixture, for I will eventually take the same injections. They are designed as a catalyst to the regrowth of the spinal cord tissue."

"Regrowth?" Johnny began to shake his head again.

"In a very simplistic sense, you could say the catalyst starts something much like heating the ends of two candles so that when you put them together they adhere to one another."

"Please, mister," Johnny begged. The tears started pouring from his eyes.

"Johnny, I told you that you had nothing to worry about. We will take great care to make certain that you remain healthy. It's to my benefit, if that will persuade you any better. I told you—you are to be my point man. You will undergo the process for us to observe until I'm ready to undergo the process myself." As Waverly paused, he smiled again, this time a small smile, and he spoke humbly, almost self-deprecatingly. "If part of your objection is thinking your head will be carried by my old body, I can assure you that is not my plan."

Johnny looked at the monkeys. He shook his head again.

Waverly couldn't keep from grinning. "No, Johnny, you will not grace a monkey's body—our process is not yet that advanced. We will soon have a bed partner here for you—a young man with a body every bit as healthy as yours."

Johnny still shook his head, but he was looking up into Waverly's face now. "You're . . . insane," he said in a quivering voice.

"No, as a matter of fact, I'm quite brilliant. I realized that at about your age. But to the point of why I'm here. As soon as your bed partner arrives, we will begin the process. And, by the way, he won't be so lucky as you without us being able to take the time to first give him a few days of injections—but I want to move on with this before you deteriorate from being kept bound and unmoving. I told you that your health is of a prime concern to me.

"Our potential problem comes in having to move you from this bed to the operating table. Experience has taught us that even with a strong heart and high blood oxygenation rate, the success rate of the surgery is highest if we don't administer an anesthetic until the last moment. We will of course give you Valium to take the edge off your nervousness. But that will not keep you from resisting if you're of that mind-set. And should that happen there could be serious consequences. In fact, one monkey—" Waverly glanced at the cages. "—a brother of the spider monkey, resisted to the point of being injured severely, making himself useless to us. That's why we had to make do with the gray langur. If you resist, it's quite possible you'll also ruin yourself for the later observations we must make. If that happens . . ."

Waverly walked to the black box between the beds. Johnny couldn't get his head far enough to the side of his mattress to see down toward the box as Waverly undid its latch and opened it back. A terrible stench washed by his face.

". . . You'll end up like this," Waverly said, lifting a rotting human head into the air by its hair.

Johnny moaned and wet himself in his fear.

The monkeys screamed.

Waverly sat the head down on the other bed, positioning it upright, where the sunken eyes faced Johnny.

"I purposely kept it in anticipation of it making enough of an impression on you for you to forgo trying to resist."

Waverly stared at the head for a moment, then spoke without looking at Johnny. "This particular item isn't the result of a mistake, by the way. The unfortunate man who wore this was not so lucky as you; he was needed only for routine observation of a detached head prior to the final step with you. It was crucial to know if there were any complications I hadn't thought of in keeping a human head alive for the amount of time required between severing and reattachment. We will need about two hours. It should give you a measure of comfort to know it survived a full four hours. And, incidentally, gave no indication that there would have been any difficulty if we had wished to go longer before turning it off."

It wasn't until Waverly looked back at Johnny that he realized the teenager had passed out.

▲ CHAPTER THIRTY-TWO

The room where the personnel records were kept was down a hall past the hospital's main lobby. The door was locked.

"Do you have a credit card?" Shannon asked.

Michael reached into his hip pocket for his billfold.

His Visa card was stuck down in a slot behind his driver's license.

As he handed it to Shannon, she said, "Amazing what I've learned from my clients. I was locked out of my office and my receptionist hadn't gotten there yet—and here this shifty-eyed, break-in artist comes by wanting to know if I'll represent him. You should see me with a piece of wire and a dead bolt."

As she wiggled the card into the crack between the lock and the doorknob, Michael glanced up the hall. Though it was empty, anyone stepping into it could see from end to end.

"Do you have a client who can teach us how to break out of jail?"

"It's not that serious," Shannon said as she continued to wiggle at the lock without looking back at him.

"Breaking and entering?"

"We're not going to steal anything."

"I hope there is another emergency department somewhere that needs a doctor."

"You don't need a job," she said. "You're going to

be a congressman. There." The door swung open.

She turned the lights on from a switch inside the doorway. He stepped inside behind her and quickly closed the door.

A counter twenty feet away divided the room from front to back and ran from one side wall to the other. Behind the counter, a solid mass of cabinets extended several feet up into the air.

"I hope everything is in alphabetical order," he said. It was.

Under P—for personnel records.

The wide cabinet door with a P on it was unlocked.

Shannon opened it. Folder after folder were crammed tightly together, three shelves high. She lifted the first one out. It had the name Ronald Edens typed on its tab. He was a maintenance worker.

She reached for another folder. Michael pulled out the one next to it.

The first physician's folder was that of Charles Lee. Michael recognized the doctor by the identification photograph clipped to the inside cover of the folder. He was a radiologist. The information under the photograph indicated he had come from China, via six years in Tampa, Florida, and had received his education at the University of Tennessee, and Vanderbilt Medical School.

Michael nodded knowingly. "Look at him," he said, pointing toward the photograph. "A Chinese Communist spy if I ever saw one."

Shannon frowned. "Why don't you start looking instead of making smart remarks?"

"Looking for what?"

Shannon turned to the next page in the folder. "I'm glad you're not a cop I'm counting on to protect me," she said.

"And the thought behind that?"

"Because if you came upon a crime scene, you'd just throw your hands up in the air and quit because no one left a note behind confessing. You have to search for clues, Michael. You won't know if there are any until one hits you in the face." She closed the folder and reached to the shelf for the next one.

Michael took the one beside it.

Fifteen minutes later, they had gone through half of the folders. Michael heard the door opening first, and looked across his shoulder. A tall, uniformed, hospital security guard with long, slicked-back black hair stared at them.

"Oh, it's you, Dr. Sims," he said. "Excuse me."

Still staring in their direction, the guard stepped back out into the hall and pulled the door closed in front of him.

"You didn't lock it?" Shannon whispered.

"You came in after me," he said.

"I did not."

He recalled she was right, but didn't admit it. He looked down at the folder he had opened, and placed the tip of his forefinger in a blank space at the center of the top sheet. "Here it is. A written confession: 'I'm guilty of stealing spinal cords from dead bodies at the Coastal Regional Hospital.' " He nodded. "Yep, case closed."

"Michael, why do you keep being a smart aleck?"

"Because it bothers me when I can't get something done I'm trying to do."

She stared at him a moment. "You do believe my father was murdered, don't you?"

"Hell, I don't have any idea—and this is crazy."

As she continued to stare at him, her lip trembled. "I'm just trying," she said.

Feeling guilty, he reached for another folder. "Hell, it's only that I have no idea what we're looking for—and you don't either."

*   *   *

A few minutes later, Shannon tugged at his sleeve. She pressed her forefinger against the typing under a photograph of Dr. Marzullo. She had a questioning look across her face. "He performed my father's bypass surgery. It says he came here from Los Angeles."

"I knew he was from California," Michael said.

"Michael, Los Angeles was where the pathologist was from who stole the tissue that brought about the hearings."

"Yeah, Shannon, and I just read that the head of neurology came from New York. But that doesn't mean he bombed the World Trade Center."

"Michael, he's the one who told me about how depressed Daddy was—that he should have known he . . . He told Everette, too. He was the reason I even started wondering if maybe there might have been more depression than I thought." Her eyes narrowed. "He was making certain everybody knew Daddy was depressed."

"So are you saying Waverly had some credentials forged for Marzullo—yet didn't think to list him as coming from somewhere other than Los Angeles?"

"Maybe. That's not so difficult to believe. I represented a man once on an armed robbery who was masked but wore his old football jersey."

"Don't tell me—his name was on its back?"

Shannon nodded.

"You win that one?"

"No, I didn't. You couldn't have either."

He pointed to the typing above where she had placed her finger. "It says Marzullo was employed at the medical center there. You can call and ask about him."

"No, there could have been a Marzullo who practiced there and not be the same doctor who's here. He could have assumed the name to give him a background."

"Okay, then fax them his photograph, Sherlock. Or have them fax you his out of his file there. I'm sure you can think up a reason that will sound convincing."

"I have a better idea," Shannon said. She walked to the telephone on the counter and lifted the receiver. "Can you get an outside line on this?" She was already punching in a number.

She placed the receiver to her ear. "It's working," she said. She glanced at her watch. "I don't know if he's had time to get back to Washington yet."

A few seconds later she said, "Is Mr. Samples in?"

She listened a moment as the party on the other end of the line said something. "Can I have his home number then, please?"

She immediately frowned. "Well, if you don't have the authority to give it to me, then will you call him yourself and tell him I want it—Shannon Donnelly. I'll call back in ten minutes."

She waited a moment. "Of *course* this is important," she said. "Fine, I'll hold . . . Shannon Donnelly. D-o-n-n-e-l-l-y."

Michael saw her glance at him. "Some ditzy . . ." she started, and shook her head.

Then Samples came on the line so quickly Michael wondered if he were actually in his office and not taking calls.

"Robert," Shannon said, "I need a favor again."

"Shannon, I told you the last time that I—"

"No, it's nothing that will cause you a problem. Daddy had a set of the old Waverly hearing files here. But all he had was the transcripts. I need a photograph."

"A photograph?"

"Of the pathologist who lost his license after the hearings. I'll bet there's one in the files there. If there isn't, I know there'll be some newspaper clippings— something with his photo in it."

Michael heard a sound in the hall outside the closed doors. He listened closely. It sounded like a stretcher rolling along the tile floor.

"Robert," Shannon said. "I told you I thought my

father was murdered. You get me the photograph I need and, maybe, just maybe, I might be able to prove it. The hearing files are public record anyway. Please."

She nodded and smiled at whatever the administrative assistant said. "That's fine, Robert. However long it takes for you to find one. I want you to fax it to me at my office."

As she replaced the receiver, she looked at the photograph of Marzullo, then tore it loose, keeping it in her hand as she slid the folder back in among the others in the cabinet.

▲ CHAPTER THIRTY-THREE

WASHINGTON, DC

Samples stared at his desktop for a moment after finishing the telephone conversation with Shannon in Biloxi. He had felt so down at Lawrence's death that he had been sitting around the office for days, mostly doing nothing, only interrupting his doing nothing for the quick trip to Biloxi for the funeral. Lawrence had not only been his boss, but his closest friend. He just couldn't make himself do anything. And adding to his depression was the knowledge that his career was over. At sixty years of age he wouldn't be retained by whoever won the election.

His wife had wanted him to retire anyway, so maybe the time had come. But that's not what he was thinking about at the moment. What currently occupied his mind was his having enjoyed a reputation of efficiency all during his time as an administrative assistant. He didn't want the new congressman coming into the office and seeing that nothing had been done since Lawrence's death, that everything since the suicide had been allowed to stack up and go unanswered.

That's not how I'm going to be remembered, falling apart at the end, he had thought as he flew back from Biloxi in the quiet solitude of the private Learjet. As soon as the plane had landed, he had come to the office to start clearing up what business he could. He looked up at the attractive, dark-haired young intern who stood across the desk from him. She cradled a thick folder of papers against her chest.

She smiled at him.

"Sylvia," he said. "Put those in the chair and go into the files in the storage room. Under the W's there's a stack of Waverly hearing folders. If you don't mind, start bringing them to me. One by one," he added wearily.

The young lady nodded, and turned toward the door leading back into the office's reception area. "And then look in the rolodex on Carl's desk," Samples added. "Look under FBI for Special Agent in Charge Caroline Sanderson's home number. Tell her I'm faxing a photograph to Mississippi, and I'm going to fax her a copy, too."

As Sylvia walked out the door, he leaned back in his chair. Shannon had kept asking for more and more information. She didn't think Lawrence had committed suicide, and from all she had now requested in the last few days, she obviously had in her mind that someone at the Biloxi Waverly Center might have been involved in his death. That she had those thoughts hadn't bothered him initially. She was a daughter deeply disturbed by the death and he could understand her reluctance at first in not wanting to accept what had really happened. He had been glad to humor her—especially for Lawrence's sake.

But now she was still at it. *You get me the photograph I need and I might be able to prove it.*

A photograph of a doctor who had once worked for the Waverly Research Centers.

The thought that there could be a connection between Lawrence's death and what she asked for seemed inconceivable.

But if there was, she could be getting herself in deeper than he thought was wise. That wouldn't be how

Lawrence would want him to leave his daughter. All on her own.

"Sylvia, when you get Agent Sanderson on the phone, I'd like to speak with her myself for a moment."

BILOXI

When Michael and Shannon stepped from the records room, closing the door behind them, the tall security guard walked down the hall in their direction. He nodded as he passed by, saying, "Dr. Sims." He looked at the door they had closed, kept his gaze on it for a moment, and continued down the hall.

Michael stared after him. "He's going to mention we were in there. Do it casually at first to one of the file clerks or Clark; casually until he finds out for certain we weren't supposed to be in there, and then he's going to tell what he saw us doing."

He shook his head as they started down the hall. "You don't have an opening for a paralegal by any chance? I might be needing a job."

She smiled. "I'll hire you."

"From a doctor, to a private investigator, to a paralegal," he mused. "Up, down, and then starting back up again. How long does law school take? I guess I could try that."

"You can't be accepted into law school in Mississippi if you've been convicted of a felony."

"A felony? I thought you said what we were doing wasn't that serious."

"I wasn't under oath."

"What about law schools in another state?"

From the end of the hall, Daryl walked toward them.

"Damn," Michael said as he glanced back toward the record room. "Now my best friend is going to end up being forced to testify against me."

As Daryl stopped in front of them, he smiled at Shannon and said, "If Michael can't find anyplace better than this to take you, you should try a night out with me."

He looked at the photograph Shannon held down at her side. She turned Dr. Marzullo's face against her skirt. Daryl's eyes narrowed. "What in hell are you two up to?"

"You don't want to know," Michael said.

"Guess not. You're not going to tell me anyway. You remember that stripper who was being brought in? The one with the broken leg?"

"Yes, Daryl."

"Turned out to be a damn female impersonator in town for a show at one of the clubs. What's the world coming to?"

Shannon smiled. "You didn't take a close look at the contusions?" she asked.

Daryl smiled. "Hell, Michael, she's got a personality, too. If you're short change to take her out somewhere other than here, I guess I could loan you some."

"Why are you still on duty?" Michael asked.

"Because that prick Dean didn't want to miss seeing his son play in a Little League All-Star game. I can promise you that's the most expensive game he's ever seen." Daryl rubbed his thumb and forefinger together, implying how much money he was making off of Dean by covering his shift. "And he's got two more hours of paying through the nose. He better be here in two hours or I'm going to quadruple the charge." He looked up the hall behind them. "Well, somewhere back there is a new candy machine. According to Olga. Sugar keeps me going." He looked at Shannon and winked. "All kinds of sugar." He stepped around them and continued up the hall.

As they walked from the hospital and started toward the Expedition, Shannon said, "Remember, not—"

"A word about this," Michael finished for her. "I wonder which is worse—going to jail or getting shot."

Shannon smiled.

The stocky figure came running at him from the darkness off to his side. He caught the movement out of the corner of his eye and whirled toward it.

The woman screamed, crazed, with her mouth wide and her teeth showing like an animal. She held her purse out to the side with both hands as she ran, clutching its strap as if she was going to swing it like a bat.

As she came by Shannon, Shannon slammed her palms hard against the woman's shoulder, knocking her off balance to the side, where she caught her foot against her ankle and tripped, sprawling to the blacktop and skidding across it with her momentum.

Shannon jumped toward the woman, and raised her own purse over her head.

"*No!*" Michael yelled.

The woman, her legs splayed, her skirt ridden up her thighs, started sobbing against the pavement. Her purse lay beside her. She reached for it, but stopped her hand and beat her fist against the hard blacktop. Michael leaned down and gently caught her shoulder.

"Mrs. Whitaker."

She looked up at him, tears flooding down her cheeks. "I want to kill you," she mumbled. "I want to kill you. You lied to me and then let Johnny die." She shuddered, a great convulsive shudder that shook her entire body. He tried to help her to her feet.

She pushed his hands away. "I've prayed you rot in hell," she said in a cold voice. He pulled gently on her shoulders. She resisted another moment, then came up, letting him help her to her feet, and faced him.

"I hate you," she said, tears running down her face to drop from her chin. "I hate you," she repeated, and shuddered again.

A security guard came sprinting across the pavement.

"I'm sorry," Michael said. "I'm so sorry Johnny died. But it was ... there wasn't any way to predict ..." He shook his head. "I'm so sorry." He put his hands to the sides of her shoulders. Her red and swollen eyes stared into his, the tears still running down her face. He gently pulled her toward him.

She suddenly stepped forward, turned her face against his chest, and started sobbing convulsively, shaking all over. He held her gently.

"I'm sorry," he said.

The security guard looked at him. Michael shook his head. The guard glanced at Shannon, looked back at him, then started slowly back toward the hospital, glancing across his shoulder as he walked away.

The woman's sobs came silently now. "I hate you," she said.

"I know," he said softly.

In the surveillance room at the Waverly Research Center, the stocky security guard had heard a woman's loud scream of rage. A shuffling noise he couldn't interpret had followed. There had been some low talking, far enough away from the Expedition that he couldn't understand what was being said, then silence.

A full five minutes passed, then he heard the Expedition's doors open and close, then the sound of its motor starting.

"*I wasn't going to hit her,*" Shannon said. "*I thought she might have a weapon.*"

"*I know,*" Michael said in a voice so low it was hard to hear.

Then there was silence again.

Seconds once again turned into minutes, still without the sound of anyone speaking.

The guard turned up the speaker volume.

Nothing but the roar of the engine and the whine of the tires as the Expedition moved along the pavement.

He leaned closer.

"*Damn it, move over so I can pass!*"

The Expedition's horn roared with the volume of a freight train racing by the guard's face. He grabbed his ears and jerked his head back from the speaker.

His coffee cup rattled against the saucer.

On Highway 90, Shannon shot an irritated glance at the man in the slow-moving pickup who had pulled over to let her pass. "I hate slow drivers hogging the road," she said.

Michael nodded without saying anything, still thinking about Mrs. Whitaker.

"I hate that she did that to you," Shannon said.

When he still didn't say anything, she turned her face back toward the windshield.

Underneath the ashtray in the Expedition's dash, the small, round, highly sensitive listening device recorded every sound, even that of the heavy utility vehicle's tires rolling against the pavement.

The device also recorded the Expedition's location.

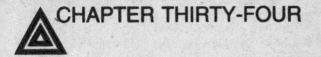

CHAPTER THIRTY-FOUR

Waverly stood in Lobb's room at the rear of the detention area. He lifted the telephone receiver on the bedside table, pushed it down into the grooves of an oblong, plastic device that resembled another telephone base, then punched a long series of numbers into the keypad at one side of the instrument.

The call was transported by satellite to a deserted island among the hundreds of deserted islands in the Bahamas. This one had recently been purchased by the Waverly Corporation through a shell corporation set up in the Cayman Islands—and was no longer deserted.

Heavy earth-moving equipment sat at rest in the darkness. A few lights still gleamed from windows in the prefabricated dormitory where the work crews from Colombia were housed.

A bright Caribbean moon shone down through the clear skies against a wide cement block and concrete building already completed. A sprawling, three-story home under construction was half completed fifty feet away, and was connected to the smaller building by a covered walkway. Hundreds of potted plants and flowers in full bloom were stacked side by side in the bed of an aging dump truck.

The sound of a telephone ringing came from the back bedroom of a rust-streaked house trailer.

A heavy-set man in his mid-fifties rolled to his back in the queen-size bed and reached for a cellular telephone lying on the bedside table.

"Yeah, what is it?"

A screeching, meaningless sound came through the receiver.

The man quickly swung his feet to the floor. In only a few seconds he had locked the receiver's earpiece and mouthpiece into the molded sockets on the descrambler on the table.

"Okay, Jonathan, go ahead."

"How is it coming down there?"

"Surgical suite and recovery is completed. Your home will be ready in a month. They're planting the flowers now."

"Good, Barry. You know you're going to have a guest in a couple of days."

"The doctor from Hungary?"

"Yes, and his assistants."

"They'll be impressed with the surgical facilities."

"My health's going fast, Barry."

"You want me to get in a larger work crew to finish the house?"

"No, a month's fine. A year's fine. It's only that we're going to have to go ahead before too much longer. I get this bill passed, and at least get the funding going in the right direction, and I can rest a little easier. You know a couple of the rats didn't come all the way back. There's still more we need to know. We get the bill passed, we can throw money at it—especially the aging of the circulatory system. I think we'll be fine. You know, Barry, if we had been able to get the joint venture passed the last time, we would have reached this point years ago—surpassed it."

"Yeah, Jonathan. You don't know how badly that makes me feel."

"Won't be long after the funding passes you'll have to come here to take over the trusteeship."

"I'm ready, Jonathan. I've been going over every paper you sent me. I know where you want each dollar spent."

"My father trusted his life to your father, Barry."

"Yeah, I know—and he's been well rewarded."

"There's more difference in our ages, Barry, but we've been family ever since we were kids. You know in the long run I'm trusting you with my life."

"It's an honor, Jonathan."

"You know I'm really counting on you. I won't be able to come back for a while—maybe a year, maybe longer."

"I know, Jonathan. The trusteeship will be yours as soon as you come back."

Jonathan chuckled over the line. The descrambler wasn't programmed for that and made a series of high-pitched chirping sounds. Barry knew what they meant. "Glad you're in a good mood, Jonathan. You sounded down, right at first."

Waverly chuckled again. "I was just thinking how there'll be no sunbathing with my new figure. Even after the face-lifts, couldn't you just see that—my face and a twenty-year-old body? Especially with the muscles. My body is going to have a lot of muscles."

"You do that, Jonathan."

Dancing yellow light from bonfires on the beach reflected off Murphy's face as he sat in his car staring at a mixture of scantily clad to full-clad young men and women and boys and girls walking slowly along the white sand.

One youth in his late teens or early twenties turned away from a bonfire and walked alone toward the highway.

He waited at the side of the pavement for a line of cars to pass, then started across it toward the Holiday Inn.

Murphy opened his door.

As he did, his cellular telephone vibrated.

He tugged it out of his pocket and lifted it to his ear.

"We've already taken care of business," Lobb said. "Come on back."

Every so often the smoke detector on Shannon's office wall gave off a chirp, the high-pitched sound irritating Michael. He stared at it, then walked to the bookcase built into the wall across from her desk. It contained hundreds of legal texts, from wafer-thin books to some that were three inches thick. He glanced at his watch and walked to the doorway leading out into the hall.

Shannon, holding Dr. Marzullo's photograph by her side, remained by the fax machine, thumping her fingers against its top.

Michael glanced at his watch again.

The machine rang.

Then it clicked, made another sound, and paper began emerging from its rear.

Samples had set his fax on the lowest speed in order to afford as much detail as possible in the photograph. It came agonizingly slowly.

Michael waited.

Very slowly, the top part of the head of the man in the photograph came into view.

Michael looked at Shannon. She was staring intently at it as it slowly inched higher and higher. But he already knew it wasn't going to be Dr. Marzullo. Dr. Marzullo had light-brown hair. The hair of the man in this photograph was notably blond, almost white-looking in the fax.

The eyes appeared.

The deep, dark, sunken eyes.

The puffy skin around them.

Michael tightened his eyes, staring closer.

The nose appeared.

The lips.

All on a narrow face.

The sideburns and beard weren't there, but there was no doubt. Shannon looked dejected. He touched her arm and mouthed, "It's Dr. Lobb."

Before she could say anything, he placed his hand over her mouth. She nodded.

They made their way out of her office to the front door and stepped outside into the cool night air. He walked a little way from the building before he turned to face her.

"He's the pathologist from L.A.," he said. "He's dyed his hair and grown the beard, but he's the pathologist. As crazy as I thought you were, Shannon; as crazy as I thought I was becoming, you were right."

"It has to be tissue they took, doesn't it, with him involved again?"

"It's something they're doing."

"That's not good enough, Michael. I have to know what."

"Let the sheriff figure it out. You have enough to go to him now."

"You're forgetting Waverly's money. That means high-priced attorneys. An army of them. James can't just arrest him because Lobb's working at the center. There has to be an investigation. When that starts, Waverly will flush everything. We need the tissue in our hands to prove it was really taken again."

"In our hands?"

"Without it all we have is a crazy theory that we can't prove—we don't even know if it *is* tissue."

"Shannon, England saw something when he was at the hospital. If they stole tissue again, it had to be from either the man or the woman who died while he was there. The police can exhume the bodies. The incision will be noticeable."

"What if neither one of the bodies has incisions, Michael? We're real close. We're almost there. Yet if we say something wrong . . . if it turns out that the tissue wasn't taken, we're going to be *so* wrong that nobody will listen to anything we have to say."

"You'll have Lobb in any case."

"Have him? Have a former doctor somebody at the center felt sorry enough for to give a job baby-sitting mental patients? So he's passing himself off as a psychiatrist? Who cares? It's going to be a great big nothing unless one of the bodies does have tissue missing. We have to . . ." As Shannon stopped speaking, her lip suddenly trembled. She turned away from him and stared toward the street.

"What?"

She shook her head and spoke without looking back in his direction. "I don't give a damn about anybody but Waverly. And what do we have even with this photograph? Damn it, what will we have even if it turns out one of the bodies has tissue missing? How am I . . . how am I going to prove Waverly had anything to do with Daddy's . . . How . . . am . . ." She shook her head back and forth. "Damn it, Michael, I'm not going to be able to prove . . ." Her voice broke and she couldn't say any more.

He stepped up close behind her and cupped her shoulders in his hands. A police car passed on the street. The black officer behind the steering wheel glanced in their direction.

"Why don't you give the sheriff a try at it, Shannon? You've done all you can. Let him take over and see what he can do now. If one of the bodies is missing tissue, you have Lobb for certain. If it's something else they've done, he's still going to have a problem—impersonating a psychiatrist, probably some other charges the sheriff can stick him with. This is your father's county, Shannon. The sheriff, the judge, whatever it takes, they're going to turn the screws. Lobb might be willing to talk to stay out of prison."

Shannon leaned her head back against his shoulder. "There has to be something else I can do," she said. "I can't stop now." She turned out of his arms to face him. "*We* can't stop now, Michael." There was a look of renewed determination on her face. "We're not going to stop. First, we're going to see for ourselves if tissue is missing from one of the bodies. If there isn't, then we'll think of what to do after that." She was staring directly into his eyes. "You're going to help me, aren't you?"

He suddenly realized what she meant. She had said *We're going to see for ourselves*. See.

"Not on your life."

"We've found out so much, Michael. We only have a little way to go. Please."

He shook his head. "Not on your life."

"Michael, it's just this last step."

"Just?" He shook his head again. "Not on your life."

Thirty minutes later, they stood in the Gulfport Wal-Mart. Shannon held a shovel in each hand.

"You're crazy," he said. "You're really certifiably insane."

"Nobody is going to know he was murdered unless we prove it. I can't afford to tell Everette one of the bodies is going to be missing tissue, and then he digs it up and it's not."

"You're going to end up losing your law license," he said.

"How? If the tissue is missing, I'm not going to be in any trouble—maybe a little embarrassed at how I went about finding out, but that's all. No one would press charges. If it isn't missing, then there's just going to be a desecrated grave. They'll think devil worshippers did it."

"Devil worshippers?"

"I'm going to prove Daddy was murdered, Michael, and I'm not going to take any chances of telling Everette something that he'll find out is not true. I'm going to know for certain."

"If there is tissue missing, the defense attorneys will be able to claim you're the one who took it—you dug up the grave and took it. You know that's going to happen."

"You can't tell the difference in when it was taken?"

He reluctantly nodded. "Yeah, you could."

"I thought so. I'm going out there. So one more time, are you going with me?"

He shook his head no.

"Okay," she said. "Then all I need from you is for you not to say anything to anybody about what I'm doing. I can handle the rest myself."

"Dig up a grave all by your lonesome—maybe two graves?"

"I told you all I need from you," she repeated. "Where do you want me to drop you off?"

Olga Lindestrom stood in one of the rooms at the back of the ICU. She smiled pleasantly down at the young man lying in the bed before her. They shared a common heritage of sorts. He was Jackie Johansen, a fourth-generation American whose family came from Norway. She was a third-generation American from Sweden. They both had blond hair, though none of his could be seen with his head completely swathed in bandages. A plastic bag hanging from the rack next to the bed ran a clear saline solution through an IV tube into his arm. His vital signs were good, his blood pressure 116 over 78, his temperature only a couple degrees above normal, and his heart beating with strong, steady thumps as measured on the cardiac monitor mounted above the bed.

Olga looked across her shoulder. The nurses' station was empty. The only other nurse in the unit, a noticeably overweight black-haired woman, stood with her back to the room as she sipped coffee from a Styrofoam cup near the door to the hallway. "This is about your last injection," Olga said to the young man.

He rolled his eyes as if he didn't believe her, smiled, and turned his head to the side as she leaned forward, felt for the vein in the crook of his arm, found it, and inserted a hypodermic needle expertly into place.

She looked back across her shoulder again as she reached inside the pocket of her scrubs. She lifted out a syringe filled with a yellow-colored milky liquid and attached it to the needle. The faint backflow of the man's blood turned the liquid pink in the bottom of the syringe, showing the needle was properly in the vein. She injected the blood and the liquid back into his arm and quickly replaced the syringe in her pocket.

Her gaze went to the cardiac monitor.

In only seconds, the jagged up-and-down peaks being sketched across the screen began to spread farther apart. A few seconds later, they began to lessen in height. The man's eyelids fluttered. His arm twitched. His fingers, cupped toward his palms, began to relax. As his eyes closed, not to open again, Olga turned and walked in the direction of the nurses' station.

In a moment, she was engaged in conversation with the other nurse near the unit's entrance.

In one of the rooms, an aging male patient with IV tubes running into his body in several places said something, and the nurse walked away from Olga toward his door to see what he needed.

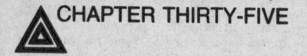# CHAPTER THIRTY-FIVE

They came silently through the night between the tombstones, statuettes, and small markers. Shannon carried a flashlight, switched off. He carried the two shovels. She wore a dark sweat suit, and he was still in his green scrubs, so they both blended into the darkness. *Like camouflaged commandos on a mission behind enemy lines*, Michael thought. *Or crazy people.*

"This is absolutely insane," he said. "Incredibly insane. No, there's not a word for it. I'm going to lose my license. You're going to lose your license. We're both going to end up in jail. Under the jail."

"Shhh," Shannon said.

All around them were the oaks, magnolias, and cedars growing thick across the manicured grounds. A few hundred feet to their left, the bright headlights of slow-moving traffic passed by on the street running alongside the cemetery.

Michael wondered if they had come too far across the grounds. He was having trouble with the directions Bobby Showers's wife had given him. At Shannon's urging he had made the call this time, and said he was with the National Guard. Showers's chart showed that he had belonged to the Guard. Without even asking him why the National Guard needed to know the location of the body, the woman had told him the directions as best she could. They had chosen Showers's grave first because he had been on the same hospital floor as England. Michael squinted his eyes, trying to see better. The clouds cutting off the moonlight didn't make it very easy.

Then he saw the dim outline of the statue of an angel with spread wings at the head of a grave directly in front of them. Shannon saw it at the same time.

"His wife said about fifty feet to the right of the statue," she said.

They angled in that direction.

A few seconds later, they nearly walked over the small group of flat markers.

"I *think* that's it," he said.

He pointed toward a grave off by itself.

As they neared the plot, the lack of thick grass growing across a rectangular-shaped piece of ground made it apparent it was the right one. There wasn't a headstone yet, only the marker put there by the funeral home until the stone was engraved.

They stood in silence for a long moment.

"Well," Shannon finally said, looking at him.

"Well," he said back to her.

She stared a moment more. "This is crazy," she said in a low voice. Then she laid the flashlight on the ground, took a shovel from him and pushed its point into the ground at the edge of the grave. She looked at him. "We don't have all night. If this isn't the one, we have one more to go."

"One count of grave robbing isn't enough for you?"

He was speaking like he was making light of what they were doing. But he knew there was nothing light about it. He still didn't know how he had let her talk him into coming along with her in the first place. He came closer than he ever had in his life to not doing something he had agreed to. He looked back across his shoulder to where they had parked the Expedition, and almost walked off and left her. But he was almost as certain as Shannon that one of the bodies was going to have tissue missing.

He began digging.

Despite the fresh, relatively uncompacted dirt, it took them over two hours of hard labor. She was sweating. He was sweating. They were down in the hole they were excavating, digging themselves deeper and deeper with each shovelful of dirt they threw up over their shoulders. His shovel hit the casket first. Shannon raised her eyes to his at the metallic sound. Her head was barely even with the top of the hole. She pushed down on her shovel. It hit metal. She began moving the blade back and forth to scrape the remaining dirt off the coffin.

Soon it was uncovered.

They had only to dig down a few more inches at the casket's front to completely uncover the lid.

Michael used the back of his hand to wipe the dampness from his forehead. He looked over the edge of the grave toward the headlights moving up and down the road alongside the cemetery—and caught movement out of the corner of his eyes.

It had been a fleeting movement back to his right, across the ground between a pair of cedars.

Shannon saw him looking into the dark. "What?"

He continued to stare.

"What?" Shannon repeated, her voice lower.

He saw it again as it came out from behind the cedar.

Small, unrecognizable in the darkness, only a low shape hugging the ground.

Now it turned in their direction, and came trotting toward them—a small shape.

A dog.

"Damn," Shannon said. "Scare us to death."

At her words the animal stopped and stared at her face, sticking barely above the lip of the grave.

It was a beagle.

It suddenly barked—loudly.

"Shhh!" Shannon said.

The beagle raised its muzzle toward the clouds and howled.

Shannon stamped her foot. *"Dog. Shut up."*

The beagle tilted its head sideways, looking at her from an angle.

"Go away," she said.

The beagle's tail wagged.

The animal took a step forward.

Now he growled, a low-pitched, sinister sound.

"Damn it, dog," Shannon said.

The beagle froze with his paw forward, and growled again. Then he tilted his head once more.

Michael couldn't help but smile. "Your turn, Shannon."

The beagle took a step closer.

Michael pulled himself up onto the edge of the grave. Sitting there, he held out his hand toward the animal.

It wagged its tail and took a step closer.

Michael slid his eyes in Shannon's direction. "You brain him with the shovel when he gets close."

Shannon frowned.

"Come here, girl," Michael said.

"It's a boy," Shannon said.

"You have good eyes. Come here, boy."

The dog trotted toward him. Its tail wagged wildly back and forth now. As the animal stopped in front of him, he patted its head.

The beagle's ribs showed against its thin sides.

"Tell you what, boy. You keep an eye out for the posse and warn us if they come, and I'll buy you a bone."

The metallic sound of Shannon's shovel scraping against the coffin made Michael serious again.

She threw a shower of dirt out of the grave, and pressed the shovel back down into the ground at the coffin's front.

Michael slid back into the hole.

In a moment they were where he could get the point of his shovel into the narrow slot where the lid fit against the body of the casket.

"You can't lift me, too," Shannon said and caught the lip of the grave and pulled herself up onto the bank.

Michael jammed the shovel blade into the slit and pried. The shovel slipped. He jammed it hard back against the narrow slit, and pried again. He heard the latch snap. He laid the shovel aside, straddled the coffin, caught his fingertips in the slit, pulled up on the lid, and pushed it back.

Bobby Showers lay in silent repose in a dark suit, his eyes closed, his hands crossed over his stomach.

Michael could hear Shannon's breathing above him.

The beagle stepped up beside her and looked down at him.

He reached his hands down inside the coffin and moved his fingers past Showers's face and around behind his neck.

The skin gave slightly. He couldn't feel an incision or the stitches where an incision might have been sutured closed.

He undid the tie, unbuttoned the collar, and ran his hands down inside the back of the shirt, feeling along Showers's spine.

There was nothing.

He moved his hand a little to one side of the spine, feeling for an incision made farther away from the spinal column.

His hand came up against the shoulder blade.

It felt . . .

He pressed his fingers against the bone.

He pressed harder.

He moved his hands back to the front of the body and quickly unbuttoned the shirt.

He ran his fingers down the rib cage.

"Give me the flashlight," he said.

Shannon knelt at the end of the hole, leaned over it, and handed the flashlight down.

He switched it on, spread the shirt wide across Showers's chest, and pressed against the sternum with his hand.

It gave slightly, like it was supposed to. Yet there was the feel of something different.

"What?" Shannon whispered down to him.

He pressed harder—and felt the abrupt resistance.

He forced his fingers between the ribs, and dug them into the skin—and felt the solid resistance again.

He thought of something to probe with.

Damn, he hadn't brought anything. He picked up the shovel. He hesitated a moment, then placed its pointed end against the stomach just above the belt line.

He pressed down hard.

The skin gave.

He pressed harder. The shovel stopped against something solid. He might as well have been pressing the blade against a steel plate.

He was *pressing against a steel plate.*

He was certain of that now.

He raised the shovel several inches above the body, gripped the handle tightly in both hands, and slammed the point of the blade down hard into the stomach.

"Michael!"

The skin parted beneath the sudden driving force.

And the shovel clanged against steel.

"Michael?"

He plunged his hand down into the wide slit.

The interior of the body was empty. He felt the steel reinforcing plate running where the spine should be, welded to the metal ribs.

"We haven't committed a damn felony," he said. "We haven't committed a damn anything. It's a mannequin."

CHAPTER THIRTY-SIX

Michael scrambled up out of the grave, rolling over its edge onto the ground and coming to his feet.

Shannon wiped her forehead with the back of her hand, leaving a smear of grime above her eyebrows. Her cheek was stained with dirt and streaks of it marked her sweatshirt.

"They stole a whole body?" she questioned, looking down at the replica of Bobby Showers. "Why?"

Before he could say anything, she added, "England didn't see them removing tissue at the hospital. He didn't see them doing anything there. The body had to be switched at the funeral home; somebody there had to be in on it. Everything had to be done at the funeral home." Her eyes came around toward his. "What did he see?"

"Bottom line is you have enough now to let Everette take it from here—he'll figure it out. He'll know your father was murdered."

This time Shannon nodded without asking further questions. She put her hands on his forearms, squeezed them gently, and raised up on her toes, kissing him on the cheek.

"Thank you," she said.

Leaving her hands against his arms, she turned her face toward the grave, looking down inside it again. She was silent for a moment. "England wouldn't have waited long to call his wife after he saw something." She had spoken in a low tone, almost as if she were thinking aloud rather than speaking to him.

Her eyes came back to his. "Michael, England made his first call to his wife at eleven fifty-seven. You said the chart showed Showers was pronounced dead just before midnight."

He nodded. "Eleven fifty-four."

"England saw something right then. It had to be then. If he had seen something earlier, he would have called her as soon as he saw it. He saw something, went straight to the phone, and called her—three minutes after Showers was dead."

Michael looked at the mannequin now. What he was thinking seemed inconceivable. But it had seemed inconceivable that Shannon's father had been murdered. *Showers saw England die?*

Saw him murdered?

But why wouldn't he have called the police rather than his wife?

"What?" Shannon asked.

"There wouldn't be any reason to murder someone," he said, arguing with his own thoughts.

"What?"

"If they were going to steal a body, they would simply wait until a patient died and was delivered to the funeral home. There was no reason to murder anyone."

"Michael," Shannon said, her voice low again. "In the hearing files there was more than Lobb simply bribing the family to remove spinal tissue. Remember— though it was never proved who was responsible, the second autopsy the committee authorized indicated the patient had been receiving spinal injections while he was still on life support."

That was where her father had come up with the phrase "living tissue." Working on living tissue. "Michael, I saw a segment on TV once. I didn't watch all of it because I don't like to see things like that, but some doctors at a research institute were working on laboratory rats afflicted with cancer. They injected them with cancer-fighting agents, then waited a few days and dissected them to see what effect the agents had against the tumors. They had to kill the rats to know."

At Shannon's Expedition, Michael waited while she lifted her purse off the seat, opened it, pulled out her cellular phone, and held it out to him.

He walked far enough away from the Expedition not to be overheard if there was a listening device, then punched in a number. When the woman who served as the hospital operator at night answered, he said, "Third floor, east."

Seconds later, a feminine voice answered and he said, "This is Dr. Sims. Is Luanne on duty?"

"Just a moment, Doctor."

Luanne must have been standing close to the other nurse at the station, because she answered almost immediately.

"Luanne, a little over a week ago a Mr. Bobby Showers expired on your wing. Do you remember him?"

"Yes."

"Who pronounced him dead?"

"Dr. Marzullo."

"Do you remember Joe England? He was on the floor, too."

"No."

"Thank you, Luanne." He punched information into the phone and asked for Marzullo's residence number.

"What are you doing?" Shannon asked, balancing the squirming beagle in her arms.

"Dr. Marzullo is the one who pronounced Showers dead. I know he wouldn't have thought anything unusual about the death or he would have requested an autopsy. But I want to ask him anyway."

"What are you thinking?"

"Shannon, nobody would have made a mannequin up unless they knew for certain a patient was going to die—and which one."

She stared at him for a moment. "And *when* he would die," she said in a low voice.

He nodded. "One thing that is out of the ordinary is for a patient to be far enough on the way to recovery to be moved up to the floor from the ICU and then expire."

Marzullo's number came across the line and he punched it in and raised the phone back to his ear.

Shannon looked back across the cemetery in the direction of Showers's grave. A quizzical expression crossed her face, her brow wrinkled, and her eyes narrowed in thought.

"Michael," she said as she looked back at him. "Remember in the records room I told you about Dr. Marzullo telling everybody Daddy was dead. When Marzullo called me, why didn't he simply just say he was sorry? Why would he go into the reason my father killed himself—it wasn't the time to be doing that, was it? Shouldn't he have just been offering me his condolences?" she repeated.

Marzullo's number was still ringing. Michael lowered the phone to his side. Marzullo had pronounced Showers dead. He had also pronounced Johnny Whitaker dead—and had said there was no reason for an autopsy in Johnny's case.

What there was no reason for was Johnny's dying.

"Do you have a gun?" he asked.

"At the office, in my desk. Why?"

He disconnected the number. "Because I'm going out there."

"Out there? The center?"

He nodded. "The blow to Johnny's chest shouldn't have been enough to kill him."

And she wasn't able to ask him who Johnny was or what Michael meant, because he turned at the same moment as he spoke and started back toward the Expedition, moving too close to it for them to speak.

Carrying the beagle, she hurried after him.

The first faint rumble of thunder could be heard in the distance out over the Gulf.

The *click-click-click* of the linen cart's wheels as it came down the hall carried into the ICU.

Olga turned to the nurse writing in a chart on the counter. "How does coffee and donuts sound?" she asked, and smiled as the noticeably overweight woman looked back at her.

"Olga, don't do that to me." But the look on the woman's face said she didn't have any willpower.

Olga reached inside her scrubs' pocket and pulled out a handful of change.

The woman said, "Your punishment is paying for mine, too."

Olga smiled and counted out a dollar and a half. "I'll start the coffee," she said.

"A regular devil," the woman said, and walked toward the unit's exit.

When she stepped out into the hall she nodded at the dark-skinned man pushing the linen cart.

He smiled and nodded back at her, then turned the cart and pushed it inside the unit.

△ CHAPTER THIRTY-SEVEN

"Yeah, what is it?" Lobb asked into the telephone. He looked at Blue, standing at the bars in his cell, staring across the floor at him with a cold glare.

"You need to come over here," Murphy said. "Right now."

Lobb replaced the receiver, looked toward Blue again, and walked into the medical supply room.

The door-sized section of wall stood open.

Under the bright lights, clear plastic tubes coiled across the operating tables, the smaller tubes running up to IV bags full of clear solutions hanging from a rack, and the larger tubes snaking down toward box-shaped heart-lung machines the size of a wide trunk. Lobb used the small garage-doorlike control to cause the section of wall to swing shut.

Blue's eyes followed him as he stepped outside the supply room and walked across the floor to the desk. There, he pushed a button on the panel at the side of the desk.

A metallic clank came from the steel door leading from the detention area, and the door swung open.

Lobb walked toward it.

Blue's eyes didn't quit following him until he had passed out the door and it had shut behind him.

Then Blue looked back toward the shadow under his

bunk and said something without any sound coming from his mouth.

The linen truck, its headlights turned off, backed into the darkness cloaking a door at the rear of the hospital.

The door opened.

A cart laden with sheets and towels was pushed outside.

A man in a custodian's uniform stepped down from the passenger side of the cab and hurried to the rear of the truck.

In a moment, the cart had been lifted up into the bed.

Within seconds, the truck's headlights had flashed on and, moving slowly, the blocky vehicle disappeared around a corner of the hospital.

Dr. Lobb used a magnetic card to unlock the door and stepped inside the surveillance room.

"Yeah, what is it?" he asked.

Murphy, his wide shoulders slumped under the material of a dark windbreaker, a frown across his face, stared at the wide bank of radio speakers. Dr. Lobb stopped beside him.

"Listen," Murphy said.

All the receivers carried sound. One, the low hum of the air conditioner running in Shannon's apartment. One, the occasional chirp of the smoke detector in her office. One, the whine of the Expedition's tires rolling rapidly along the pavement.

"*Michael, you want to get something to eat?*"

The voice was Shannon's, clear and almost too loud with the speaker's volume turned up high.

"*I'm not all that hungry.*"

It was Michael's voice.

"So?" Lobb questioned.

The scowl remained across Murphy's face. "Nothing but small talk," he said. "Jerry said ever since they were at her apartment, the only thing they've mentioned that has anything to do with us is something about you being a psychiatrist. I think they've figured out that we might have them bugged. It's that bastard screwing up at the marina and getting seen—they're not saying anything they don't want us to overhear." He looked into Lobb's face. "What I'm wondering now is have they figured out more than we think? Look at this." Murphy stepped to the visual monitor beyond the speakers. It was the size of a big-screen TV, and brightly lit with a glowing map of the Gulfport-Biloxi area depicted in blue and white.

He pressed his thick forefinger against a red line running alongside the bright blue line that depicted Highway 90. "That's them on their way from her apartment to the hospital. Then to her office." He kept tracing his finger along the route the Expedition had taken. "Stopped at the Wal-Mart, then . . ." He ran his hand ahead of the line and pressed his fingertip against a spot where the Expedition had moved off the highway.

"That's the cemetery where Showers is supposed to be buried," he said.

Lobb stared at the spot.

"They were there for over two hours," Murphy said.

The sound of a horn honking coming from a speaker caused Lobb to look in its direction.

"Over two hours," Murphy repeated.

Lobb looked at the route the Expedition currently traveled. The end of the red line moved slowly north a short distance off I-110. It stopped moving.

"Back at her office," Murphy said.

The sound of the Expedition's motor coming from the speaker ceased. There was the sound of the vehicle's doors opening and closing.

A few seconds of silence followed.

The sound of another door opening and closing. "They've gone inside."

Murphy pushed a button on a speaker at the top of the bank.

There was only silence.

He turned the volume control as high as it would go.

They heard the sound of shuffling feet.

A drawer opened.

It closed.

The smoke detector chirped.

A small dog barked.

"Shut up, dog," Shannon said clearly.

The sound of shuffling feet again.

Lobb ran his gaze across the map back to the cemetery.

"Get out there and take a look at the grave," he said.

CHAPTER THIRTY-EIGHT

Shannon didn't speak until they were outside her office and had closed the door behind them. And when she did, she kept her voice low. "You said we should go to James now."

Michael shook his head no.

"If there's a place out there where tissue is stored—if there is *anything* stored out there—by the time he gets through the gate they might be able to dispose of it—you said so yourself."

"You don't have any idea where they would keep anything if it is there."

"I think I do. The main plant runs twenty-four hours a day. There's only one entrance. They'd have to carry a body past everyone working there. There's not many supervisors to a shift, but I can't believe they're all in on this—England wasn't. The care facility might not have anybody in it at night but Lobb. And it has curtains over the patients' windows."

"Curtains?"

"Thick curtains that can cut off the patients' view into the lobby. Lobb said that was how they punished them." He paused a moment. "Now that I've said all that it's still only fifty-fifty that I'm right."

"Coincidence," Shannon said, and smiled feebly. "One out of two buildings."

"It's better than no chance at all. I'll have Daryl call

the sheriff after I have enough time to get in position. When I see Everette coming, I'll go over the fence. Hopefully, if it is the right place, they won't have time to flush anything—if I can get in there quickly enough."

"And if there's anything actually there," Shannon said.

She was the one who was reluctant this time to do something—and it showed in her face. "They're going to see you coming on the cameras."

"By the time anybody can get there from the robotics plant I'll already be inside."

"How?"

"I can get through a door."

"Not the one in the detention area—you said it's steel."

"Wasn't it you who kept telling me how you had to keep trying if you were going to get anywhere?"

"But I wasn't talking about getting shot."

"With the sheriff at the gate they're not going to shoot anybody."

"Who are *they*?" she asked. "Lobb? Whoever made the mannequin to look like Showers has to be involved. Some of the security guards—if not all of them."

"They're not all going to be in the building. When I get inside, there's no way any of them are coming after me."

"It's Waverly this time, too, isn't it? It couldn't happen twice at his centers and he not know about it. I knew it was him."

Michael slipped the tape recorder he had taken from her desk into the breast pocket of his scrubs. He kept the snub-nosed revolver she had given him in his hand.

"Daddy bought that for me right after I started practicing law," Shannon said, looking at the weapon. "He told me if I was going to have criminals in and out of my office all day I needed something. It made me uncomfortable—knowing what I might have to use it for. I wish I had two now."

They fell silent and started toward the Expedition.

*   *   *

He wasn't breathing. His pupils were unreactive and he had no pulse. Olga Lindestrom watched as Dr. Marzullo pulled the sheet up around Jackie Johansen's neck.

"You can tell the family to come in. Then have the body moved to the morgue."

"Yes, Doctor," Olga said.

Two nurses in their mid-forties, one of them noticeably overweight, stood in front of the nursing station. She was the one who had gone for the donuts and come back as the cardiac monitor alarm had gone off. She shook her head. "A heart arrhythmia," she said. "I've been working here for twenty years and I would have bet every year of that experience that he was going to be okay. I couldn't even figure out why Dr. Marzullo had admitted him here."

"Nancy," Olga called from Jackie's room, catching the woman's attention. "Will you please tell the family they can come in to view the body."

Nancy nodded, though she immediately felt a surge of irritation. She had plainly heard Dr. Marzullo instruct Olga to inform the parents of their son's death. Olga had only passed the duty on to her because she didn't want to have to face the unpleasant task. Nancy turned toward the hallway leading toward the visitors' waiting area. She lifted the remainder of her partially eaten donut up off the counter when she walked past the nurses' station.

Olga remained close beside Jackie's bed.

Dr. Marzullo came out of the ICU and walked slowly past the waiting room where a priest was trying to comfort Jackie's sobbing parents.

He turned down the hallway leading to the hospital's front entrance, still walking slowly. He held that pace as he moved outside the building toward his black BMW in the doctors' parking area. Every now and then he glanced anxiously at his wristwatch.

Michael looked at the blinking low-battery light on Shannon's cellular telephone.

"Damn," she said. "Don't any kind of batteries last?"

Michael held his finger to his lips for quiet. He pointed to a service station off to the right of the highway, and Shannon drove the Expedition into the parking lot and stopped. They stepped out onto the concrete and walked to the bank of pay telephones at the station's side.

He lifted a receiver and punched in a number.

It rang several times before he hung up. "Daryl's not home—or has the ringer turned off. What about your receptionist?"

"She went out of town for the weekend. Surely Daryl isn't the only doctor you can trust."

"Which one do you want me to trust?"

"You grew up here, Michael. Think of somebody else."

"You *didn't* grow up here?" he asked. "You don't want to call anybody for the same reason I don't. They'll think we've gone crazy. What about your mother?"

Shannon shook her head. "I love her to death. But she's not strong enough for something like that. I don't know what she might do—maybe call the sheriff, too. What about your mother?"

He knew she would do anything he asked. But, damn, he hated to put any more on her. He lifted the receiver, deposited the change, and punched in his cellular number.

His mother answered on the third ring.

He took a deep breath before he spoke. "Mother, I have something very important for you to do."

"Michael, where are you?"

"Listen, Mother. This is going to sound crazy to you.

But do exactly as I say. First of all, I'm not going to be in any danger."

"Danger?" The sudden alarm in her voice was evident. "Michael, what do you mean, danger?"

"Listen. Write the time down right now. Wait exactly one hour. Then call Sheriff Everette and tell him to get out to the Waverly Research Center as quickly as he can. Tell him I have broken inside the complex."

"Broken inside . . . Michael, what are you—"

"Mother, listen. Tell him I'll be inside the mental-care facility. Tell him exactly this—that if he doesn't come right then, somebody might get killed."

"Michael!"

"Mother, nobody would really get killed. I only want you to tell him that to make certain he comes right then. If he doesn't, that's the only way I could get hurt."

"Michael, you're scaring me. You're worse than scaring me."

"And tell him that Shannon Donnelly is with me."

"Shannon Donnelly? Michael, what has she—"

"Just do as I say. It's real important."

"Michael?"

"Yes."

"You're going to go ahead and do this no matter what I say?"

"Yes."

"Then I'll do what you told me."

"Thank you."

"Michael, I'm scared."

"I know. I'm sorry. I wish I had time to explain. You'll understand when I talk to you later tonight. Just trust me that everything is okay."

"Michael, I love you."

"I love you, too. One hour, exactly—not sooner and not later, and I'll be okay."

He replaced the receiver. Despite the cool breeze coming in off the Gulf, he felt the perspiration that had formed at the back of his neck.

"Damn, you don't know how bad I hated to do that," he said. "But I was afraid if I didn't tell her all that, she'd call Everette right now."

Marjorie's hand trembled as she placed Michael's cellular telephone beside Howard's. He stood in front of her.

"What's wrong?" he asked.

"Michael's acting crazy. I don't know what's happening. He said that he was going to break into the Waverly Research Center. He said for me to call the sheriff in an hour and tell him. He said if the sheriff gets out there before then that . . . Michael said that he could get hurt. He's with Shannon Donnelly, the congressman's daughter. She's done something to get him into this."

"He wasn't speaking about me," Howard said.

"What?"

Howard walked to the control station, opened the panel next to the steering wheel, and pulled out his revolver.

When he turned around he held the weapon up in front of him, its long barrel pointing toward the overhead.

"He didn't say I had to wait an hour."

Murphy, his dark windbreaker and jeans rendering him nearly invisible in the night, strode quickly across the cemetery toward Bobby Showers's grave.

It was directly ahead of him. He passed the statue of the angel with her wings spread. He began trotting.

He was almost at the grave when he saw the mound of dirt surrounding it. He rushed up onto the mound and stared into the hole.

The mannequin, its coat and shirt pulled open across its chest, lay exposed in the open casket.

Murphy turned and ran toward his car.

◭ CHAPTER THIRTY-NINE

A thousand monkeys chattered in low voices. A million ants crawled within his backbone, biting, sending jolts of pain lancing down his spine to radiate out into his arms and legs. Lost in the hazy, uncomprehending world of the sedative Dr. Lobb had given him, Johnny moved his head slowly back and forth, sobbing silently in the darkness, crying for his mother to come and get him.

The overhead light flashed on.

The monkeys screamed.

Dr. Lobb stepped into the room.

The monkeys grew silent when they saw the syringe. The black eyes of the spider monkey's head and the opaque eyes of the langur's head locked on the long needle.

Johnny didn't even turn his eyes toward Lobb as the doctor's hand pushed his head to the side and the needle started into his neck.

Waverly came in the door.

Between them, they undid the straps binding the teenager to the bed, lifted him to his feet, and started with him toward the door.

When Waverly glanced at the monkeys, they rose in their cages and opened their mouths wide, silently brandishing their pointed fangs.

*   *   *

Something made a noise ahead of them in the trees.

Michael touched Shannon's arm and stopped.

They listened.

Nothing.

Then, barely perceptible, the sound again.

Like something scratching at the ground.

Michael raised the revolver.

Shannon glanced at it, and then ahead of them into the darkness between the thick oak trunks.

The sound continued.

Michael took a step forward. Slowly. Another step. Shannon followed behind him.

The scratching sound continued.

It grew more frenzied—then ceased.

Two more slow steps, then three, and Michael stopped when he saw an armadillo the size of a large house cat raking its claws among the twigs and leaves under a tall oak.

Across the open ground beyond the armadillo, the chain-link fence surrounding the Waverly Research Center rose eight feet into the air.

They dropped into a partial crouch and moved past the animal, which ignored them as it continued its search for night-crawling insects. They dropped even lower as they neared the end of the trees.

Within the fence, the sprawling robotics plant was brightly lit. No one moved outside the building. He wouldn't be bothered by anybody from there. If any of the supervisors were to leave, they would exit toward the far side of the building where the employee parking spaces lined that side of the structure. They wouldn't be able to see him even if he was already running toward the smaller building. If any employee arrived, he would be able to see their car or truck headlights as they approached the gate in time to avoid being seen. He looked to his right toward the care facility.

Its steeply pitched roof and blocky, square shape gave it the appearance of a giant, dark monument, stark and forbidding underneath the cloudy sky.

The patients' wide windows were darkened. A thin, barely perceptible glimmer of illumination marked the two slitlike openings near the rear of the structure. They were the barred windows to the cells, with Blue's the farthest to the right. Did the glow shining from behind the openings mean the lights stayed on all night, or was someone inside the area at the moment?

He moved to his right.

Shannon kept close behind him.

Crouching low, stopping momentarily behind the thick tree trunks along the way, they made their way farther and farther to the right, until the care facility was directly in front of them.

The fence was fifty feet away. The blocky building sat a hundred and fifty feet inside the fence. Two hundred feet of open ground to cross—two thirds the length of a football field. Michael hadn't remembered the distance he would have to run being that far.

He settled onto his haunches behind the cover of the last thick oak trunk before the open ground began.

Shannon crouched beside him.

"I'll wait until I see the sheriff's cars coming," he said. "The moment I do, I'm going over the fence. You stay here until the sheriff is inside the complex and you know there's not going to be any trouble."

"How are you going to get inside the building?" She had asked that outside the office.

"If I have to I can shoot the lock off the front door." He still didn't know how he was going to get inside the detention area. "Maybe I'll be lucky and Lobb will simply come out wondering what I'm doing there."

"Uh-huh, coincidence," Shannon said.

"All I want is two minutes alone with the bastard and we won't be wondering what's in there anymore."

"What are you going to do?"

"I'm going to shoot him."

There was no levity in his tone. He didn't mean for there to be any.

"Michael?"

He pulled the tape recorder from his pocket. "If I get to him I'm going to show him this. I'm going to tell him he has five seconds to start admitting what they've done—what they've been doing, and that Waverly is behind it. If he doesn't, I'm going to shoot him in the leg and ask him again."

"You're serious?"

When he didn't say anything, she said, "Michael, you can't use a forced confession in court."

"It's not going to be forced."

"You shoot him—he's obviously been forced. And you—"

"I'll lie. I'll say I shot him because he attacked me. Who are they going to believe, me or him?"

"Michael, I appreciate all you're—"

"It's not for you now, Shannon."

She stared at him for a moment, then turned her gaze back to the building.

To the south, a jagged streak of lightning raced across the sky above the Gulf, followed by the distant sound of thunder rumbling.

"Daddy didn't know what they were doing," Shannon said. "I know the Englands told him whatever it was that made him think something was going on, but it couldn't have been about bodies being stolen or he would have told the police. England would have told the police. Whatever England saw, it had to be just enough to make him suspicious. He didn't know for certain something was wrong. He told Daddy, and Daddy called Waverly. Waverly gave him some excuse, and he believed it enough that he told Waverly who had told him—Daddy wouldn't have wanted rumors going around about the corporation. It could hurt him, too. He assumed Waverly would get it straightened out. Then, when the Englands were killed, even in a car accident, he had to wonder. Like I wondered. He came here. I believe he talked to Waverly about it. Waverly gave him some excuse again, but I don't believe it played that time. I believe it was obvious to Waverly or someone that Daddy was going to have the police investigate. Michael, he had known Waverly for nearly thirty years—he trusted him. That's why he told him about England."

Michael nodded. "It wasn't his fault. He couldn't have known what would happen."

"You don't have to say that. He knew he was responsible. I just wanted you to know how I believe it happened, and that he intended to do something about it."

Murphy had driven fast. But now he began to slow his car. He looked at the portable tracking unit the size of a laptop computer lying on the passenger seat. The screen glowed a light green. The red line that had moved off the highway and gone down the dirt road into the thick woods behind the center, had stopped and remained motionless.

He spun the steering wheel, driving off onto the rutted road. Not much more than a bumpy trail, it wound through thick oaks and past low areas spotted with narrow sloughs filled with algae-covered, stagnant water. The tracking unit showed the Expedition stopped around the next curve.

Murphy slowed the car, brought it to a stop, and climbed out onto the spongy ground.

Seconds later, stopping beside a clump of bushes and a hundred-year-old oak draped in Spanish moss, he leaned forward and stared at the dim, blocky shape of the Expedition setting off to the side of the road in the direction of the center.

Murphy angled into the trees.

From somewhere close off to his side, a pair of

ducks, disturbed from their roost by his movement, quacked loudly as they flapped up into the air.

"I'm telling you," Howard said. "You better listen to me and let me get out there now."

Marjorie nervously shook her head back and forth. "Michael said to wait an hour. He said he could get hurt if I didn't wait an hour."

"Marj, how's my being out there going to cause him to get hurt? I want to go out there to make sure he doesn't get hurt."

Marjorie still shook her head. "Michael said an hour. Oh, I don't know. I'm so scared."

Howard glanced at his watch. "It's been thirty minutes already."

"Oh, Howard, I don't know what to do."

CHAPTER FORTY

The gate began to roll back before the linen truck reached the fence. The blocky vehicle's headlights swung to the left toward the care facility, illuminating the building and the area around it—and the front end of the white limousine, nearly completely concealed in the darkness on the far side of the building.

"Waverly," Shannon said.

Michael stared at the bumper and front portion of the hood sticking out past the building. Then his gaze was drawn back to another set of headlights turning off the highway toward the complex.

Seconds later, he could distinguish the outline of Marzullo's black BMW. Michael's stomach tightened. He knew he was right about Johnny Whitaker now. And Showers. And how many others? They weren't going to be the only ones.

The BMW came through the gates and drove to the care facility, parking next to the entrance as the linen truck turned in a short circle in preparation for backing to the building.

Dr. Lobb came outside. Marzullo stepped from the car and walked toward him. The truck, now only a few feet from the door, stopped, and the driver climbed out of the cab and hurried to the vehicle's rear.

A moment later the double doors were opened and the driver and Lobb reached up into the truck bed.

When they stepped back, Shannon and Michael could see them lowering the end of a stretcher toward the ground.

A body dressed in a hospital gown lay on the stretcher.

"Michael," Shannon whispered.

Another man jumped from the rear of the truck.

Jonathan Waverly appeared in the doorway of the building as the stretcher rolled toward it.

As the stretcher stopped, the man lying on it slowly lifted his hand toward Waverly. *"My God,"* Shannon gasped. "He's alive."

Waverly pushed the hand aside, and the man's arm fell back by his side.

The stretcher was pushed inside the building.

"Michael, how did . . . ? *My God,*" she said again.

Michael glanced at his watch and then looked toward the narrow blacktop leading from the complex and at the highway beyond it. There was no traffic, no sign of any more approaching headlights.

"I'm going in now."

Shannon clasped his forearm. "A few more minutes and Everette will be here."

"I don't know what's going on, but that guy might not have that much time."

"There's Waverly, and Marzullo, and—five of them we can see. And the cameras—remember, they'll see you coming."

"There's a gap in the coverage," he said, causing her to look back toward the building.

He had watched the cameras as they swept back and forth. The two on the corners of the building facing him moved in sync, each panning a separate section of ground—but moving in opposite directions. First they would turn slowly toward each other until their fields of view crossed, then they would start swinging back to the outside. As they panned farther and farther away from the grounds fronting the building, they left an area uncovered by the lenses for a full thirty seconds before they started back toward each other again.

Shannon took an audible deep breath and nodded. "Okay, but you keep saying *I*—and that's not how it's going to be. I'm going in with you."

"Shannon, don't start now. I don't have time to argue. Be logical—you would just be in my way."

"I'm going to be right behind you. This all started with me. That's how it's going to end. Besides, name something I've done up to this point that's logical anyway."

He looked at her, knew how useless it would be to argue. He nodded and came to his feet. "When the cameras swing back far enough I'll say *go.* We're going to have to move fast. I hope you can keep up."

"I knew you were a male chauvinist," she said and grinned. "You are obviously unaware of the fact that I won the district hundred-meter dash in high school—two times."

She actually grinned broadly now.

He looked at her and shook his head. "You really are crazy."

Then he turned his face back toward the care facility as the truck began to drive away from the building. The man who had gone inside with the stretcher now came trotting back outside, hurrying up beside the truck, opening its passenger door, and climbing inside. The truck turned toward the gate.

"Three in the building now," he said. "Waverly, Marzullo, and Lobb."

"That we know of," Shannon said.

A drop of water hit her on the forehead. She looked up at the dark clouds overhead just as a jagged bolt of bright lightning raced across the sky.

The quivering, blue-white illumination cast them in bright relief. She glanced back across her shoulder in the direction they had come.

As she did, she heard the loud quacking of ducks, startled from their night's sleep, flapping up into the air.

Murphy frowned in the direction of the ducks, then stopped walking as a flash of lightning illuminated him among the trees. Then it was suddenly dark again. He held his automatic out at a relaxed arm's length in front of him, and started forward once more, moving slowly now. The edge of the trees was fifty feet away.

▲ CHAPTER FORTY-ONE

Murphy moved slowly, now holding his automatic in both hands. When another bolt of lightning darted across the sky, he moved the weapon quickly from side to side, sliding his eyes back and forth in sync with the pistol's movement, trying to catch a glimpse of Shannon and the doctor in the quivering illumination.

The rain started coming down more noticeably now, drop after drop splashing against his hands and face. He stepped past a thick oak trunk and felt the cold steel of a revolver barrel press against the back of his neck. He froze in place.

Michael pressed the barrel harder against the towering man's neck. Murphy let the automatic fall from his hand. Shannon came quickly out from behind the trunk and lifted the weapon from the ground. "On your knees," Michael said.

Murphy, his lips compressed, glanced back across his shoulder.

Michael pressed the weapon harder. Murphy slowly dropped to his knees. Michael raised his foot and drove the flat of his shoe hard into Murphy's wide back, knocking him sprawling forward, hitting the ground on his chest, his arms splaying out awkwardly to his sides.

His anger showing across his wide face, he looked back over his shoulder.

"Put your hands behind your back—cross your wrists," Michael said.

Dr. Marzullo pushed the stretcher through the open doorway into the detention area.

Blue, clad only in the shorts that stretched around his thick hips and bulging thighs, stared from the front of his cell. His big hands clasped the bars.

Jackie Johansen, his hands secured by straps to the sides of the stretcher, widened his eyes when he saw the huge, nearly naked man. He tilted his head backward to look at Marzullo and tried to speak. But he was not yet completely out from under the effects of the sedative Olga had administered, and could not make his words come.

Marzullo moved the stretcher in front of the steel door leading into the medical supply room. Lobb opened the door.

The section of wall to the side of the room stood open.

Jackie's eyes widened again at the sight of Johnny Whitaker, clad only in a pair of white Jockey shorts, lying on the operating table just inside the next room—and the sight of the empty operating table beside the occupied one.

"Nooo!"

Lobb leaned over him, loosening the strap that bound one of his wrists to the stretcher. Jackie, suddenly shaking his head back and forth, tried to pull his arm away from Lobb's grip, but his weakened efforts had little more force than those of a child.

Lobb unstrapped the other wrist, Marzullo stepped forward and they lifted the young man to a standing position.

His feet dragging, they pulled him to the operating table and lifted him up onto it, laying him on his back.

A moment later they were securing him by the straps hanging from its sides.

Waverly walked up beside them. Jackie glanced at Johnny lying across from him on the other table, staring at him. He forced a slurred statement from his mouth. "Wha' . . . doin . . . me?"

Dr. Lobb reached for the mask hanging on the metal cylinders past the head of the table. Marzullo walked to the heart-lung machine.

"Go," Michael said and sprinted for the fence.

Behind them, Murphy lay face-down on the wet ground, his wrists tied behind his back with his shoelaces and tied a second time with his belt. His shirt had been stripped from his wide upper body, looped around his ankles and knotted. One sleeve of Shannon's sweatshirt was tied so tightly around his thick neck he had difficulty breathing. The other sleeve ran to the shirt tied around his ankles and was knotted there.

Michael reached the fence several steps before Shannon, and frowned back at her for lagging. "*Sprint champion,*" he mumbled as he grabbed her by the hips and boosted her up the barrier. She grabbed the wire and clawed toward its top.

He scrambled up behind her.

She perched at the top of the fence for a moment, swayed as if she was going to topple backward—and leaped toward the interior of the complex.

She hit the ground hard, sprawled on her face, and grunted, her hands splaying out to her sides, but somehow she managed to hold on to Murphy's automatic.

Michael landed behind her, went to his knees, and came up running after her as she sprinted for the building.

Under its eaves, the cameras neared the end of their swing toward the sides of the building, and began to slow their movement for their return journey.

Shannon was sprinting with her head down now.

A hundred feet to the building.

Eighty.

The cameras started back toward them.

Sixty.

Michael slowed slightly and pushed against Shannon's back.

"You're going to make me fall, damn it."

The T-shirt she had worn under her sweatsuit was smeared with dirt and damp from the rain. Her arms pumping wildly, she ran as hard as she could.

Michael looked toward the cameras. They were a third of the way back in their arc and seemed to be moving much more quickly than he had calculated.

Forty feet.

Twenty feet.

Shannon slammed into the building.

Michael hit beside her, turned his back against the concrete blocks, and looked up at the nearest camera.

It was panning the ground they had just covered, but with its lens angled too high to pick them up against the building.

"So far, so good," Shannon whispered.

Three hundred feet behind them, a camera perched high in the limbs of an oak outside the fence, clicked and brought them into focus. It clicked again, and its lens revolved, adjusting to a close-up shot.

In the surveillance room near the front of the robotics plant, a stocky security guard stared at the close-up images filling the screens at the bottom of the bank of video monitors. He watched Michael's dim figure lift the revolver into sight and, Shannon following close along behind him in her white T-shirt, start moving slowly down the wall of the mental-care facility toward its entrance.

Outside the building the rain began to fall harder.

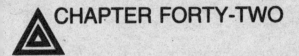# CHAPTER FORTY-TWO

Rain pelted Michael's head and ran down his face as he tried the doorknob at the entrance to the building, and it turned.

He cracked the door open slowly.

The spacious lobby between the patients' quarters was darkened except for the faint glow of a solitary night-light.

He stepped inside.

Shannon, her T-shirt mud-streaked and clinging to her slim body, closed the door behind them and locked it by its deadbolt. There wasn't an orderly in sight. To their sides the curtains were pulled tightly across the windows of the patients' rooms.

"There should be an orderly," Shannon said.

There should be somebody, Michael thought. He felt his hand perspiring around the handle of the automatic, and clasped it tighter.

They moved quietly past the card tables.

Murphy, wet from the rain and smeared with a mixture of dirt and sweat, rolled up onto his side and worked his hands harder, twisting his wrists against the shoelaces binding them behind his back. He felt his head spin from lack of oxygen as Shannon's sweatshirt sleeve dug tightly into his throat. He forced his hands farther up his back, relaxing some of the tension, and began twisting his wrists again.

A loop of the shoelaces slipped over his knuckles, and the binding loosened.

Michael stopped in front of the steel door leading into the detention area. He raised the revolver in front of him, reached for the doorknob, and tried it. It turned, and his eyes narrowed.

"If they're watching, they know now," Shannon whispered, looking at the camera pointed down at them.

He threw the door open and lunged into the brightly lit area. He swept the revolver back and forth.

Blue turned his head toward them from his cell.

The door to Lobb's room and the one twenty feet away from it at the rear of the area were closed. The door to the medical supply room was cracked open. Light showed behind it.

Michael moved forward. Shannon held Murphy's automatic in both hands. They neared the door. He slowly reached out, caught the doorknob, took a quiet breath, and threw the door open—lunging into the room with the revolver ready.

To the right of the room, a section of wall in the shape of a door stood open.

Past it, cast in the bright illumination of a pair of large flood lamps, two near-naked forms dressed only in their underwear, lay strapped to the operating tables.

The voice came from behind Michael.

"Lay your pistols down or I will shoot both of you."

He whirled to face a nine-millimeter automatic pointing around the edge of the half-open supply room door.

"Now," the voice said.

It was Dr. Lobb.

Michael's heart raced, his revolver was pointed toward the door. He couldn't fire through the steel.

Lobb's automatic was pointed at Shannon. Slowly, he lowered the revolver, bent his knees, and placed it on the concrete floor. Shannon laid Murphy's automatic next to it.

Lobb opened the door the rest of the way. Shannon stared at the man she had seen in the photograph. Behind him, Waverly and Marzullo stepped into view.

"Puh . . . lease," a slurred voice moaned from the operating tables.

Michael looked through the opening in the wall and felt a shock that hit him like a wave when he saw Johnny Whitaker staring at him.

"Puh . . . lease," the teenager begged.

Waverly lifted the revolver and automatic from the floor and stuck the automatic in the waistband of his pants. He kept the revolver in his hand.

Then his voice, cold and directed at Shannon, pulled Michael's attention away from Johnny's wide, pleading eyes.

"Your father, and now you. And you, too, Dr. Sims," Waverly said.

And then in one motion Waverly pointed the revolver toward Dr. Marzullo and pulled its trigger.

The sound of the gun firing was like an explosion in the confined room. Michael flinched. Shannon gasped. Marzullo doubled forward from the force of the slug tearing into his stomach. Waverly pulled the trigger again. The slug caught Marzullo in the chest, knocking him backward to the floor.

Waverly looked down at the cardiologist, holding his bleeding stomach, and pulled the trigger three more times.

Marzullo shuddered as each slug tore into his body. Then he lay still.

Shannon covered her mouth with her hands.

Michael watched Waverly's gaze come to his. "I have a standing offer of a million dollars for any scientist who makes a breakthrough I deem worthy in nerve research, Dr. Sims. It once again appears that what I intended to be an incentive turned into a temptation for Dr. Marzullo. That's what I will tell the sheriff when he arrives—and I'm certain that you have made sure he will arrive. So we don't have much time, do we? If you'll step out here, please."

"Puh . . . lease," Johnny echoed from the operating table. The young man next to him stared now with his eyes wide and his mouth gaping. Long, clear tubes glistened in the bright overhead lights. They were coiled on a pair of box-shaped metal oxygenators and pumps sitting on each side of the tables.

"You know what you're seeing?" Waverly asked, and Michael looked back at the aging billionaire. "The final test before I undergo the process myself. Switching my head to a healthy body. If you were a physical anatomist I think you would be overwhelmed with the miracle, but even an emergency department physician should have some idea of my brilliance."

Shannon was shaking her head back and forth in shock.

"Not madness," Waverly said, looking at her. "Of that I can assure you."

Michael knew the clear liquid in the plastic bags hanging from racks at the heads of the tables would contain heparin in a sterile solution, an anticoagulant that would keep the patient's blood from clotting as it ran through the heart-lung machine. Ran through the machine while the patients were alive—Johnny and the other young man were staring at him with horrified looks on their faces.

"But as I said," Waverly repeated, "I'm certain the sheriff is not far away. So would you please step outside now?"

Michael pushed against Shannon's arm, urging her toward the door as she stared at the operating tables. Waverly held her revolver toward Lobb.

"Clean my fingerprints off of it."

Lobb took the weapon and used the tail of his lab coat to begin wiping it as Waverly pulled Murphy's automatic from his waistband.

"Now fire a shot into Blue's cell," he said.

Lobb's eyebrows knitted questioningly.

"Fire the shot," Waverly repeated.

Lobb pointed the weapon toward the cell, looked at Waverly, then back at the bars, and pulled the trigger.

The firing sent the revolver's last bullet into the wall at the rear of Blue's cell. Blue's head jerked toward the shower of bits of concrete and dust exploding from the wall. Then he slowly lowered his gaze to the dark shadows under his bunk, and turned around to face through his bars again, his eyes narrowed in Lobb's direction. His lips parted.

A sound almost like that of a snake's hiss traveled across the floor.

"It looks like your first shot missed Blue when he came out of his cell," Waverly said. "That you didn't miss with the automatic will be obvious when the sheriff gets here. I will see to that later. But it took too long for Blue to die—too long for you." He grinned. "You were a fool to try to match wits with me," he said. Without another word, he turned and walked to the steel door at the very rear of the area.

He used a magnetic card from his pocket to unlock it. It swung back, and he stepped inside.

Michael saw Shannon's eyes come around to his. She glanced at Lobb and back to him. He understood what she intended. But it would be suicide to try to jump Lobb while he pointed the pistol at them. If they waited, there might be an opportunity. Michael shook his head at Shannon, and noticed Lobb raise the automatic toward her.

Waverly reappeared in the doorway at the rear of the area. As he did, Michael felt a sensation he would never be able to explain sweep his body. Waverly's hand was held down and out to his side. Candice, wearing a new, bright blue dress, her blond hair framing her face, an Oreo cookie in one hand, her other small hand held by his, stared across the concrete floor.

Pulling Candice along beside him, Waverly walked from the doorway toward the steel door leading back into the main lobby of the building.

Michael took a step toward him. "Why?"

Waverly stopped. Michael saw the child look at Shannon, and then her eyes come to his.

"I told you during your tour," Waverly said. "Fetal tissue is the key to the regeneration, but repeated rat studies have made me virtually certain the fetal tissue will be most effective when combined with implants from the already formed and rapidly growing tissue of a child's spinal cord."

Michael shook his head. "No."

"Not now," Waverly said. "For me—later."

"No," Michael repeated, and started walking toward the aging billionaire. "No."

"Michael," Shannon called behind him.

Waverly raised his pistol.

"Michael!"

Shannon's yell penetrated Michael's rage. He stopped, looked back across his shoulder at her, then looked toward Candice again.

The child's brows knitted. A smile slowly crossed her face. The same smile she had shown him in the trauma room. A smile of recognition now.

"Is Mommy here?"

Waverly pulled her toward the door leading from the area.

"Michael," Shannon said again, softly.

She came toward him. Lobb pointed the automatic at her back. Michael hurried to her, catching her shoulders and looking at Lobb.

Waverly stopped at the open steel entry door into

the area and nodded toward the heavy desk against the back wall.

Lobb hurried to it and stopped next to the metal panel of buttons on its far side, lifting his hand above the panel.

"Wait!" Waverly suddenly said.

Dr. Lobb stopped with his finger poised above a button.

"Clean the prints off your weapon, take the clip out, then throw it to them," Waverly said.

Lobb stared.

"We need their prints on the weapon they will shoot Blue with," Waverly said.

Lobb lifted the tail of his lab coat, quickly cleaned the weapon, then turned it sideways, ejected the clip into his hand, and flipped the pistol through the air.

It clanged against the floor, bounced and slid to a stop at Shannon's feet.

"Pick it up," Waverly said.

When Shannon didn't reach for the weapon, Waverly raised his pistol. Candice looked up at him. Michael stepped forward and lifted the automatic from the floor.

Waverly looked at Blue, hesitated, staring into his son's eyes for a moment, then looked back at Lobb and nodded again.

Lobb pressed a button on the panel.

There was a buzzing sound, then a metallic clank as the thick bolt in the lock to Blue's cell slid back.

The door swung open.

Lobb dashed toward Waverly.

Waverly raised Murphy's automatic toward him.

Lobb stopped abruptly.

"There had to be somebody here for Dr. Marzullo to conspire with," Waverly said. "And this is where you make your home. And you were guilty before. It had to be you."

"No," Lobb said. "I—" Blue rushed through the cell door, grunting, and raced toward the doctor.

Lobb glanced back across his shoulder, and ran toward Waverly despite the pointed pistol.

Candice jerked her hand loose from Waverly's and ran toward Michael, her path carrying her toward a collision with the charging Blue. Michael's blood surged in shock. He dashed forward, his mind recording what followed in the slow-motion view of an adrenaline-charged mind.

Candice running toward him. Blue taking great loping steps, coming at an angle from his cell on a course that would take him to her. Ten feet apart. Michael racing to get between them. Too late. Blue's huge hulk bore down on her. The sound of Shannon's scream of horror from behind them.

Blue passed by Candice and raced toward Lobb. Michael grabbed the child.

Jerking her from the floor into his arms, he turned and raced back toward Shannon as she ran toward him.

Waverly stepped backward out of the detention area and closed the door in front of him. There was a metallic clank of its bolt automatically locking.

Lobb grabbed for the doorknob. He spun and stared with wide eyes as Blue grabbed for him, the big hands catching his face, driving his head back into the door.

Blue grunted, moaned, and lifted Lobb up the hard steel, twisting his head to the side. Lobb tried to fight, his fingers clawing at Blue's face.

There was the audible snap of a cervical vertebra. Lobb's hands fell to his sides. Blue caught him by the belt and, his other hand still clasping a side of Lobb's face, pulled him away from the door.

Raising his hands, Blue turned the limp body upside down, and smashed Lobb headfirst into the concrete floor.

Johnny Whitaker moaned from the operating table. Shannon rushed into the supply room.

Blue leaned forward, caught Lobb's shoulder, and turned him over onto his back.

He stared down at the open, unseeing eyes. He touched the pupil of one. When the eye didn't blink, he pressed the tip of his finger harder into the pupil.

Then he straightened, and slowly turned his head toward his cell, staring into the dark shadow underneath his bunk.

A bare, almost imperceptible grin crossed his wide face.

Then he looked toward Michael and Candice.

Shannon was hurriedly releasing the straps binding Johnny Whitaker's arms and legs to the operating table. Michael looked toward the cell where Blue had been. The door was standing open.

The cell's thick steel bars would be a protection against even Blue's strength—if the door locked automatically when it was closed. Maybe Wayerly forgot. If they could get to it . . .

"Shannon, quickly, get to—"

But it was too late.

Blue charged.

◢ CHAPTER FORTY-THREE

Johnny Whitaker sat on the operating table, mumbling to Shannon as she unstrapped Jackie from the other table. Michael dumped Candice roughly to her feet on the floor, slammed the steel door to the supply room, and grabbed the doorknob. It wasn't the type that could be locked from the inside.

Behind him, the scraping sound of the operating table being pushed through the opening in the wall toward him.

Shannon, the strain evident on her face, pushed from the far end of the heavy table. Jackie Johansen had come down off it and was now trying to help her by pulling at its end while Johnny Whitaker pulled from its side.

Michael braced his shoulder against the door and waited.

Blue slammed into its other side, causing it to vibrate.

The table neared Michael.

Blue slammed into the door again, this time the steel vibrated hard enough against Michael's shoulder to cause a jolt of pain to race down his arm. He knew that if Blue only thought to turn the doorknob, and then slam into the door again, that his force couldn't be stopped.

Blue crashed into the door again.

Michael grasped the end of the table, helping pull it against the door, then leaned over the table. Still grasping the doorknob as tightly as he could, he pressed against the door with his shoulder again. Jackie and Johnny used their hands pressing against the door to help him. Candice stared at them.

"Michael," Shannon said.

She had grabbed one of the metal straight chairs from the operating area, come back into the supply room and was climbing up onto the top of the table.

She raised the chair above her head and rammed its legs upward into the plaster. White dust sprinkled her arms. She tried to pull the chair back toward her, but it hung in the ceiling.

"Damn it!" She tugged so hard her feet lifted from the table. The chair legs pulled loose, and she sat down hard on her heels and hip onto the table. Bits of plaster and dust showered down across her head and shoulders. Candice stared at her. Johnny let go of the door and dashed into the operating area for the other chair.

A moment later, carrying the chair, he climbed up beside Shannon as she rammed her chair into the ceiling once more.

Michael realized Blue had not slammed into the door again.

Blue whipped his head back and forth, staring from one side of the detention area to the other. His hands began to shake. His gaze fixed on the video monitor which was on the desk against the far wall. Its screen showed Waverly, standing outside in the patients' area, his ear close against the steel door, listening.

Blue rushed to the desk, grabbed the monitor, and lifted it high into the air, and slammed it into the concrete floor, smashing it into a thousand pieces. He caught the computer, and in the same sweeping motion, hurled it across the area where it crashed to the floor in an explosion of glass and plastic.

Blue's eyes fixed on the heavy desk itself.

A moment later, he was pushing it toward the storage room door.

Above Johnny's head, a jagged hole in the ceiling exposed the thick planks of the ceiling joists, creating a rough entrance to the attic. He rammed the chair legs into the plaster again. Shannon punched with her chair. White dust covered their arms and hands and faces, and plaster showered around them.

Through the door, Michael heard the scraping sound of something heavy being pushed toward the room.

The scraping sound suddenly increased in intensity, and came rapidly toward him. There was a tremendous crash. Pain shot through Michael's shoulder. A metal hinge pulled partially loose from a holding bracket.

"Michael," Shannon said.

Johnny swayed as he held her by her hips up toward the hole in the ceiling. Jackie lifted Candice and climbed unsteadily up onto the table with her.

Outside the room, the sound of the desk's legs being pulled back from the door. Then the quick scraping noise as it came forward again.

Michael braced.

The desk slammed into the door. The hinge came loose from its bracket. Shannon grasped a rafter and pulled herself up into the hole. Outside the door, the desk was being pulled backward again. Johnny lifted Candice by her hips toward the ceiling. Shannon reached down for her. Jackie balanced Johnny on the chair as the teenager came up on his toes. Candice looked back at him. "Reach, damn it," he yelled.

Candice started crying, but she looked up at Shannon and lifted her arms toward hers. Their hands clasped, and Candice, swinging, was jerked up through the hole. Johnny bunched his muscles and jumped. He caught a joist and pulled himself upward. Michael jumped onto the table. Jackie reached for Shannon's hands. Michael grabbed the young man's waist and strained to lift his weight into the air. Shannon clasped Jackie's wrists. Michael lifted him higher, and pushed up on his thighs. Jackie grabbed Shannon's shoulder. She slid forward as if she were going to be pulled out of the hole. Johnny grabbed her, and Jackie scrambled up across her back and disappeared into the attic. Michael stepped onto the chair.

Behind him, a tremendous crash and the door tore off its hinges, hit the end of the operating table with a loud metallic bang, and bounced to the side, clanging to the floor with the sound of metal against concrete.

Blue crawled over the desk on all fours toward the table.

Michael bunched his muscles and jumped. His hands caught the joist. One hand slipped, and he dangled, swinging sideways.

He raised his hand, trying to reach back to the joists, and Shannon caught his wrist, pulling on it. His hand clasped the plank, and he pulled himself toward the hole. Shannon and Johnny caught his shoulders and tugged him toward them.

Blue leaped onto the operating table and grabbed for Michael's legs, catching his ankle and pulling his shoe off.

Michael's feet disappeared up into the dark hole.

Blue stepped onto the chair and reached upward. His thick arms too short for his hands to reach the hole, he rose up on his toes and flexed his legs, trying to stretch himself higher. He lost his balance as the chair tilted under his shifting weight and turned suddenly out from under his feet, and he fell, crashing down hard on his side across the operating table.

The chair fell to the floor and bounced with a metallic clang, then rolled to the wall.

In the stifling heat of the musty-smelling attic, Michael, carrying Candice, hurried behind Shannon across the joists leading toward the front of the building. She tore cobwebs out of her way with waves of her hand. Jackie stumbled behind them and lost his footing. Johnny bumped into him and was knocked backward, sitting down hard across a plank; his foot crashed through the ceiling.

In the detention area, Blue stared at the white dust drifting to the floor and the hole where the foot had momentarily come into view, then disappeared up into the blackness again.

He ran toward the spot and stared up at the hole.

He shook his head and exhaled loudly.

At the front of the attic, Michael stared at a solid wall of concrete blocks rising to the exposed underside of the high-peaked roof, blocking their progress.

Above him, four-by-eight-foot sheets of plywood were nailed to the rafters. Exposed ends of nails stuck through the plywood where the tar shingles covering the outside of the roof had been nailed directly into the thin wood. Michael looked to his right, where the roof angled down to meet the joists' ends. Next to him, a thick two-by-six support beam angled up to the roof.

He shifted Candice to his side and pulled on the beam. It barely gave. Shannon grasped the board next to his hand. Jackie took hold of the beam and joined in its shaking. It wasn't giving where it was joined to the joists at their feet. Michael stepped around to its outside, and kicked it above where it was nailed.

He kicked it again.

Shannon kicked it.

Johnny lowered his head and slammed his shoulder into the board like a football player making a tackle, and it popped loose.

Johnny backed across the attic, pulling the end of the plank with him, trying to pry it away from where it was attached overhead. Above him, nails made a screeching sound, and the heavy board, stringing spiderwebs behind it, crashed down onto the joists and bounced in a cloud of dust.

Michael handed Candice to Shannon, grabbed the plank at its center, and drove it into the plywood planking where the roof sloped down to meet with the floor joists. The plywood splintered, and the end of the board burst through to the outside.

He twisted the plank back and forth, widening the opening.

Rain dripped inside the attic.

Blue stretched his hands up toward the jagged hole where Jackie's foot had stuck down into the detention area. But his clasping fingers were more than three feet short of the ceiling. He looked at Lobb's body. He shook his head and lifted his eyes back toward the hole.

He was only a few feet from the rack of restraining straps and the pinning tool that hung across pegs at the side of the wall—and now his gaze went to the rack.

He ran to it.

Using the rack like a ladder, he scrambled up to the ceiling. He swung his thick forearm upward, smashing a hole in the plaster, and was covered in a white cloud of dust and ceiling fragments raining down across his head and shoulders.

Johansen pulled Shannon through the hole in the roof and she scrambled onto its steep angle. She leaned away from its edge, having to stay low, shifting her weight toward its crest to keep from sliding down the slippery, rain-soaked shingles. Johnny came through the hole, then reached back to catch Candice, being held out to him by Michael. As Michael lifted himself out of the attic into the pouring rain, Blue popped up out of the detention area into the attic and stared toward the breach they had made.

*   *   *

Murphy jammed on the brake pedal and his car slid to a rocking halt in front of the gate. He looked toward the mental-care facility as the gate began to slide open. Lightning flashed, and in its quivering illumination he saw the figures on the roof. He jammed the accelerator to the floor. The car jumped forward. Its left bumper caught the edge of the sliding gate, bending it backward as the automobile roared past it.

The gate jammed and quit moving.

In Murphy's headlights, Waverly came running out the front door of the building and around its side, looking up though the rain at the figures climbing for the roof's crest.

Blue's head and shoulders burst through the shingles.

He looked toward the crest of the roof at Michael and the others scrambling away from him.

He came out of the hole, and turned toward them on all fours, clawing up the rain-soaked roof like a grizzly bear lunging up a slippery mountainside after fleeing campers.

Waverly fired a shot.

Jackie Johansen groaned and grabbed his shoulder. His feet slipped out from under him, and he slid down the roof and off its edge toward the ground.

Murphy grabbed an automatic from his glove compartment, threw his car door open and, his wide upper body mud-streaked and bare, sprang outside with the weapon raised.

The roar of Howard's Mercedes coming through the gate pulled Murphy's attention in that direction. He turned to face the Mercedes.

Behind Murphy, Waverly fired.

Michael, carrying the crying Candice, at the same time pushing Shannon over the crest of the roof toward the protection of its far side, felt the shot rip into his leg, and fell against the shingles. Johnny came back over the crest of the roof to help him.

Murphy aimed his automatic at the Mercedes' driver.

Marjorie screamed as she ducked under the dash. Howard fired his revolver through his windshield, and didn't quit firing.

Murphy never got a shot off.

The automatic falling from his hand, he crumpled backward to the ground.

On the roof, Blue reached for Michael and Candice, lying on the shingles staring up at him. Johnny swung at the huge man, then dodged backward at Blue's return lunge.

Michael swung his good leg, kicking Blue's feet out from under him. Blue slammed into the shingles on his side, and slid toward the roof's edge. He tried to stop, slapping his big hands against the roof, but he couldn't get a grip on the wet surface and, his body beginning to turn with his feet revolving up toward the crest of the roof, he slipped off its edge and plummeted backward, headfirst toward the ground.

Waverly looked across his shoulder at Howard, jumping from the Mercedes. Howard raised his revolver and pulled the trigger.

The hammer clicked on a spent cartridge.

Waverly raised his weapon.

Howard dove for the protection of the front seat.

Waverly fired twice, one bullet slamming into the Mercedes grill, the other zipping through a gaping hole in the shattered windshield and bursting out through the glass of the rear window. Blue roared behind Waverly.

Waverly spun and fired at the wide shape coming at him through the pouring rain with arms raised and hands spread like claws.

Bullets slammed into Blue's chest, but still he grabbed Waverly's head, lifted him off the ground, and shook him like a wild dog killing a cat.

The automatic flew in one direction. Waverly's arms and legs swung wildly—then, suddenly, limply.

Blue dropped him, stared at the Mercedes, took a step toward it.

Marjorie yelled and came out the passenger door, running toward the gate.

Howard stared, transfixed as Blue took another step toward him, then faltered in his movement. He swayed, forced one big foot out in front of him again—then, with a loud burst of exhaled air, toppled face forward into the wet dirt.

◭ CHAPTER FORTY-FOUR

Flashing blue lights from Harrison County Sheriff Department cruisers reflected off the mental-care facility and illuminated the last drops of rain, now diminished to not much more than a light mist. Two medics in yellow slickers carried Jackie Johansen on a stretcher toward the rear of an ambulance backed up to the facility's entrance. The bullet wound in his shoulder was painful, and he had broken his arm in the fall from the roof, but he was smiling.

A police car sat outside the jammed gate, blocking any of the robotics plant's employees from leaving. Deputies searched the woods around the complex for anyone who might have fled on foot. Nearly a dozen supervisors and security guards in dark windbreakers were being questioned one by one in the front offices. Some would be totally innocent of any wrongdoing that had taken place at the complex, like Joe England had been. Some would be implicated to one degree or another. Murphy had survived Howard's shots and quickly started implicating everyone involved, in the hope that his cooperation would spare him from the death penalty when his case came to trial. Sheriff Everette spoke on his car radio. He was checking to see if Olga had been taken into custody yet, since Murphy had implicated her with the first words out of his mouth.

Michael, refusing to lie down, sat on the edge of the stretcher in the back of an ambulance. "Dr. Bacon wouldn't have had any reason to examine the bodies when they were brought into the hospital morgue. He would have just checked them in and then back out when the hearses came after them. The mannequins looked more than real enough to fool anybody who just looked at them—especially when it was supposed to be a dead body that was already cold."

Candice, though still irritated with Johnny for yelling at her to climb up into the attic, wasn't as irritated as she had been before he went back inside the detention area and brought her the last of the Oreo cookies. She had two left, one half eaten and on the way to her mouth again as Shannon held the child in her arms.

There had been a conspirator at the funeral home. Murphy had already told that, too. In fact, one of Waverly's corporations owned the home. A patient had been picked for experimentation only when it was known that if he died at the hospital he was going to be sent to that particular place. That wasn't hard to determine in the tradition-driven South, where families tended to use the same funeral home time after time as each of their loved ones passed on. To make certain, it wasn't hard for Dr. Marzullo to verify through casual conversation that the family members were indeed still happy with the particular establishment they had been using.

The switching of the mannequin for the victim was easy. A mannequin was delivered to the hospital in an already laden laundry cart, and then put in bed in place of the patient when Olga was able to get any other nurse on duty with her to leave the ICU temporarily, as she had by sending the nurse for coffee and donuts after Jackie Johansen had been sedated.

This combination of conspirators had provided Waverly with one or two bodies a year: the number that were sent to the funeral home from Coastal Regional in the normal course of that home's regular business, a

number more than sufficient for Waverly's purposes—
and a number that didn't cause any suspicions from too
many sudden deaths at the hospital.

Except at the very end. That was when a combination of circumstances had Candice Schilling and Johnny
Whitaker coming into the hospital the same night—and
sets of parents saying they would use the same funeral
home. And coming in at the same time that Waverly
was ready to proceed with the final trial run—an actual
transplanting of human heads. Johnny would have been
one of the donors in the final trial. Candice would have
been taken to the Caribbean with Waverly to later provide the young, actively growing spinal tissue that
would have been used for the spinal implants. The only
thing lacking was a reciprocal donor for Johnny. Waverly had decided on an actual abduction and murder of
somebody off the street, and Murphy had been prepar-
ing to take care of that when Johansen had luckily arrived at the hospital as a patient.

"How many murders?" Shannon asked.

"All the graves will have to be reopened to see which
ones are mannequins."

"How did they copy a patient's likeness so quickly?
It was less than twenty-four hours for Johnny and Candice, even less for Johansen."

"Maybe with something high-tech. Maybe with just
an old-fashioned mold. Murphy might know, but he
hasn't said anything about that yet."

"Dr. Sims," Johnny said, leaning into the back of the
ambulance. "My family's here. My mother asked me if
it would be okay if she said something to you?"

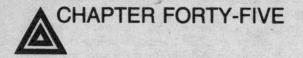# CHAPTER FORTY-FIVE

They stood beside her father's grave.

"I promised you I would," Shannon said softly.

She bent her knees and laid her hand on the soft ground.

When she stood, she walked around to Michael's good side—he held a crutch with the other—and slipped her hand around his waist. He moved his arm around her shoulders and they walked slowly in the direction of the Expedition.

"I spoke with James this morning," she said. "They exhumed six mannequins; three over the last five years, and Showers, Johnny, and Candice over the last few days as Waverly rushed to the final test. Johansen's was still in the morgue."

She shook her head. "It looks now like Waverly obtained his software patents by killing, too. At least the first major patent. Murphy said that a man came to Waverly looking for financial help to market a program he had invented. I guess the most ironic thing is it turned out Waverly was a good manager. He hired top personnel—in particular top scientists when he moved into the medical research field. They made some breakthrough discoveries that earned him a fortune. The discoveries grew into the Waverly Research Centers and added to his billions."

Shannon released his waist and walked toward the

driver's side of the Expedition as he limped on his crutch to the passenger side.

She climbed in behind the steering wheel and waited for him to get settled and push the crutch into the back seat.

"Anyway," she said as she guided the Expedition out into the traffic passing by the cemetery, "according to Murphy, Waverly started thinking about what lay ahead for him—his aging. He was a health freak and, even though he was only in his thirties when he first started thinking about aging, it was bothering him that he wouldn't look like he did then forever. Even worse, his dad had died at fifty-two. Waverly had always gotten everything he wanted. He decided he didn't want to die of old age. He didn't want an old body. He still had a problem with the circulatory system he knew would continue to age in his head even after the transplant— that would have limited him to not much more than thirty more years of life. That was the main thing he wanted the research funds for—after he got control of them he meant to flood circulatory research with billions of dollars and as many scientists as he could gather." Shannon shook her head as she paused. "Always had his way. Bet he was a bully in grade school."

Michael smiled. "No, too little."

She leaned toward him and rested her hand on his shoulder. "What did England see?"

Michael shook his head. "Even Murphy doesn't know from what Everette said. All he knew was Waverly ordered him to kill England. And his wife, in case he had told her anything. My guess is England, being on the same floor as Showers, recognized the man pushing the linen cart from when he had seen him out at the care facility, and saw him go into Showers's room. Soon after he came back out, Showers supposedly died. Maybe England did see something for a moment through an open door—but not actually see Showers being lifted into the cart. Maybe he saw the linen man doing something at the bed with him. Maybe it didn't even start at the hospital, but England saw something out at the care facility—or thought he saw something. Maybe the linen man was there at the time, and then, again, England saw him go into Showers's room just before he died. Take your pick of what happened—or none of the above. Whatever it was, it was just enough to make England very suspicious, and he had his wife call your father."

Shannon nodded, but didn't say anything for a while.

When she finally did, she smiled a little. "How does it feel being a doctor again?"

"When did I ever stop?"

"I mean about your outlook now?"

"Everybody has their bad days," he said.

It was only a few minutes until they were back at the yacht harbor.

Shannon parked next to Howard's Mercedes.

When they stepped outside, the beagle barked at them from the bow of the *Cassandra*.

"Be quiet, dog," Shannon said, "or I'm going to feed you to the sharks."

Howard leaned over the *Howard*'s rail toward them. Marjorie stood next to him.

"How much longer on that crutch, Michael?" he asked. "I remember a boar hog getting a tusk into me in the woods one day. Made a lot bigger hole than the bullet that hit you. Dad said I didn't need no crutches—said it would get in the way of my work."

"Be quiet, Howard," Marjorie said. "The doctor told him to stay on it for a week."

"Okay," Howard said. "Okay. It is a different generation. In my day, I wouldn't have—"

"*Howard,*" Marjorie warned.

He shrugged.

"Getting ready to throw it away today," Michael said. "Just been enjoying Shannon babying me."

"Well now, that's different," Howard said. "You're not as thick as I thought."

"Male . . ." Marjorie started. "What do you call them, Shannon? Male chauvinists?"

The beagle barked again.

"You tell 'em," Shannon said.

The dog barked again, growled in a low tone, then tilted his head to the side and waited for what Shannon was going to say next.

"Michael," Howard said, his tone more serious now. "Me and Marj have been thinking about cruising down to the Bahamas for a few weeks—if you don't object."

"*Together?*" Shannon questioned in a fake, shocked tone.

Marjorie shook her head. "Oh, no," she quickly said. "Not like that. I mean . . . not living in sin—not that kind of thing. Just Howard and I, uh, cruising together as friends."

Howard winked.

Marjorie saw it, and pinched his side.

TURN THE PAGE FOR A SNEAK PREVIEW
OF CHARLES WILSON'S NEW THRILLER,

GAME PLAN—

A JANUARY HARDCOVER FROM
ST. MARTIN'S PRESS!

PROLOGUE

She came silently down the wide corridor, moving swiftly, but not running. The only things that took away from her youthful beauty were two tiny blemishes spaced a few inches apart on her forehead, and the United States Disciplinary Barracks garb she wore—shapeless trousers and shirt in faded blue colors. Six months since she had been brought to this place, and they still made her wear the hated garments. Six months and she could still visualize the razor wire of Leavenworth, still smell the concrete walls. She had been sentenced there after killing a sergeant who thought he could use her and then treat her as he wished. And she died a new death every day she was there, trapped in the confining space.

And now, after volunteering for the experiment for which she had been brought here, she was treated no better than she had ever been. The guards still snapped their orders, still stared at her as she walked by—despite how insignificant they were now and all she had become since the surgery. She stepped over the body of the military policeman lying on the floor. His arms were splayed and his features were frozen with the agony he had suffered going to his death. She dropped the gas mask she had been carrying since removing it at the entrance to the corridor, and it landed next to his outstretched hand.

To her sides, steel walls painted a light green reflected the illumination cast by the overhead fluorescent fixtures, spaced thirty feet apart. The military hadn't bothered to veneer the ceiling; it still consisted of the solid rock left when the passageways and rooms had been carved out of the bowels of the wide hill rising above the ground. The door at the end of the corridor was closed, but not locked, and she pushed it open.

Two doctors in surgical scrubs, their plastic face shields still in place, lay sprawled on their backs on the tile floor. A male nurse in similar scrubs lay on his side, past the operating table.

On the table, Enriquez, covered to the waist with a sheet, lay bathed in the bright glow of the operating lamps. He was unmoving but not dead. The endotracheal tube protruding from his mouth and funneling oxygen into his air passages had protected him from the gas that had filled the complex moments before. He slowly turned his face in her direction. The two small, round incisions in his forehead had not yet been stitched closed. Blood seeped from the wounds and trickled across the skin. The look in his eyes told her that he was confused by the new thoughts racing through his mind. It was always that way at first, she knew. It had happened with her, and it had happened with the others. He moved his hand slowly out from his side and held it toward her in a pleading motion.

Then his features suddenly contorted into an expression of obvious fear.

He knew. Despite his confusion, the new power surging through his mind was such that he had reached a conclusion without even knowing how he had come by it. This sudden realization wasn't based on any form of psychic ability, but rather a logical conclusion coming from information streaming out of the data banks he now possessed. It was logical that she and the others would have to run when they reached the surface, he had realized. And he knew that even with their enhanced physical strength, they could not carry him and run for long.

He didn't make another gesture. But every second now his ability to control his mind would improve. He would soon realize what had to happen after they left. He would try to fight through the lingering effects of the sedation and rise from the table to escape before it was too late. But it was already too late for him. She turned from the room, leaving him staring after her.

Ahead of her now, from beyond the open doorway at the far end of the long corridor, she heard the clanging sound of the grill that had covered the air shaft dropping to the floor. That meant that the others leaving with her had finished piling the folders containing the experiment's research records into the halls and setting them afire. The only thing left was to crawl up the steeply inclined shaft to the freedom above. She keep walking, despite feeling an urge to increase her pace.

She passed one of the old ether barrels, placed against the wall under a wide steel support beam holding up a section of limestone ceiling. Ethers, phosphates and other chemicals found in the laboratory storerooms had been mixed together quickly, put in similar containers, and placed in strategic locations throughout the complex. The timers were already set. The resulting explosion and firestorm would put to shame the power of the ordnance being tested on the range above the ground as a cover for the site.

As she reached the end of the corridor and turned into an intersecting passageway, she saw that the other four, dressed in the brown garb reserved for male prisoners, were already starting up the air shaft.

In only moments, the last one's scrambling feet had vanished from view. And the urge to move faster suddenly turned into a growing nervousness.

It was her emotion trying to take over. That she still could feel that kind of sensation didn't surprise her. She still had all the feelings and mental processes she had possessed in the past. The new artificial power she had been given had only combined with the old, superseding it, but not erasing it. And now, the old burning desire to be free of confinement had combined with her keen awareness of the explosives to cause the feeling. The timers were ticking, all set by men she wasn't certain of, set by men who had sent her to see if Enriquez had recovered enough from the anesthesia to escape with them—although they had known that was highly unlikely. And now they had scrambled up the shaft without waiting for her. If she had brought Enriquez with her, they would have needed to help her get him up the shaft. They had known that, too.

And she suddenly broke into a run toward the opening, hating them for feeling the need to hurry even as she ran faster and faster.

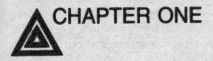

CHAPTER ONE

TEN YEARS LATER

The rain came down hard, hammering the roof of the governor's mansion, splashing against the sides of the buildings along Capital Street, and forming shallow pools spreading across the pavement. Alfred Wynn drove his Mercedes in what most would consider a reckless manner, weaving around the slower traffic, slashing through the puddles, the sleek vehicle's tires throwing wide sheets of water out to the sides.

But he knew what he was doing. He knew he was absolutely safe under the conditions—the amount of water his tires cut through, the drag that the water caused, the weight of the Mercedes resisting the pull. He knew all these facts without even thinking, and the speed he could drive safely up to the very mile an hour.

A flashy diamond ring on his hand and his large frame encased in an Armani suit, he gave the appearance of someone who knew what he was doing in his business life, too. Obviously rich, the look on his chiseled, square face was one of complete confidence, absolute total confidence; the confidence that came from knowing all there was to know—and being able to instantly assimilate it all into complex thought that served whatever purpose he desired.

He didn't show a sign of panic when out of the corner of his eye he caught the image of a furniture transport truck running the red light at the intersection he should have been safely passing through. All he did was raise his arm against his face for protection, a primitive, instinctive gesture that came from somewhere deep in a part of his mind he had almost forgotten was there.

And then there was the thunderous sound of the truck's front slamming into the steel of the Mercedes' side.

At that moment, on the top floor of the tallest office building in the city, two large men in their mid-forties, dressed in nearly matching tailored suits, sat across from each other near the end of a long conference table. The larger man suddenly flinched. The other man's mouth gaped.

"What . . ." he started, ". . . a truck . . ."

Then their faces swung as one toward the far wall, as if they knew where the collision between the Mercedes and the truck had taken place, many stories below and several blocks away—in the direction they were looking.

Two miles away, Spence Stevens turned his aging Ford Bronco toward the rear of the main teaching hospital located at the center of the sprawling, 160-acre University Medical Center complex. He parked out of the rain by stopping under the protection of the second floor of the hospital extending out over the emergency department entrance. But he was already soaked. His white shirt clung to his shoulders like a T-shirt damp with perspiration from a game of hospital-league basketball. Even his jeans and sneakers were damp. A droplet of water trickled out from under his hair and moved slowly down his face. He used his knuckle to wipe the drop away, pushed open the driver's door, and stepped outside. Rolling his damp shirtsleeves up his forearms, he came around the front of the Bronco and walked toward the emergency department doors.

As they slid back and he walked inside, an older couple standing in a small waiting room off to the left stared his way. The woman smiled at his appearance. Ahead of him, a tall security guard standing beside the next doorway leading into the heart of the department looked at the wet clothes and smiled, too.

"Left my raincoat at my apartment this morning," Spence explained as he passed the man.

"No kidding," the guard called after him.

As he continued across the floor, doctors and nurses dressed in surgical scrubs went about their business around him. An older cardiologist wearing a suit and tie and standing at the nurses' station off to the left, looked at him, staring at the wet attire for a moment, and then went back to writing orders in a chart. Dr. David Lambert waited in the corridor past the rear of the department. The aging pathologist wore a white, knee-length lab coat over slacks, a dress shirt, and bright red tie: about the only combination of clothing Spence could ever remember seeing him in. Always the red tie. In fact there was almost nothing ever different in the old man's appearance, Spence caught himself noting for at least the fiftieth time in the few years since he had been a medical student and Lambert one of his professors. Lambert's slight build had not seemed to vary a pound over that period of time, his thin neck always making his shirt collars look too big. And, most memorably, he was still possessed of those ever-alert, piercing dark eyes that seemed to stare right into you and know all there was to know about you. Not many things could make a beginning student so nervous as meeting Professor Lambert for the first time and being a recipient of that piercing stare. Lambert smiled as Spence walked up to him and stopped.

"You swam?" the old man questioned, looking at the wet clothes.

"Forgot my raincoat," Spence repeated.

"Good thinking, son," Lambert said as they shook hands. Then the old professor looked across his shoulder down the hallway in the direction of the morgue. "Can you believe he carried a donor card?" he asked, remarking on the peculiar fact that the man delivered there earlier that morning, a man guilty of at least two prior murders and a record of abusing others all his life, could otherwise be so caring as for such a bequest to have been found on his body.

Shaking his head in amusement, Lambert turned down the hall, and Spence followed after him.

With the elevator stopping for passengers at nearly every floor, it had taken the two men four frustrating minutes to get from the suite of offices on the top floor of the office building down to the lobby area. When the elevator door opened, they pushed past an old man starting to step outside. He stared after them as they hurried toward the building's entrance, but didn't say anything. They were large, obviously strong men, both of them a good six-feet-two and well over two hundred pounds, and it would be foolish to cause a scene with a pair already proven to rudeness at the least. And their tailored suits and shiny shoes spoke of wealth and power. The shoes especially, the old man knew. He was a shoe salesman. The shoes were Vallys—easily a thousand dollars a pair. He didn't need any problems.

The two disappeared into the heavy rain falling outside the building.

From a few blocks away came the sound of the bells atop St. Peter's Cathedral. It was twelve o'clock in the city of Jackson, Mississippi.

The morgue was fifty feet wide by a little over twenty feet deep, with most of its rear blanked from sight by a tall wall of metal body drawers. A small work area to the right of the drawers contained a white porcelain sink, a washing table, and the stocky body of Tommy Small, lying on his back on a gurney. Shorn of the blood-stained jeans and a shirt he had worn when rolled into the morgue, he was naked except for a towel laid across his stomach and tucked up under his wide hips like a loincloth. Dr. Lambert, his thin, straight white hair hanging down across his forehead, stood on one side of the gurney. Spence, now wearing a black disposable full-body apron over his damp jeans and shirt, his hands clad in a double thickness of latex gloves, stood on the other side. In addition to the two jagged holes where police bullets had exited Tommy Small's chest, the left eye, partially protruding from its socket, showed where a round had entered his head from the rear and lodged itself just behind the orbital socket. The force of the shot had caused the cornea to disintegrate, leaving a slight amount of clear-colored pulp at the corner of the eye.

"The right one was usable for a transplant," Dr. Lambert said, sliding a pair of glasses with thick lenses from his lab-coat pocket. "You're the only person I know who would be interested in the other one."

Spence hoped the optic nerve wasn't damaged. From the angle the shot entered the head it didn't appear that the trajectory of the bullet itself would have done any damage. But the concussion could have severed or damaged the nerve beyond use even in his experiments. He lifted a scalpel from the stainless-steel instrument cart next to the gurney.

His first incision was at the very inside corner of the eye, as close to the bridge of the nose as he could get it.

On Capital Street, only one car at a time was being let through the eastbound lanes at the scene of the accident. The Mercedes' side was caved in and the furniture truck's cab had ridden up on the sleek car's top. Firemen standing in the driving rain were using hoses to spray the gasoline away. There was no ambulance in sight.

The two large men stared through the windshield of their Mercedes, brought to a crawl in the slowly moving traffic. As the car neared the intersection, the larger man slowed it even more, lowered his window and leaned his head outside toward a young fireman directing a wide spray of water under the truck.

"Where did they take him?"

The fireman glanced across his shoulder but hadn't quite caught the question.

The Mercedes suddenly stopped. The man threw open the door and stepped outside into the rain. "Where did they take him?" he snapped.

A police officer directing traffic through the intersection stared at the man. The fireman hesitated a moment, then said, "The truck driver wasn't hurt. He—"

"The one he hit, you fool!" the man shouted. "Where did they take him?"

The young fireman's lips tightened. He started to come back with an even louder voice. But then realizing he must be facing someone important, considering the way the man was acting and the Mercedes he drove, he held his tongue. He had just received his position on the fire department a month before. He certainly didn't need to jeopardize it.

"They took him to University."

As the man slid back inside the Mercedes and it sped past the policeman directing traffic, the fireman stared after the car. As he saw the policeman glance at him, he felt a little embarrassed at having taken the abuse he had. Powerful figure or whatever, he wasn't certain now. But there was *something* he had sensed in the big man's demeanor.

Spence dug the scalpel farther down inside the orbital socket and past it, cutting carefully, even deeper, around the optic nerve, into the brain.

Dr. Lambert, eyes blurred behind the thick lenses of his glasses, smiled his approval at the dexterous movement of the sharp blade.

"You learned well," he said. "You remind me a lot of myself when I was younger."

Spence glanced at the older man. Lambert wouldn't be a bad model to emulate when it came to working with a scalpel. And not only when he was younger. His skill with operating instruments put him more in the mold of a neurosurgeon than a pathologist. There couldn't be anyone who was more skilled by steadiness and hand-eye coordination—and that intuitive feel that a person who was going to be a skilled surgeon possessed long before he entered medical school.

Of course I'm biased about anything that has to do with Dr. Lambert, Spence thought. He knew that started just after finishing the second year of his neurology residency, when he began to think about making his career one of research rather than joining one of the private practice groups in the city. "You're crazy," everyone had said. "Only two years from beginning a private practice that will set you up for life—and you want to give that up for a researcher's salary and a state pension that will hardly pay off your house before you die." Only Dr. Lambert had said that if research was where he wanted to be, the hell with what anyone else thought. By that time Spence already knew where he was headed, but it was nice for the old doctor to add his encouragement. And he did so repeatedly after that, right up to the day Spence remembered ending his residency and starting work in research the very next day. He smiled a little at his next thought.

"What?" Dr. Lambert questioned, looking across Small's body.

"I was thinking about how you helped talk me into research. I was just wondering what I'm going to be thinking of you about the time I start drawing my pension."

"Hell, son," Lambert said, "the others will have their millions, but you'll have the good feeling." There was the inkling of a smile at the corners of the pathologist's lips. "Of course not much else," he added.

Spence lifted the eyeball, complete with the optic nerve ending in a clump of severed brain tissue, into view.

Siren wailing, the ambulance swerved off North State Street through the rain into the University Medical Center complex. The driver followed the narrow pavement circling around the helicopter pad toward the emergency department at the rear of the main hospital. The paramedic in the back of the ambulance, a slim female in her late twenties wearing a yellow rain suit, performed her life-saving actions almost by instinct, she had done them so many times before—though she knew this time they were of no use. If nothing else, the inch-wide flat piece of steel driven into the Mercedes' driver's forehead just above his left eye told her that. It had been driven into the skull when the side of the Mercedes had virtually exploded when hit by the loaded transport truck. A couple of inches of the metal, jagged on one edge and smooth on the other, protruded above the skin. How deep it went she could only guess, but it was obvious it had gone *too* deep. The profuse amount of blood that came from a head wound had quit running around the metal. There was no movement of the heart to pump the blood. He was in full cardiac arrest. He was asystolic into ECG leads. She had intubated him, started an IV, and given him a total of five milligrams of epinephrine and three of atropine—all without results. Mr. Alfred Wynn, the forty-two-year-old senior vice president of Computer Resources Incorporated, according to the identification in his wallet, would be DOA at the hospital. He was already dead.

Then, directly below the protruding piece of metal, Alfred Wynn's eye opened.

The paramedic's eyes widened.

The blood began pumping out around the metal.

The paramedic jerked her head toward the read-out on the electrocardiogram monitor.

The man driving the Mercedes suddenly tightened his eyes. He stared over the steering wheel through the top of the car's windshield as if he were looking for something in the heavy, dark clouds overhanging the city.

"He was back," he said.

He looked across the seat. "John," he said, a questioning tone to his voice, a tone that was almost never present in either of their voices.

John had seen the same thing. He looked toward the clouds. But that was only where his idle stare went as he concentrated. What he was seeing was inside his head. The image had come back, for just an instant, and blurred, and then it was gone again.

Now it was back again.

This time a clearer picture—a woman's face, her features twisted into an incredulous expression, looking down at Alfred's face. She had long blond hair tied back in a ponytail. She wore a yellow rain jacket over a light-blue uniform shirt . . . a small hose running from Alfred's face toward a round, steel cylinder . . . the scene bouncing.

An ambulance.

A paramedic.

The flash of the building off to the side.

The emergency room entrance.

The blond paramedic came outside the rear of the ambulance, reached back inside the blocky vehicle and pulled the gurney toward her. Its legs popped down to the concrete, and the body of Mr. Alfred Wynn, strapped to a spinal board, came outside. Her partner, a male with his dark hair damp and draping across his forehead, had hurried out of the driver's seat to the rear of the ambulance, and now used the flat of one hand to pump on Alfred's chest while using his other hand to pull the gurney toward the open emergency department doors. The blond rapidly compressed the ambu bag, forcing oxygen down the endotracheal tube into Alfred's lungs. A pair of nurses dressed in blue surgical scrubs met the gurney, grabbing its sides and helping pull it hurriedly inside the department.

"He was gone," the blond paramedic said to one of them. "He opened his eye—he could see, I know he could see. No pulse. No cardiac rhythm, no breathing . . . he could see."

As they passed through the doors into the department, a slim, unusually young resident in green scrubs met the gurney.

The eye popped open again.

The eye beneath the section of jagged metal driven into his forehead. . . .

WITH HIS TAUT TALES AND FAST WORDS, CHARLES
WILSON WILL BE AROUND FOR A LONG TIME. I HOPE SO."
—JOHN GRISHAM

Paleontologist Cameron Malone has discovered a
500,000-year-old man, so miraculously preserved that
some scientists call it a fraud. But Malone firmly believes
in his find—and so does another man, renegade scientist
Dr. Noel Anderson, who has plans for the Ancient Man.
Plans that will prove the theory his colleagues ridiculed,
and shatter the very foundations of modern science.

When Anderson steals some tissue from the frozen corpse
and uses the still-viable DNA to create a modern Ancient
Man, his experiment succeeds beyond his wildest
dreams—and transforms into a waking nightmare. Only
one man, Dr. Cameron Malone, can stop these horrors of
genetic engineering. But can he do it before they are
unleashed on mankind?

DIRECT DESCENDANT
Charles Wilson

Six-year-old Paul Haines watches as two older boys dive into a coastal river...and don't come up. His mother, Carolyn, a charter boat captain on the Mississippi Gulf Coast, finds herself embroiled in the tragedy to an extent she could never have imagined.

Carolyn joins with marine biologist Alan Freeman in the hunt for a creature that is terrorizing the waters along the Gulf Coast. But neither of them could have envisioned exactly what kind of danger they are facing.

Only one man knows what this creature is, and how it has come into the shallows. And his secret obsession with it will force him, as well as Paul, Carolyn and Alan, into a race against time...and a race toward death.

EXTINCT
by Charles Wilson

"Eminently plausible, chilling in its detail, and highly entertaining straight through to its finale."
—DR. DEAN A. DUNN, Professor of Oceanography and Paleontology, University of Southern Mississippi

"With his taut tales and fast words, Charles Wilson will be around for a long time. I hope so."
—JOHN GRISHAM